WORDS FROM THE HEART

"I am falling in love with you," JoAnna said. "And I want to know if you could love me back?"

"JoAnna, you cannot mean this. I am Navajo . . . you are bilagaana. This is forbidden among your people."

"Does love have a culture or color, Notah? Everyone laughs and cries in the same language, is it any different with love?"

For all her casualness in their friendship, JoAnna doubted she had concealed her true feelings from him. She knew she loved him with all her heart.

"You should stay with your people, JoAnna. Find a man among them who will love you and give you children."

"Your people have become my people. I cannot go back to the greedy men and narrow-minded, bigoted women of my race who cannot see beyond the color of a person's skin in order to judge their worth. All I'm asking is that you just let me stay near you . . ."

Books by Carol Ann Didier

APACHE WARRIOR

NAVAJO NIGHT

Published by Kensington Publishing Corporation

Navajo Night

Carol Ann Didier

ZEBRA BOOKS
Kensington Publishing Corporation
http://www.kensingtonbooks.com

ZEBRA BOOKS are published by

Kensington Publishing Corp.
119 West 40th Street
New York, NY 10018

All Kensington titles, imprints, and distributed lines are available at special quantity discounts for bulk purchases for sales promotion, premiums, fund-raising, educational, or institutional use.

Special book excerpts or customized printings can also be created to fit specific needs. For details, write or phone the office of the Kensington Special Sales Manager: Attn. Special Sales Department. Kensington Publishing Corp., 119 West 40th Street, New York, NY 10018. Phone: 1-800-221-2647.

Zebra and the Z logo Reg. U.S. Pat. & TM Off.

ISBN-13: 978-1-4201-0377-9
ISBN-10: 1-4201-0377-6

First Printing: September 2009
10 9 8 7 6 5 4 3 2 1

Printed in the United States of America

This book is dedicated to Joann,
who first introduced me to the real
Apache and Navajo people;

to my STAR friends who encouraged me:
Karlene, Frances, Mia, and Petrina;

and lastly, to Karen Kay and Lucia St. Clair Robson
for their wonderful contribution to the world of
Native American history and romance, and
who inspired me to try my hand at
writing about them, too.

Prologue

Dinétah, Navajoland
New Mexico Territory
Summer 1851

The young Hataalii raised his fist and yelled his grief and frustration to the heavens. Why call him to be a holy man if his prayers would not be effective to save the one person who meant everything to him?

The agony of it washed over him.

Squash Blossom, his precious wife of a year and a half, the mother of his twins, had come to him, both as the holy man of the Navajo, and as her husband to cure a stomach ailment or maybe a female illness neither could diagnose.

He had prepared the sand painting, placing her in the center of it, burned the incense, prayed, sung the Blessing Way song—*all ninety-six stanzas*, he thought—but had he? The *sing* had to be done exactly right to work the cure. Had he become tired toward daylight; had he left out a verse or maybe some words?

He racked his brain trying to remember every detail of the past four days, the allotted time for a healing sing. What had he done wrong or omitted doing? How had he displeased his gods?

No answers came to him.

He'd watched her die in agony and fear, calling out to him to help her, and he hadn't been able to. She died in his arms while he held her close, his tears mingling with the last of hers.

In his pain he leaned over his wife and viciously scrambled the sand painting until the design and colors all ran together. As soon as he had done it, he knew a moment of panic. One *never* wantonly destroyed a sand painting. There was a proper ritual to be followed. The sand must be swept away in a reverse order of how it was created. The sand would then be buried outside or scattered to the four directions. Failure to destroy a sand painting, or attempting to reverse any part, could bring blindness or death to the transgressor. And he had just transgressed badly.

He waited for the gods to retaliate for his misbehavior. Sweat poured off his forehead. *How could they ever use him again?* He regretted his hasty action and hoped the gods realized it was from his anguish over not being able to save Squash Blossom that he had struck out so violently.

When after several minutes passed and nothing happened, he relaxed. Maybe the gods were just going to wait for another time to take their revenge for his actions. But for now, it seemed he was going to be allowed to live. However, as he sat there he made a sacred vow to himself and the holy ones, *if* they were still listening.

Never again . . . *never again* was he going to let another member of his clan die because of his inadequacies. He made an oath that from now until his last breath, he would study to show himself approved by the present Hataalii. He would learn every verse in every sing and prayer the Navajo used. He would learn all the colors to use in the sand paintings and he would never smudge or mess one up, ever again. It had been a sacrilege to do so in such a rage.

His conscience smote him that he could rail against the gods as he had. It was a wonder they had not struck him dead on the spot for his irreverence.

He also made another vow. He would *never* marry again. He would never love that deeply again, and he would never encourage anyone to care for him in such a way either. Squash Blossom had left him a part of her in their children—Bella, the girl who so resembled her, and Bacca, her twin brother, who took after him. That would be enough. He would give them all the love and attention they needed; and somehow they would go on, the three of them, and he would never let the twins forget the wonderful mother and wife she had been.

Thank the gods the twins were just six months old and would not remember much. He would get Old Woman and one of the nursing mothers to help with the babies, and in return he would hunt for them and keep their hogans warm in winter.

Notah stepped from the ceremonial hut and called for help in preparing his wife's body for burial. That would be done correctly, and with all the ceremony it deserved.

Chapter One

New Mexico Territory
1860

The warrior sat astride his pinto pony overlooking the valley. The wagon traveled slowly and tortuously over the rocky, parched terrain below him. Had the travelers been looking up they might have seen him silhouetted against the clear, blue sky—the hair of both horse and man blowing in the breeze that caressed the higher elevations. In the valley, no breeze moved at all. It was only hot and dry.

Where had these people come from? Spirit Talker wondered. The man had a woman with him, so maybe he was not hostile. Why were they on Dinétah, Navajoland, and where did they plan to go? There were no white settlements out here. The nearest town where the bilagaanas lived was the Spanish settlement of Santa Fe.

He decided to follow them awhile to see what they did and where they camped for the night. Perhaps then he could discern their ultimate destination or plans.

In the valley, the lone wagon ambled on. It didn't seem to be in any hurry, as if it had no real destination in mind. The man, in his middle years, driving the wagon leaned over and patted the petite, pretty blue-eyed girl beside him to reassure her that all was well.

Dr. John Lund knew a moment of regret for bringing his twenty-one-year-old daughter to this godforsaken wilderness; but at the time, he felt it had been the right decision to make. It would take a long time for his past to catch up with him out here.

"Are you getting tired of sitting, JoAnna? We could stop and get out and stretch if you want to."

"Yes, Father. A walk might help get some of the kinks out. Do you think there is any water around here? I would love to find a water hole big enough to take a bath in. It was never this hot or barren in Virginia."

Another pang of unease hit him. Had he been right to deprive his daughter of the finer things of life just to soothe his hurt and pain? Surely, she was suffering the loss of her mother just as much as he was suffering the loss of his wife.

"I know, dear. Possibly we'll come across something soon. That looks like a patch of green up ahead. Hopefully, that signifies water nearby."

He slowed the wagon to a stop and helped his daughter down. He noticed she had taken off several petticoats that society dictated a well-bred woman wore in this year of 1860, but it was so beastly hot, he wondered how she managed in the long-sleeved blouse and skirt as well as she did. She had a big floppy straw hat on her head to shield her face from the sun, but even so, she was developing a lovely golden tan.

He began to feel like a fool. She should be going to balls and afternoon teas, not walking on a hot desert floor without any prospects for a future out here. But when he'd told her of his desire to come to the New Mexico territory, she had said, "If you think that is best, Father, I will come." How selfless she had been, and how selfish he was.

JoAnna walked to the back of the wagon to their two thoroughbred horses they had brought with them. She talked to them, rubbing their noses and scratching behind their ears.

"Poor Prince and Princess. This is nothing like the green grass and sweet-flowing springs of Virginia, is it?"

They bumped her and rubbed their heads on her shoulder as if they agreed with her.

It had been hard on them, walking hundreds of miles. Then trying to keep the stallion from nipping at the mare was a constant struggle too, but John would not leave them behind. They were too valuable and he hoped to use them for breeding.

Dr. Lund had the grace to be embarrassed. Surely though, with other white men coming west, new settlements would be starting up out here soon. Eventually there would be a need for a preacher with doctoring skills. JoAnna was fast becoming almost as good as he in diagnosing illnesses and knowing how to treat the sick. She'd helped him for several years in the infirmary that had been attached to the back of their home. On Sundays, he led the faithful in worship, and did his doctoring during the week. It had been a good life.

He'd been so blessed when Rebecca Jameson of the Norfolk Jamesons had defied her parents to marry a struggling preacher-doctor. She had though, and he had loved her with a deep abiding love that time would never destroy. JoAnna was their only child. Rebecca grieved that she could not have more children, but the three of them had been content and complete as a family, until that fateful day when their world was ripped apart.

He'd never forget the anguish of Robert Foster when his son had died from a riding accident. Father and son had been riding to the hounds when the son took a jump too high for the speed he was going. His horse hadn't been able to lift up soon enough and had crashed into the timber and bramble thicket on the other side, tangling in branches and vines and falling on top of Buddy Foster.

They'd brought Buddy to John as quickly as they could, but his legs were broken in several places. A branch had pierced his lung and Buddy had died on the operating table while he and JoAnna were still working on him. Foster's grief was a horrible thing to see. Buddy was his heir, his pride and joy.

He started drinking heavily and eventually lost all ability to reason.

One Sunday after church had let out, he came racing up to the church waving a pistol and shouting for John to come out. Knowing how Robert was hurting, he'd gone out immediately, as had Rebecca and JoAnna. They wanted to be of whatever comfort they could to the tormented man and long-time friend. But something went awry, and Robert started shooting wildly, saying *"How would you like it if you lost your daughter?"* and he'd pointed the gun at JoAnna.

Rebecca had screamed, *"Nooo, Robert,"* and jumped in front of her daughter, taking the bullet meant for JoAnna. To everyone's horror, Robert Foster then shot himself in front of the congregation who had gathered on the front lawn of the church.

Everyone was too stunned for a moment to react; then everyone went wild, screaming, grabbing up the children and running for their buggies.

John was bent over his wife, calling her name, oblivious to anything else going on around him. JoAnna lay stunned from having the breath knocked out of her. When she realized she was all right and that her mother was bleeding, she'd cried out her own fear and anguish as well. While her father lifted Rebecca, she ran ahead to the infirmary to prepare the operating room.

But it was too late. It had been a clean shot, right to the heart, and Rebecca had died instantly.

Shock and disbelief hung in the air between father and daughter.

Lovingly, John bathed the blood away and folded Rebecca's hands on her chest. Then he laid his head there as well and cried. JoAnna didn't know what to do to console her father. She was still reeling with the magnitude of the horrible incident herself. She knew that Robert Foster, in his right mind, would never have done such a terrible thing, but she was getting a first-hand lesson in what grief could do to a person just by watching her father.

She'd sat down hard on the bench in the waiting room and wondered how you recovered from something like this. That was why she hadn't been surprised when her father came to her a month later and told her he was giving up the church; that he wanted to make a fresh start in a new land. She had obliged him by saying she would go wherever he wanted to go.

But, oh, all the way to the newly established New Mexico Territory! The only things out there were wild animals, Mexicans, Indians, trappers and miners; no civilization to speak of, but when her father told her she could stay behind with the Jamesons, she knew she could not let him go alone. She feared she might never see him alive again if she did, so she had agreed to come.

All of a sudden, her weak ankle gave out and JoAnna stumbled but righted herself before she fell. Curse this twisted right foot. It had been damaged in birth and had never straightened out correctly. It curved to the inside when she walked and wasn't very noticeable unless she stood on it too long, walked too far, or tried to move too fast. It had also been the cause of her mother not being able to carry any more children.

In her younger years, some children had been unkind and called her *pigeon-toed,* and *cripple,* but her father's Bible teachings had helped her to forgive them and her gentle, loving spirit eventually won them over as they grew up. JoAnna had no hopes of getting married though. She knew no man would want her with a deformed foot. So she had decided to become a nurse and her father's assistant. She'd been studying about plants and herbs and their healing properties and had even created several concoctions that had worked in helping patients heal or relieved their aches and pains.

Now she would have to learn a whole new realm of plant life. There weren't too many textbooks on the west in general, and none on plant life, in particular. She wondered if the Native Americans who lived here, should she get to know any, would be willing to teach her about the plants that grew in New Mexico and how they might be used in healing.

So far, they hadn't seen anyone for days. She had never envisioned a land so vast and unpopulated. She was beginning to realize just how big America was and how widely diverse in its landscape and topography. They'd been traveling for months now and didn't seem to be any closer to a destination than when they'd first set out. She didn't want to rush her father, but she longed to find a spot to settle in.

Just then, her father called to her to come get back in the wagon, and he pointed up ahead.

On the trail, blocking their way, sat an Indian brave. JoAnna had seen some Indians on the way west, but she had never seen one who looked like this. He both frightened and intrigued her at the same time. He sat there like a prince, tall and proud in the saddle.

She hurried over to the wagon and her father pulled her up on the seat beside him.

"I'm not sure what tribe he is," John told her, "but I believe we're in Navajo country now. He doesn't look like he means us any harm, but get the pistol from under the seat and hide it in the folds of your skirt. My rifle is beside me, already loaded."

JoAnna hoped it wouldn't come to bloodshed. He was too magnificent to die. Of course, she didn't want to die either, but she prayed they would be able to come to some sort of understanding to let him know they meant him no harm. Her heart began to race the closer they came to him.

He did not move out of the way, just waited for them to reach him.

Chapter Two

John stopped the wagon about five feet from the Indian. He raised his hand, palm out and pointed to himself. "Hello. My name is John Lund."

When the Indian didn't respond, John tried Spanish, as many of the tribes close to the Mexican border knew that language as well. He'd been picking up a little of the language as they traveled west and never hesitated to learn new words as he went. At one town, he had even conversed with another preacher who had started a primer using Spanish words to help teach the Mexican children in his flock. He'd written out the English word and the Spanish word side by side. John had found the little homemade book invaluable the farther west they traveled.

"Buenos Días. Mi nombre, John Lund."

The man answered, "Buenos Días." When he looked at JoAnna, he noted that she was not a little girl as he had first supposed from a distance, but a very tiny, full-grown woman.

Seeing the direction of his gaze, John said, "This in my niña, JoAnna."

Ah, thought Notah, *not the bilagaana's wife, but his daughter.* For some reason he was pleased by that but didn't stop to reason the why of it.

"Where are you going?" Notah asked John in Spanish. "Where have you come from?"

"We're from the land of the rising sun. We left many moons, ago. I am a doctor and we're looking for a place to settle down."

"What is this *doctor*?"

"Oh, I suppose you could say like a shaman or medicine man among the Indian tribes. I try to heal people who are sick, or hurt, set broken limbs, things like that. The Spanish word for doctor is *médico,* I believe." He used his hands as he tried to get his statements across.

"Ahh," Notah acknowledged. "I, too, am a 'doctor' to my people. Our word is *Hataalii* or holy man."

"Why, how wonderful," John exclaimed. He was excited to think that he may have found a kindred soul in this man before him.

"Should we find a place to settle around here, would you be willing to teach me and my daughter about the healing properties in the plants out here? JoAnna is quite good with the making of herbal remedies and unguents from native plants."

Umm, another healer, thought Notah. There were always Native American women who were wise in the healing arts as well as the holy men of the tribes, so he did not find JoAnna's interest as unusual as a white man would.

Notah began to think ahead. They did not seem as though they brought any danger to him or his people and, as he was quick to discern the character of a person, he knew this man might be an asset to him. He'd desired to learn more about the bilagaanas as more and more were coming into his territory. Some homesteaded, some raised cattle, and some mined Mother Earth for the ore she held in her bosom. Perhaps this John Lund and he could learn from each other.

He remembered a quiet valley up ahead and said, "If you are truly ready to settle down, I know of a little valley at the edge of Dinétah that has a small spring running through it and is at a crossroads for travelers going to the Spanish city of Santa Fe."

John was amazed at the offer. While the Navajo had been talking, John had been sizing up Notah as well. He felt relief in knowing that the man held no animosity toward him, but rather would even be willing to help them relocate out here.

"That would be fine," John answered. "My daughter is getting plumb weary of living out of a wagon and would love to have a place to call home, a *casa* of her own."

John then turned to JoAnna and explained what had been discussed between him and Notah. He asked her, "What do you think, JoAnna? Would you be willing to follow this Navajo and see what the valley looks like?"

JoAnna had been avidly listening and trying to follow the conversation between this compelling

Indian and her father. She hadn't learned as much Spanish as her father, so she hadn't gotten the gist of the whole conversation, but when her father asked if she would like to see the valley, she was ecstatic.

"Oh, yes, let's, Father! What did he say his name was?" she asked.

"He didn't say," John answered. "He only gave me his title. Apparently, he is considered a holy man among his people and practices healing."

Turning back toward Notah, he asked, "Sir, I would like to know your nombre if you don't mind giving it."

He wasn't sure the man would answer truthfully. John had heard some tribes were very skittish about giving their real name to anyone outside their culture. Some fear of having power over them by the use of their name, or something like that. He was surprised when the man answered.

"My name is Notah Begay. I am of the Kayenta Clan. We call ourselves *Diné, The People,* and our land is called Dinétah. You are in Dinétah now. If you will follow me, I will, lead you to the valley."

John quickly agreed and finally relaxed his hold on the rifle by his side. He looked over at JoAnna and smiled.

He knew another moment of guilt for dragging his precious daughter halfway across the country because of his inability to cope with the loss of his wife. Yes, it was past time he stopped this aimless wandering and made a home again for JoAnna.

JoAnna was caught up in her own daydream and hopes. The Navajo was the most fascinating and interesting man she'd seen since they'd headed west. His voice was low but carried a vibrant sound to it that made her warm all over just listening to it. His dark eyes were intelligent and filled with a peace she'd never seen in a man's eyes before. It must be true that he was a holy man. She felt he would always be in command of himself in any situation. He radiated confidence and a sort of power. Crazy as it seemed, she felt *safe* with him.

JoAnna wondered what he thought of them. Was he married? Did he have a family? How old was he? How did one learn things like that from an Indian? You could not just ask such personal questions upon a first meeting.

She noted how tall and straight he rode in his saddle. A beautifully colored, woven blanket covered the horse's back. Surely, some woman must have made it for him. He wore his hair to his shoulders but clubbed off evenly all one length. A colorful band of cloth covered his forehead and was tied in an intricate knot on one side of his head. A tunic of what looked like velvet fitted over deerskin leggings to complete his outfit. Sturdy-looking leather moccasins were on his feet and a beautiful squash blossom necklace of turquoise and silver hung from his neck. A wide silver belt studded with turquoise was at his waist. He had a wide silver band on one finger. She wondered if that signified a wedding ring.

All in all, he looked like a very prosperous person, not like some of the Indians they had encountered traveling west. She found herself anxious to learn more about him and hoped they would be settling near him and his village.

After traveling for another hour, they neared the entrance to the valley. John noticed two trails leading off—one to the east and one to the south.

He called out to Notah, "Which one of these paths leads to Santa Fe?"

Notah stopped beside the wagon and pointed to the one going east. "This is the one that leads to the Spanish town. It is about a five suns journey from here."

"Umm," John murmured. Apparently, it was fairly well traveled and he took this as a good omen. Maybe he could make a go of something here after all if he could entice people to come in off the trail to visit his trading post (a thought that was just now forming in his mind), have a drink of water, and exchange local gossip.

They entered the valley by passing through a small, red-rocked canyon. At the end of the canyon, they came out into a beautiful grassy meadow with some willow and juniper trees in the distance.

At once, John felt a peace steal over him and for the first time in a long while, he felt like he was coming home.

Turning to look at JoAnna, he saw tears in her eyes and heard her sigh . . . a sigh of relief, maybe?

"Well, what do you think, JoAnna?"

"Oh, Father, I like it already."

Notah watched the exchange between father and daughter and thought it bode well. Riding over to the wagon, he pointed and said, "There is a small hogan, our name for our dwelling places, near the stream. It is deserted now but was used by an old sheepherder. When his daughter thought he was too old to keep living alone, she bade him move in with her and her family. It has stood empty now for many moons, but I think it can be made habitable again."

Together they rode farther into the valley for another half-mile until they came upon the octagon-shaped dwelling. There were gaps in the wall where the chinking had come out and the roof certainly needed fixing, but it looked sturdy enough for all the wear and tear of weather upon it and for its being abandoned so long.

Notah dismounted and ground-tied his horse. He waited as John helped JoAnna down from the wagon.

Taking JoAnna's hand, John followed Notah to the entry of the hogan, which he noticed faced east. There was no door but it looked like a woven blanket or some skins had once covered the opening.

Inside it was much the same. The room, which was approximately ten feet around, contained very little of the man's former life, just a few rags, some pottery and a woven basket in a corner were all that was left. A smoke hole in the center of the roof over a depression in the middle of the floor, ringed with stones, was apparently for the fire. In the west wall was a small opening that served as a window, again with no covering over it.

It was a far cry from their house in Virginia, but it could be made livable until John could build them a real one.

Turning to JoAnna, John said, "I know it's not home, but what do you think, sweetheart?"

"I think we can make do, Father. We've lived so long in the cramped quarters of the wagon that this seems like a mansion."

Not for the first time, John was ashamed of what his selfishness in running from Virginia had cost JoAnna. Somehow he had to make it up to her and he vowed he would.

Looking over at Notah, he said, "Mr. Begay, you have yourself a deal. May I purchase this land from you or pay you with something from my wagon?"

At first, Notah was offended. *No one bought or sold Mother Earth.* The Diné believed they were only stewards of the land, no one owned it. Then he realized that the white man and the Mexicans thought they had a right to own the land, fence it, and call it theirs.

It was such a foreign idea to the Navajos. Yes, each clan lived in a certain area and each respected the rights of the other clans to occupy their section, but no one said, "Stay off this piece, as it is my land." If another's sheep wandered onto someone else's campground, they penned the sheep up and let the owner know where to find them. They didn't keep them or kill them.

"The land is not mine to sell," Notah answered John.

Not understanding what he meant, John replied, "Well, to whom does it belong? I would be happy to meet with them and pay them for it."

"No, you do not understand. We do not own the

land—we only take care of it. It belongs to all the Diné. You may use it for as long as you want, and then when you leave, someone else may come along to use it again. That is the way of my people."

"Oh, excuse me," John finally saw what Notah had been trying to tell him. "Then I would be honored to live here and take care of it until such time as I leave," he answered him.

"That is good," Notah replied.

Going back outside, John noticed a thatched roof over a brush arbor, open on all sides, out in the backyard. A fire pit was at one end. He surmised that most of the cooking was done out there in good weather. The supports looked in good shape but, again, the roof needed repair.

"You will need a corral and shelter for the animals" Notah remarked. "I will return in a few suns with some of my people and we will help you build it. You will need a strong one for when Ghost Face walks the earth. You have arrived at a good time. We have a couple of moons to prepare you for the cold to come. You are sheltered from the strong winds here in the valley, but it snows much and this will be isolated for many suns at a time. For now I will show you what plants are edible in the valley and stay the night to help you settle in. Then I must get back to my people."

"That is more than I could ask for," John gratefully replied. "And if your people will help me, we would be most blessed and grateful."

Notah nodded.

JoAnna watched their exchange, noting the

direction of their gazes and the motions of their hands. She was determined to learn more Spanish as quickly as she could, and Navajo as well. She noted the gleam in her father's eyes and the satisfied look upon his face.

Yes, she thought, *he has finally decided to stop looking for some elusive thing, and is willing to make a home once more.* And she was glad . . . so very, very glad.

Walking back to the wagon, she let the tailgate down to get to the goods inside. First, she wanted her broom, rags, and a bucket for water. She'd noted the cobwebs in the hut and knew she'd have to clean it before they moved in, which might not be until tomorrow. But that was all right, one more night in the wagon wouldn't kill her. She was just so thankful to be stopped somewhere.

She saw the men were busy unhitching the thoroughbreds, and the two mules that had pulled the wagon, as she gathered up her things.

The stream was about fifty yards behind the thatched shelter, so taking her bucket she headed in that direction.

Notah saw her heading away and walked in her direction.

When JoAnna became aware of his nearness, she looked up and said, "I'm going for agua," as if it wasn't obvious.

"Sí, I know," Notah answered, "but this is new territory for you, and you must be careful of snakes and scorpions, so watch where you walk." He tried to show her by hand signs the dangers he was speaking of, realizing she did not understand as much as her father did.

"Oh, I never thought of that. Muchas gracias, Notah, I will be careful."

Nodding, he turned back. He felt she would be fine, so he let her go on. He could see her from where they were and if anything happened to her, he would be right there. As she walked away, he noticed she favored her right foot and had a slight limp to her step. Not that it detracted from the rest of her because the more he saw of her, the more he was aware of her beauty. She also exuded a calm and sweet spirit, two qualities he admired very much as a holy man.

He wondered for a moment about her foot. Maybe at one time, she had broken it and it hadn't healed properly, or she may have just twisted it recently; but somehow it looked more permanent than that to him. Well, he knew no one was perfect and this did not detract from her comeliness at all . . . and that thought bothered him. He didn't want to be attracted to any woman—ever again— and certainly not a bilagaana woman.

Turning abruptly, he went back to help John set the horses and mules to grazing, but first they needed to be watered. Admiring the fine lines and sleek muscles of the horses, he knew they came from superb stock. He wouldn't mind having one of his mares bear a foal from John's stallion.

"I'll take the horses down to the stream for agua, then come back for the mules. I'll stake them over there to graze," he said, nodding off in the direction of a flat, grassy spot.

"Fine. Thanks, Mr. Begay. I'll unload a few things while you're doing that. I know JoAnna's going to want to clear the hogan out before we move in, so I'll give her a hand with that."

Notah dipped his head in acknowledgment, then took the horses by their leads and headed to the stream. Not because he wanted to see the daughter again, surely not, but he did want to keep an eye on her to make sure she was safe from any harm. With dusk falling, the night-prowling animals would be coming out and stopping by the stream to drink.

Chapter Three

JoAnna filled her bucket, and seeing how clean the water was, couldn't resist the urge to wash her face and arms. The stream delighted her. It did not run swiftly, seemed mostly shallow, but in the center it looked deep enough for a bath, and as soon as she could, she fully intended to take one. Just the thought of being able to put her whole self in water again was delicious.

Hearing the clip-clop of the horses, JoAnna turned to see Notah leading them to the stream.

He was talking to them as he stroked their necks. She could tell he admired them. They were fine horses from her grandfather's stable.

JoAnna couldn't help staring at the fine physique of the man leading the horses, either. Just the sight of him moving in an easy glide over the rough ground caused her breath to hitch in her chest. Notah had a noble bearing that radiated from him. She could well imagine him as a prince of his people. What had he called them, the Diné? Yes, that was it. He said it meant "The People."

When he came near, she smiled at him, trying to show him her appreciation for all he had done for them already.

Her smile lit up her whole face and her eyes shown with her pleasure. For a moment, Notah forgot to breathe. Every expression showed her sweetness and comeliness. There was no coy flirtatiousness about her; her eyes were too honest. They talked to him as plain as the smoke signals of his people. He sensed lying would not come easily to her.

"Hola . . . hello," she greeted him.

He ducked his head, but didn't answer her. He really didn't know what to say to her anyway. She didn't know very much Spanish and he knew no English.

JoAnna tried once more, determined to hold a conversation of sorts with him.

"I cannot thank you enough for helping us today and bringing us to this beautiful spot. I know we will be happy here."

She hoped she was making herself understood but could not be sure.

"Muchas gracias." She tried again to express her joy in finally finding a place to land.

Notah got the gist of what she was saying and nodded as he stopped the horses at the water's edge. He bent down and pulled off his moccasins, then rolled up his leggings. Ordinarily, he would have stripped down to a loincloth, but not in front of this bilagaana woman.

He then proceeded to take off his necklace, belt, knife and scabbard, and his tunic and laid them on the bank.

JoAnna's eyes widened at the wide expanse of naked chest now available for her perusal. She had seen men naked before, completely at times since she helped her father in his surgeries, but she had never seen a hairless chest like this that tapered down in a vee to a smaller waist and tight buttocks. Every rib was delineated and muscles rippled when he moved.

"Oh, my stars," JoAnna breathed. He looked like a Greek statue of Adonis she'd seen in her art class.

Pretending not to notice her staring, Notah led the horses out into the stream and started splashing water on them. Taking off his headband, he unfolded it, and started wiping them down with it.

JoAnna's breath caught in her throat once more as she watched the play of muscles in his back as he rubbed down the horses. His well-defined calf was visible and showed strong development as well. She couldn't ever remember looking at a man's calf before, but her heart swelled inside her and a funny fluttering started in her abdomen. She felt herself growing warm in places she'd never been warm before, and more and more breathless by the minute.

What were these feelings he evoked in her just by the sight of him. They were all strange and new, but wonderful. She knew the basics of reproduction and about the act of love, but no one had awakened her young heart yet to the thrill of love or desire. She wondered if these were the beginnings of such feelings.

But that would never do. She knew enough about mixed-race relationships to know that a white woman falling in love with an Indian was taboo.

Anyone who had been captured by Indians and lived to escape and tell about it was looked upon with disgust, even if it had not been her fault. No, she would have to guard her heart; she could not let herself fall in love with a Navajo. Besides, with her deformed foot, no one as perfectly formed as he would want a crippled woman by his side. He might even be married as it was.

Notah surreptitiously watched JoAnna watching him. He got the impression that she liked what she saw but wasn't sure she should. He felt she was still innocent in the ways of a man with a woman. Diné maidens married much younger than bilagaanas apparently, and would have one or two children to show for it by now. He wondered why she was not married. Her size belied her age, but he thought she must be about nineteen winters old. Would she think his advanced years of twenty-seven winters too old for her? *Now, where did that thought come from?* He squelched it as soon as it registered. It did not matter what she thought of him or his age. He glanced up at her once more just in time to see a change come over her face.

At that particular moment, JoAnna was thinking she wished her mother were still alive so she could ask her about these new feelings. As always, thoughts of her mother brought a pang of remorse and a cloud of grief crossed her face.

He immediately noted the brightness leave her face to be replaced by a look of sorrow. He wondered what had caused her to become sad. Since there was no other woman along, he assumed JoAnna's mother was either dead or had decided not to come west with her husband and daughter. Maybe she planned to join them later after they had gotten settled somewhere.

He had an odd desire to comfort her. Not knowing what could have caused the change in her, he decided to let it go. If there were something to be learned about her and the absence of a mother, he would learn it over time. For now he would help them settle in and make the place livable for winter.

JoAnna watched him for a few more minutes fascinated by the tableau before her. Notah was scratching the heads of the horses and whispering soft, guttural words in their ears, apparently in his language. It was almost as if the horses understood what he was saying because they bobbed their heads up and down as he talked as if agreeing with him.

For a second, JoAnna wondered what it would feel like if he put his fingers in her hair and whispered Navajo words in her ears. Shocked at the direction of her thoughts, she blushed and looked away. Quickly, to hide her confusion, she bent down and grabbed the handle of her bucket and started back up the path to the hogan, sloshing water as she went.

When next he glanced up, he saw her heading back to the wagon. He felt her absence. Should he have offered to carry the water back for her, he wondered.

No, he scolded, *carrying water is woman's work.* Yet he still felt badly that he had not helped her.

Chapter Four

Over the next week, Notah was as good as his word. Several men and women would come by on different days to help build the corral and a shelter for the horses, and to make repairs to the hogan and brush arbor.

The women helped JoAnna cook for the men, showed her plants that were edible, even brought along a lamb one day to cook over an open fire. They brought her pounded yucca root, their version of soap, to do laundry and helped her clean and set up the hogan. A couple of the women even brought her several of their beautifully woven, heavy woolen blankets. JoAnna marveled at their intricate design and knew they would be a welcome addition in the cold months ahead. It sounded like the winters would be severe, even here in this little sheltered valley.

One day Notah brought them a ram and ewe to start their own flock of sheep. John was thrilled and humbled by their generosity. He felt this was a good beginning for a real friendship with these people.

When he'd eaten of the lamb they had roasted, he couldn't remember any fancy dinner in Virginia tasting better.

Around the end of the second week, an older woman came with Notah along with two small children, a boy and a girl, close in size and age. They rode a painted pony similar to the one Notah rode. The woman sat on a horse, too, and carried a long walking stick with a hook at the end like a shepherd's rod.

When they reached the compound of the transformed hogan and surrounding pens, Notah dismounted and reached up to lift the little girl down, while the boy jumped off on his own.

JoAnna couldn't help smiling at the little boy's show of independence. "He wouldn't need any help getting off a mere pony," it said. She was fascinated by them and wondered who they were. The woman also slid deftly off her horse as well.

It hit her then. These must be Notah's children; why else would he bring small children around a place where men were busy building and working hard. He was certainly old enough to be their father.

JoAnna felt a pang of something she couldn't identify. Loss? Certainly not! He was not hers to lose.

Taking each child by the hand, Notah walked toward a curious John Lund and a disappointed JoAnna. Why was she disappointed to learn he had a wife? It was to be expected and it should not affect her one way or the other.

The old woman followed behind Notah and the

children. JoAnna noticed she carried a basket on one arm and the rod in the other.

"Hola," JoAnna said, holding up her hand in greeting, palm out, signifying peace.

"Hola, JoAnna," Notah answered and nodded to John, who nodded back.

"What have we here, Notah?" he asked, smiling at the children.

"These are my beloved ninâs," he answered. Putting his hands on the boy's shoulders, he said, "This is Bacca, my son." Then, turning to the little girl and pulling her close, he said, "This is Bella, Bacca's twin sister, and my precious flower."

JoAnna couldn't help smiling at them. They were so perfect in every way. Surely their mother must be a very beautiful lady, she thought; and as handsome at Notah was, the result could only be beautiful children, as these were.

Notah spoke to the two in Navajo and they shyly answered JoAnna with their own "Hola," not quite meeting her eyes.

JoAnna couldn't help but wonder where their mother was as she stooped down to their level to take their hands in hers. She wanted to convey her friendship to them and make them feel welcomed.

"Mi casa, su casa," she said in Spanish, welcoming them to their home.

They met her eyes then, and theirs widened in surprise. They had never been this close to a white person before and her eyes were the color of the summer sky. They were fascinated by her and felt her gentleness reach out to them. Then, self-consciously, they hid their faces against their father's legs.

Notah gently put them from him as he turned to the elderly lady behind him.

"This is Old Woman. She has taken care of my children and my household since they lost their mother."

JoAnna noted that he said, "lost their mother," not lost his wife"—whatever that meant, if anything. However, she put all such thoughts aside, as she turned to greet the older woman.

"By what do I call her?" JoAnna asked Notah.

"She is just called 'Old Woman'."

Old Woman? How odd, surely she had a real name. But she would not be impolite and ask. So taking the woman's work-worn hands in her own, she smiled a heartfelt smile and said, "Hola, Old Woman. I am happy to meet you and am honored that you have come to visit my father and I."

Notah translated as JoAnna spoke.

Old Woman was quick to discern the young girl's warm welcome and good heart and, smiling back, she patted JoAnna's hand in acknowledgment of the greeting.

John broke into the greetings then by saying, "Well, Notah, we had no idea you had a family. These are some handsome children. I'm glad you brought them to see us. JoAnna wants to teach children once we got settled out here. Start a school, too, if possible."

"What is a school and what would she be teaching?" Notah asked.

"Oh, that's right, I guess you don't have schools as such. It's like you teaching your children the history of your people, how to count sheep, how to read sign and such. We teach our children the same. Maybe someday you would even let your children be taught our language and about our country."

"Yes, I understand. It is a good thing to learn from each other, maybe."

Notah had already been thinking along those same lines. He knew the Black Robes at the Spanish Mission held studies for the Mexican children and imagined that was similar to what John was talking about. Possibly his children should learn the bilagaana's tongue as more and more were coming into the territory. It might help them in the future to understand what was being said to them. Too many times his people had been cheated, lied to, and had treaties broken by the false promises of the white man.

"I will let my mind work on it," Notah told John.

"Good, good," John replied.

Old Woman asked Notah what they were talking about and he told her what John said about teaching the children English.

"I think it would be a good thing," she replied. "I would try to learn, too. You said he is a Medicine man and she is a Medicine Woman. I wish to learn what they know and teach her our ways of healing as well."

Notah nodded and turned back to John and JoAnna saying, "Old Woman says she thinks it is a good thing and she would like to learn, too, along with the children. She is wise in the ways of healing among my people and knows much about the plants to use in many different illnesses. She is willing to share her knowledge with you in exchange for learning some of your healing ways."

"Why that is wonderful!" John exclaimed. He turned to JoAnna and explained what Old Woman had said.

At his remarks, JoAnna's always-expressive eyes blazed with excitement. Oh, to be able to learn from these people about their healing practices and the use of the flora and fauna out here was just what she had hoped for.

"Oh, yes, yes," agreed JoAnna, barely able to keep from jumping up and down, she was so pleased. "I would be thrilled to teach them and to learn from them as well."

"Then it is settled," Notah declared. "We will start in two suns from now. The sooner we can all talk as one, the better."

John then took Notah off to discuss opening a trading post and going to Santa Fe to buy some trade goods. He wanted to know what special needs or things his people might like to have that he could supply them with.

JoAnna took Old Woman and the children over to sit under the brush arbor where they had put a table and benches. Telling them by hand signals to wait there, she hurried back into the hogan.

She didn't know why she had brought some toys with her from her younger days, but she found the box she wanted and opened it. She took out one of her favorite dolls—a brightly colored Raggedy Ann—

and a slingshot that was her father's. Probably the boy already had one, but she wanted to give each child something. In another box, she spied a flowered silk shawl that had been her mother's, so she took that for Old Woman.

Going back outside, clutching her gifts, she headed for the arbor. She hoped they would like them. You couldn't buy friendship, she knew, but she found she wanted theirs. Anyone that was important to Notah had suddenly become very important to her, too.

The children and woman were exactly where she'd left them, talking quietly in their language, waiting for her to return. She could see the curiosity in their eyes about the things in her hands but they were too polite to ask. They didn't have long to be so though, because she quickly presented them with her gifts.

She handed the Raggedy Ann doll to Bella first, saying and pointing to herself and then to the little girl, hoping to make her understand what she was saying. "Bella, this was my doll when I was your age. We had many good times together and I hope you will, too."

Bella's eyes widened and she clasped her hand over her little rosebud mouth in surprise. Through JoAnna's hand signs and halting Spanish she understood the doll was for her. She took it lovingly and stroked the red yarn hair. The clothing was different from what the Navajos wore, but they were colorful and the shoe-button eyes and red mouth smiled back at her.

"Gracias, señorita," Bella said shyly in pleasantly accented Spanish.

"De nada, you're welcome," replied JoAnna.

Turning to the little boy, she held out the leather and wood slingshot saying, "Bacca, this was mi padre's. He shot many a squirrel with it."

Reaching for it with a smile but also a smug look on his face, he accepted the gift. Did this bilagaana woman think he did not know what a slingshot was, even though it was finely made with newly tanned leather and intricate carved designs on the handles?

"Gracias," he replied. Then he jumped down and ran off immediately to find a stone and try it out.

"Well, I guess that means he liked it," JoAnna said to Old Woman and Bella. She had taught both boys and girls in her Sunday school class back home in Virginia, but she was out of her element here, and these two were so different from her experiences with children before. Maybe they seemed so serious and more mature because of the loss of their mother at a young age. However, she didn't know what age they were exactly, for Notah had not said or told how long his wife had been dead.

JoAnna turned around to see Bella happily crooning and patting her doll. She looked at Old Woman and said, "This scarf belonged to my own dear madre and I would like you to have it."

Then she folded the scarf into a triangle and showed Old Woman how it could be worn tied under the chin or as a scarf around the neck, even though she felt sure Old Woman knew what it was used for.

The older woman's eyes lit up at the lovely colored

flowers on the silk scarf. She took it tenderly and rubbed the silk through her worn fingers and along the side of her cheek. She smiled at JoAnna and nodded her thanks. Then she put it on her head as JoAnna had demonstrated.

"How I look?" she asked the bilagaana girl whom she was beginning to like very much.

"Wait one more momento," JoAnna said, scampering back to the hogan as fast as her crippled foot would let her.

Going inside she found her silver-handled mirror and took it back outside to the brush arbor.

She held it up to her face to show Old Woman how to hold it, then handed it to her.

Old Woman took note of the beautifully engraved silver handle and the glass inserted on one side. When she turned it over and saw her own reflection in the mirror with the scarf on her head, she gasped in wonder, her hand flying to her mouth in surprise, just as Bella's had done. She had never seen such a clear picture of herself before. Streams or copper kettles had never showed her face so clearly. What a wonderful thing it was!

Awed, she turned the mirror one way, and then the other, and saw how she could even see behind her. Excitedly, she called Bella to her side and showed it to her.

Bella, clutching her doll to her little chest, got off the bench she'd been sitting on and came around the table to see what Old Woman was so excited about.

When she looked at her own reflection, it scared

her, and she backed away. "What magic is this, Old Woman? Is that *me* in there? How did I get in there?" she asked worriedly.

When Old Woman turned it a little and caught her own reflection in it, as well as Bella's, she cried out again. This was indeed a fearful yet wonderful thing.

Seeing how amazed the woman and the child were, JoAnna decided to give them a mirror of their own. She couldn't part with this one that was part of her dresser set, but she had a smaller round one that she would give them on their next visit.

Just then, Notah called to the children and Old Woman to rejoin him, as it was time to leave.

"Oh, won't you stay to eat with us?" JoAnna asked. She hated to see them go.

"Another time, maybe," he answered. "The children need to go to bed soon."

Noticing the things the children were holding, he smiled and asked them what they had, realizing JoAnna had given them the toys.

Proudly they held up their gifts and excitedly told him what they were. Old Woman showed off her head covering as well.

Notah spoke to the children, "Did you thank the bilagaana for these gifts?"

"Yes, Father, we did," the twins answered.

He looked at Old Woman for confirmation and she nodded that they had thanked her properly.

Turning to JoAnna, he said, "Gracias, you have honored my children by these gifts, but it was not necessary."

"I know that," JoAnna answered, "but all little

children love surprises. These belonged to me and my father and I wanted to give something meaningful to them."

"Aha," he dipped his head at her.

He told Bacca to mount up, and then lifted Old Woman up on her horse. Lifting Bella, he placed her in front of him as it was late and he could see she was tiring.

He smiled once more at JoAnna and John, raised his hand in farewell, and rode out of the compound.

"Well, JoAnna, did you ever think we'd have such help from Indians?"

"No, Father. When we first saw Notah in our path, I was scared to death. I could never have foreseen this, but, oh, I am so glad things have turned out this way. You must be, too."

"Yes," John answered. "I truly believe we've made a good friend in Notah and I am looking forward to learning from him about this land, his beliefs, and his people. I have a peace about this, honey. I feel maybe this *is* where God wants us to be."

"I do, too. I felt a peace the minute we came through the gorge into this little valley. Old Woman told me she would help me mix up various herbs for drinking and making salves for cuts and burns.

"Oh, Father, I am really beginning to be happy that we came out here. I never realized how big our country is, or how varied. I would not have wanted to miss this, no matter what happens in the future."

John hugged her close and tucked her under his shoulder and looked into her face.

"Thank you, JoAnna. I have doubted the wisdom

of my actions many times since leaving Virginia and bringing you out here with me where there are no other white women and no creature comforts. I felt guilty for depriving you of your friends, the parties, and the chance to meet and marry a decent man, but I would have missed you terribly and worried about you every day had you not come with me."

"Father, I couldn't bear the thought of you going off without me and I would have been just as worried about you. And, if anything had happened to you, how would I have ever found out. I couldn't bear to lose both you and Mother."

"Ah, JoAnna, I don't deserve you. I've been selfish and you've been so unselfish. I love you very much, dear daughter."

"As I love you," she answered. "We're going to make a wonderful new life here. I know it. I am so happy that Notah brought his family by today. They are such beautiful children."

They turned around and walked arm in arm into the hogan to eat their dinner. An inner peace settled in their hearts at the fortuitous outcome of their meeting with the Navajo man called Notah Begay.

Chapter Five

As the months progressed, Notah visited almost as often as he brought the children by to study with JoAnna. Sitting under some willow trees near the stream, Notah decided to share some of the legends of his people with her and her father. On this occasion, John had decided to take a break from work to sit and eat lunch with them under the trees, as well.

"You have told me your story of creation, John. I would like to tell you some of our stories."

"Please do," John answered, looking at JoAnna to gauge her reaction.

"Oh, yes, I would love to hear your stories, Notah. The children have shared a little. We understand that you believe in living in *balance* and *harmony*, believing that all things are connected in nature and animal and human life. What is the word the children use?"

"Yes, we call it 'Walking in Beauty' or 'Hozho.' The holy people are all around us, the Wind, Lightning, Thunder, Sky, and Rain. We know which offerings will appease them and how to call down their blessings. If just one thing is out of balance, it affects the whole picture of Hozho and we must strive to find the imbalance and correct it."

"Well, I could see where that would be tricky and, sometimes, probably downright difficult," John remarked.

"Yes, when the gods are displeased, one must search through everything you have done or said recently to find what you did to bring the discord into your life."

John was grateful that in Jesus he was immediately forgiven if he confessed his sins and asked God to cleanse him. The only offering a man had to bring to God was himself and a contrite heart. Jesus had already done the rest. He had tried to share this with Notah, but he could see Notah, although he respected John's beliefs and his creator God, would never abandon his Navajo ones.

Notah began to speak again.

Our original world lay deep within the earth. It had no sun or moon, but dimly colored clouds moved around the horizon to mark the hours. At first life was peaceful; then the evil of lust and envy took hold and violence broke out. So the ancestral Navajo fled into exile, grappling upward through a hole in the sky to another world directly above. Here, where the light was blue, harmony again prevailed. Then again came bitter quarreling, followed by escape and a climb to yet another world, and then another.

Finally, First Man and First Woman, the direct ancestors of humankind, emerged on the present earth. Water covered the earth's surface, but sacred winds gusted in to blow it away. With the aid of a sacred medicine bundle and guided by the Diyin diné, the holy people, First Man and First Woman filled the world with all its natural bounty and beauty. First Man laid out each object in the bundle and by chanting transformed it into an animal, a plant, a mountain peak, and an hour of the day. They produced North Mountain, which is sacred to the Navajo, and fastened down the peak with a rainbow.

Everything in the new universe resided in perfect balance controlled by a spiritual symmetry. Four is a sacred number to the Navajo. There are four directions, four winds, four seasons, and four basic colors of black, blue, amber, and white. Blended together this produces our Hozho, essential harmony and our concepts of beauty, peace, happiness, and rightness.

While Notah talked, JoAnna sat mesmerized listening to the stories. She loved the cadence of his voice, the deep baritone that made even the guttural sounds of his language sound pleasant. He was a good storyteller and she could see how he would inspire confidence in those he prayed and chanted over in his healing ceremonies. So far Notah had not invited her or her father to attend one of the Blessing Way ceremonies and she was curious about them.

She followed his every hand movement and expression on his face with adoration in her eyes.

As if aware of her intense interest, Notah looked up into JoAnna's face and caught his breath. She had a rapt, dreamy expression on her face as if she had just woken from a pleasant dream, or had just been made slow, delicious love to and was looking at a lover.

Shocked at his thoughts, he looked away. This would not do! He did not want JoAnna to fall in love with him and he did not want to fall in love with her. But he could no longer deny that the fascination for her was there.

He'd found himself visiting more and more often just to hear her lilting laughter when she played a game with the children. On one particular visit, he'd heard her singing; her sweet voice had carried to him on the breeze and had stopped him in his tracks. It had wrapped around his soul and squeezed it. His heart swelled within his chest. Apparently it was some sort of a lullaby, because she was holding Bella in her lap and rocking her to sleep. He'd wondered what it would feel like to lean his head on her breast and have her croon to him and stroke his brow. He felt the stirrings of sexual arousal begin and shook himself.

Stop this, Notah told himself. *She is not for you and you will not encourage these feelings.*

"Tell us the story of Spider Woman, Father, and how she gave us the weaving of blankets," Bella asked Notah.

"Yes, please do tell us that one. I haven't heard it, yet," JoAnna added her plea to Bella's.

"All right. Two of our other gods are Spider Man and Spider Woman. It was Spider Man who taught us how to make the loom, and Spider Woman who taught us how to use it."

At once, JoAnna and John could see the comparison of weaving with a spider's web. They smiled at how the Navajo tied all their beliefs together with nature, to learn from it.

Notah continued.

In one of the stories the old ones relate, a Diné girl was walking through the barrens when she saw smoke rising from a tiny hole in the ground. Looking inside, she spied an ugly old crone who was Spider Woman.

"Come down and sit here beside me and watch what I do," said the old woman.

She was passing a wooden stick in and out between strands of thread.

"What is it that you do, Grandmother?" asked the girl.

"It is a blanket that I weave," she replied.

Over the next three days, the Navajo girl watched intently as Spider Woman wove three different blankets of wonderful designs. She then went home and showed her people all she had learned.

Later she again visited Spider Woman and told her how everyone was now busy weaving.

"That is good," the old woman replied. But she also gave the girl this warning: "Whenever you make a blanket, you must leave a hole in the middle. For if you do not, your weaving thoughts will be trapped within the material—not only will it bring you bad luck, but it will drive you mad."

And since then, all Navajo women have always left a spider hole for a way of escape in the middle of their blankets.

Little Bella clapped her hands and laughed at the story. "I am going to be Spider Woman when I grow up and weave wonderful blankets," she told the group.

JoAnna smiled in loving affection at the delightful child. She was becoming so attached to both of them. Bacca was a little more reserved in his actions toward her, but Bella had taken to JoAnna right from the start. She loved to cuddle on JoAnna's lap after lunch and take a nap in her arms.

It made her have some very treacherous thoughts. Could she be a mother to Notah's children? Would he even want her to or let her, for JoAnna realized her feelings for this wonderful, enigmatic man, were undergoing a deep change from friendship to longing and something much more.

Notah noticed the love in her eyes for his daughter. And he had noticed the love Bella had for JoAnna. She spoke often of JoAnna in their hogan at night after a visit with her. Both of the children were more relaxed and happier than he'd seen them in a long time. They laughed more and weren't so sober in his presence. Their English was improving daily and they'd even taught him a few words at night.

Of course, Bacca still had to learn the ways of a hunter and a warrior to become recognized in the clan, but he could tell the association with JoAnna and her father was having a good influence on his children.

Was she having an influence on him, too? As much as he hated to admit it, he felt she was. He knew his eyes followed her every movement when he was in their compound, even though he tried not to let her or John know it. In spite of her clubbed foot, which he had only glimpsed once, she moved with grace and a bearing that was almost ceremonial. He could visualize her as one of the Diné dancers in their healing chants, she moved so gracefully.

Again, he commanded himself to stop speculating about her. She was not for him. He had vowed never to love again and he would not break his vow, especially for a bilagaana. That was taboo in her race as well as his. He could not see how a love relationship would ever be possible between them, and for some reason that hurt, and pain constricted his heart.

When he looked at her again, her eyes were alight with her feelings for him. He could tell she was having the same thoughts as he, being a good discerner of the thoughts of others in his practice as a holy man, but he could not let them develop further.

In order to break the spell, he got up from the ground and beckoned to the children, saying, "Come, little ones. It is time to head home. Say your good-byes to our host and hostess."

After they left, JoAnna sighed out loud. Her father looked over at her and asked, "What are your thoughts, JoAnna?"

"Oh, I don't know, Father. I'm becoming so attached to the children . . . and maybe, even to Notah. Is that wrong? Is it just because there aren't any other men out here that makes him so attractive to me? He causes strange feelings in me and I'm not sure how to handle them. I wish Mother were here so I could talk with her."

Then realizing how that might sound to her father, like he wouldn't know how to help her with these feelings, she spoke quickly, "Not that we can't talk about such things . . ."

John reached over and hugged her, smiling all the while. He knew exactly the *kinds of feelings* she was having. He'd seen them brewing for some time, but what he wasn't sure of was what was brewing in Notah.

"Don't worry about it for now, JoAnna. Your father is not so old that he doesn't understand a budding attraction for the opposite sex when he sees it. I like Notah and I think he is a fine man. I know he is not what I would have looked for back east for you as a potential husband, but should something develop between the two of you, I could give my blessing to it."

JoAnna turned in his arms, surprised by his remarks.

"You really could, Father?"

"Yes, I could."

She had never dared let herself hope that her father would approve of such a liaison even though she knew he respected Notah.

"Thank you, Father. That means a whole lot to me. But at this point, I don't see anything like that happening between us. From what Old Woman has told me, he has vowed never to marry again for some reason."

However, as they turned and walked toward the hogan, she could not help the spark of hope that blossomed in her heart and soul.

Chapter Six

US Army Headquarters
New Mexico Territory
Spring 1862

The general's adjutant opened the door to usher Christopher Carson into the office of General James Henry Carleton, the new army commander for the Department of New Mexico.

"The general is ready to see you now, sir," he said, as he motioned to "Kit" Carson to enter. Then he saluted both the general and the man and closed the door behind him.

Kit Carson saluted the general and was acknowledged by Carleton.

"Hello, Kit, please, take a seat," General Carleton said, indicating the chair in front of his desk. "How are you? It's been a while since we've seen each other."

"I'm fine. I've done some prospecting while

scouting on the frontier and have been learning to live like an Indian."

"There was some talk about you going Native. Any luck with the prospecting?" the general asked. Rumors of gold and silver abounded in the west.

"A little—not enough to retire on," Carson answered, laughing. "However, I am curious as to why you've called me in."

General Carleton leaned back in his chair, steepled his fingers together, and gave Carson a piercing look.

"You haven't heard the buzz going around army circles about putting all the Indians onto reservations?"

"Well, yes and no, but that's a pretty tall order, sir, considering how many Indians there are in the west."

Kit looked at General Carleton and wondered where this was going. He knew that the general had a reputation for being a stickler for doing things by the book, yet he had been heard saying on several occasions that "Once the Indians were Christianized and made to learn farming and other industrious pursuits, that they *possibly* could become civilized." But most of all, he was known for his total contempt for them.

"If America is going to expand from sea to sea and fulfill her destiny, then something will have to be done with them; they cannot stop progress and the opening up of this country for white settlement," the general said.

"But we're not there yet, are we, General?" Kit asked. "We've just begun a civil war in the east and we've only started crossing the prairies to the Pacific Coast."

"True, but there are more and more Americans coming into the area, and depredations and hostilities are being perpetrated against them, as well as the Mexicans and Spaniards who were already here. One of the tribes we're getting more and more flack about is the Navajos."

"The Navajos?" Kit exclaimed. "I've lived with them, eaten with Chief Manuelito and his family, listened to the prayers of Hataalii, Notah Begay, and can number several friends among them. They're mostly farmers and sheepherders, not warriors."

Carleton replied, "I understand you've been involved with them to some degree but apparently, the Mexicans and inhabitants of the Arizona and New Mexico territories don't feel the way you do. We've had numerous complaints that the Navajos have been raiding farther south, stealing cattle and horses, stopping new homesteads from getting started, and keeping out new mining. Reports have come in that this area appears to be rich in copper and silver ore."

"So," Kit replied, "the Navajo is standing in the way of American enterprise and progress?"

"Yes, to be blunt. But I have another idea. If we can convert them to Christianity and teach them to become farmers, eventually they will see the benefits of conforming to our ways. I've been ordered to round up all Navajos from the four corners area of Utah, Colorado, Arizona, and New Mexico down to

Canyon de Chelley and drive them south to Fort Sumner on the Pecos River to a place called the Bosque Redondo."

"Drive them south, sir? You mean like herding cattle, and to Fort Sumner of all places! It's in the middle of nowhere! There's nothing down there but barren flats, no good grazing for their livestock, no firewood for fuel, no good water. Are we punishing them or trying to destroy them?" Kit couldn't help asking.

The general had the grace to look embarrassed, but only for a moment, as he admitted, "Probably a little of both, but only in order to break their spirit, you understand?"

"Well, it goes both ways, General," Kit replied. "For years the Mexicans and Spaniards and their priests have been kidnapping Navajo children and making slaves of them, forcing them to work at their missions, and even using the girls as concubines. So it seems only natural to me that the Navajos would retaliate with their own raids, taking food and livestock in return."

"I'm aware of those stories, too, Kit, but the Navajos can be furious fighters. There are reports that they have made frequent attacks on the people braving the Santa Fe Trail, the route that now connects Missouri to New Mexico. Also, with the army's new forts being built out here, our horses are in competition for what good grazing land is available. Horses and cattle are more valuable to us than sheep or goats."

Stunned, Carson said, "So, in other words, the

Navajo must go somewhere else. How is this to be accomplished, may I ask? Are we mounting a campaign against them?"

"That," answered General Carleton, "is exactly what we are going to do. I am hereby giving you full authority to do whatever it takes to head them south. I also offer you a new commission with the rank of colonel, if you will take on the responsibility. I'll see you have whatever men and arms you need."

"You know they don't exactly come out and fight in the open just because we're in the field," Kit informed him. "They specialize in hit and run warfare, like the Apaches, retreating into their canyons and their rugged terrain, like their cliff dwellings in Canyon de Chelley."

"Yes, but you're the most familiar with this area and their ways. You know where they hide. You will be my supreme commander in the field. I'll see that you have carte blanche to do whatever you need to do."

Carson knew he would be a fool to turn down such an assignment. He knew, also, he had just been given his marching orders; and although he had grave misgivings about the policy and the outcome, he could not disobey a direct order, even though the general had said it would be his decision. Maybe because he did know the chief of the Navajos, he could soften the blow and ease the way for them somehow. If not, he dreaded the outcome.

He stood and saluted and said, "I'll draw up a plan and make a list of supplies, men, and material I'll need and be ready to leave by the end of the week."

"Fine. I knew I could count on you," the general answered, looking relieved for he had not been sure that Carson *would* agree.

Leaning down to write something on a pad, he tore it off and handed it to Kit.

"Here is a script for anything you need from the army store. If there is something unusual or different that you need, come and see me for further authorization."

Kit saluted once more. Then taking the paper with him, he headed for the officer's mess hall where he could sit and make a plan of attack. He knew this was not going to be a walk through the park. General Carleton was right about one thing. When aroused, the Navajos were fierce fighters. He knew they were not going to take this easily or well. He worried how Chief Manuelito and Hataalii Notah would view his friendship with them after this.

Well, most likely it would end it, but it could not be helped. Orders were orders, and if he wanted to leave this man's army in good standing, he had no real choice but to obey.

Chapter Seven

Dinétah, Land of the People
New Mexico Territory
Summer 1862

In the Navajo way, all things are based on the belief that the physical and spiritual world blend together, and everything on earth is alive and sacred. The Navajo creed is that they Walk in Beauty. The Creator, with the help of the holy people, had created the natural world. They created humans, birds, and animals. All of the natural world was put in Hozho creating balance and harmony. And, Notah, the Hataalii, had just felt that Hozho shift.

He sat as still as stone and waited. He knew in that split second, an opening had happened in the underworld and something evil had slipped through before it closed again. But what, and where, he did not know. All his senses strummed to life, telling him something malevolent was let loose among the *Diné* and something bad was about to happen.

To whom, he wondered.

Something had definitely changed in the last few minutes. Nothing overt, just a shift in the *harmony* of things. Like something slipped a little out of sync. Not something you could see with your eye but rather feel or sense, making the hairs on your arms stand up.

Whatever it was, it had been felt all over Dinétah for a split second. Those who were religious crossed themselves; others said a quick prayer to whatever god they believed in; others looked around fearfully to see where the danger was coming from, but all felt *it* was dangerous.

Then, in a few minutes when nothing untoward happened, everyone breathed a sigh of relief and went back to what they were doing.

At the ranchette that doubled as a trading post on the edge of Dinétah, JoAnna and her father ceased their activity.

JoAnna looked at her father and said, "What was that?"

"I'm not sure," John answered, "but I felt it in my spirit, like a sick foreboding of something bad. But, apparently, it's gone now. Maybe it was a rockslide somewhere or a small earthquake that shook everything for a minute. After all, this area has seen volcanic activity in the distant past; maybe some underground eruptions still take place from time to time."

"Yes, I know, but that wouldn't explain the

sense of foreboding that I felt along with it,"
JoAnna answered.

"Who knows? If it was some natural catastrophe,
word will get around soon enough by the Navajo
telegraph. Nothing seems to happen in Dinétah
that doesn't reach from one end of their land to the
other in a few days time. Never have figured out just
how they spread the word, but spread it they do."

"You're right, Father, if something has happened, we'll hear of it sooner or later."

She returned to sorting through the pitiful few
new supplies that had arrived by freight wagon the
evening before. No one seemed to think it necessary to haul foodstuffs or necessities so far out of
Santa Fe, and especially if it was to benefit the
Navajo Indians. Even though the Diné were trying
to live in peace with the bilagaanas who were sneaking onto their land searching for gold or silver, or
to build homesteads in a pleasant canyon valley,
conflicts happened and people were still being
killed on both sides. It was not as peaceful a place
as her father had thought it would be.

They'd been here going on two years now in
this lonesome place. JoAnna, now twenty-three
years-old, still a lovely petite, five foot two, blue-
eyed young lady could not let her father leave
without her.

She remembered her shock when her father had
first broached the subject. Her round, expressive
eyes, had clouded up as she tried to control a feeling of dread.

"You mean leave Virginia, and Momma's grave behind? Leave Grandma and Grandpa here alone?"

He told her he'd been praying about it and seeking an answer from the Lord for some time, and it just felt *right*. For one brief moment she'd doubted whether her father had heard from the Lord at all. Then she felt guilty for having such a thought. She trusted her father's judgment. And he'd never been wrong yet.

So they left. And it had been two of the hardest, yet most rewarding, and fulfilling years of her life. She thought it was the same for her father.

He had taken to this uncompromising land in a way he had not cared for their place in Virginia, being too wrapped up in being a doctor and a minister. Here, he had no real patients to speak of; just JoAnna and some of the Navajos who would let him set a broken bone, or sew a cut. He'd tried to convert Notah to Christianity, but he could tell that was not going to happen, so he had contented himself with learning about his Navajo ways and trying to find the similarities in their beliefs and dwell on them.

And to be honest, there was much in their beliefs to recommend them. There was virtually no thieving, cursing, wanton murders, or telling lies among them. Once a Navajo gave his word, it was his bond. Honesty and bravery were revered among the People. If there was adultery among them, it was rare. A woman caught in the act, suffered great shame by the cutting off of the tip of her nose.

John had admitted to her more than once, that

the white man could learn a lot from the Navajos. In the past two years they had worked together in harmony, learning new ways of survival and living from the Navajos, as well as improving some of their ways, too.

So, here they were, trying to operate a trading post, more or less, on the outskirts of Navajoland, making friends when allowed by the Diné, and trying to be the best example of what Christian white people should be. As her father had often said, "The Bible says nothing about the pigmentation of a person's skin as far as salvation and believing in God is concerned."

You couldn't say business was booming, but travelers, prospectors, miners, trappers, the Navajo, and even outlaws came through to buy a few items. They would all sit and chaw awhile so that eventually his reputation spread for being an honest man and for his daughter's good cup of coffee.

John made the fifty-mile trip into Santa Fe every other month to the general store there to stock up on supplies. JoAnna had met only one young woman her age and that was the hardware store's daughter. Since they only went into town every eight weeks, it was hard to cultivae a friendship from so far away.

Once in a great while someone would drive out from the town with something John special ordered, but not often. However, he was becoming known in the town and people would send others by if they knew they were headed into Navajo territory. He hoped, in time, as more Americans came west, he would have gotten in on the ground floor of

America's westward expansion thereby securing an edge in the competition by being here first.

JoAnna walked over to the door and looked out. Running her eyes over the panorama of scrub brush and red earth before her, she was caught up in the view of the wide-open country. She was awed at times by the magnificence of the scene and the majestic red rock formations that dotted the landscape, formed in a time long forgotten.

And, as for forming any real friendships with the Navajo, except for Notah, his children and Old Woman, she could only count a dozen people who had come by regularly to visit. And, she wasn't sure they were truly friendly or not.

The visits when Notah did bring his children by were the bright spots in her day. He never mentioned his dead wife when he came to visit. JoAnna had wondered about that until one day Old Woman said to JoAnna, "Bad Hozho . . . wife dead. No talk about it."

JoAnna had finally figured out who Old Woman was in relation to the twins and Notah. She'd learned that the Navajo tribe was a matriarchal society. The women carried much sway in their culture and in the running of daily life, so when the older woman saw there was no woman to care for the holy man and his children, she assumed the responsibility.

Old Woman was as close to a woman friend as JoAnna could claim. She was a healer in her own right as well, and after recognizing JoAnna's skill in healing and her desire to learn more ways to heal, she began to share her knowledge about plants and cures with her.

On the plateau, Notah was thinking he'd go talk to John Lund about what had just happened, this shift in Hozho. When they had first met, something about the white man had reminded Notah of himself, and he wondered if this bilagaana might be a holy man, too. He was not aggressive and abrupt as most white men were; he did not disrupt the harmony around him.

Notah could not understand how the white man could live in such chaos, as they seemed to generate. The Navajos view of life was that everything they did, and everything that happened to them, related to the world around them. The whites never seemed content with what they had. Notah could not understand how the white man could go into another's land and then say they had discovered it, and because they had, it was now theirs to claim as their own.

His land and his people had not needed to be discovered. They were already here, and had been as far back as even the Old Ones could remember.

Over time though, and with sporadic visits to the Lund ranch, John and Notah were beginning to understand each other better every day. He'd seen the advantage of having the children learn the white man's tongue as well. Who knew what the future held for his people, and knowing English and what the white words *really* meant could not hurt.

He reflected on his vow to remain celibate and always be on call for the holy people to use him; however after meeting JoAnna Lund, he was having a hard time keeping his mind off her. He had never contemplated being tempted by desire for a bila-gaana woman, and it disturbed him that he had such ideas about JoAnna. It was creating a shift in *his* Hozho.

All that aside, and with what had just happened in the atmosphere around him, he decided to visit John and see if he had felt it, too. They had been sharing their beliefs in their gods, and he knew John to be a sincere believer in his Jesus and that he listened to Him.

Notah wondered much about the white man's God, Jesus. He had known some Black Robes from Mexico who carried this Jesus on a wooden cross. But the Black Robes didn't practice the love that John said his Jesus had come to show. They captured the Navajos and forced them into slavery and made them work on their mission houses and in their gardens. They forced the Navajo young women to lie with them, saying they were marrying them to Christ. However, this didn't fit with Lund's telling of Jesus Christ. John had said that his Jesus was not on that cross anymore, but was seated in the heavens with the Father, Creator God.

It was puzzling to Notah, but he had to admit there must be something different about the white man's god that gave them the confidence and power to take away other people's lands without any thought for the people they were displacing. It was one reason he wanted to learn more about this Jesus. Not that he would ever give up the Navajo Way or the Blessing Way, but it was never good to remain ignorant of things that should be learned and that might be of help to one in the future.

So thinking, he rode down the trail that led to John Lund's homestead.

Chapter Eight

Suddenly JoAnna felt a tingling in her spine and knew Notah was near. She hadn't figured out yet why she was so attuned to his presence, but she always *felt* him when he neared their house.

He was still very much an enigma to her . . . quiet, stoic, always polite, but reserved in her presence. And yet, she knew his eyes followed her movements, which became awkward after a while, and she hated herself for it. She didn't want to appear clumsy in front of him, but then, she didn't really know *what* she wanted to feel in front of him, either.

Notah was different from any other man she had ever met. Not only in his appearance, which was definitely Indian, but also in his commanding presence and the self-confidence he exuded that none of the men back home had exhibited.

He was not as tall as her six-foot-two father, but

closer to five-foot-eleven probably. His black hair was cut off just below his ears and worn all one length, held back from his forehead by a cloth band. His cheekbones were sculpted and his onyx eyes tilted slightly at the corners. He was solidly built with muscles that rippled whenever he moved. His lips always disturbed her, so firm and fully defined. She'd only seen him smile once, but it had been a beautiful sight and changed his whole countenance. It had taken her breath away and caused warmth to spread throughout her insides.

JoAnna always tried to behave circumspectly when he was visiting with her father. She never entered into a conversation unless asked to join them, which didn't happen very often, or she'd come into her father's study to bring them refreshments, again, only as requested. But she was always . . . always aware of him as she was now, no matter where he was in their compound.

She knew if she turned around she would find him standing in the doorway with his unreadable eyes on her. Most of the time they were cold and flat, but every now and then they would heat up and flare with something she couldn't define, but it always scared and thrilled her at the same time.

Notah coughed to let her know he was there. A Navajo never called out someone's name to draw their attention, but rather waited to be asked to enter another's dwelling. A polite cough would announce their presence and it was up to the homeowner to invite them in or not.

Understanding this was their way, JoAnna turned and put on her most brilliant smile.

"Why, hello, Notah. What a surprise to see you today. If you are looking for Father, he is in the barn checking over his favorite horse that came up lame this morning."

She moved cautiously closer to him, not wanting to scare him off, yet knowing he had not come to talk to her.

"*Ho-ta-hey,* JoAnna. Yes, I have come to see your father."

He hesitated a moment longer, loath to end their conversation, but not knowing what else to say. Then he thought to ask her about the shifting.

"May I ask you a question, JoAnna?"

"Of course, Notah. What is it?"

"A little while ago, did your father mention anything happening in the area? Did you or he feel anything strange going on?"

He did not know why he asked her that? She was a woman and what would she know about the spirit world. Although, he was aware that she shared her father's beliefs.

"Odd that you should mention it, Notah," she answered, but then thought, well . . . maybe not so odd as he was the wise man of his clan.

"Both Father and I felt something happen. We commented on it to each another. Father thought maybe a small earthquake had happened that rocked the ground for a moment. But it was gone so fast, we weren't really sure. It is interesting, though, because Father made the comment that if something had happened, the Diné would be the first to know and it would spread all over the land in a heartbeat."

Sometimes her speech confused him and this was one of those times, *"spread over the land in a heart-beat"* did not make sense, but that they had felt it did. So, it was not just isolated to where he had been at the time. He hadn't been sure.

"I will go talk to your father now about this, then. I do not think the earth moved as you think, but there was definitely a shifting going on." And with that puzzling remark he was gone in search of John.

She wanted desperately to follow him and hear what they discussed, but thought it prudent not to. Her father would be sure to discuss it with her when he came in and she would just have to wait for him to broach the subject.

Standing in the doorway, she watched Notah make his way in that silent stride of his to the barn. He was almost graceful in his walk, if that was a term you could use for a man. Well, maybe, smooth like the walk of a panther, would be more appropriate. Anyway, it caused her to watch him and his nice long legs until he entered the barn.

Oh my, JoAnna, where are your shameful thoughts taking you these days? What would her mother say if she could divulge these fanciful feelings she had for Notah to her?

Thinking of her mother always brought a lump to her throat and tears to her eyes. There were so many things she hadn't gotten to discuss with her mother, and now she never would have the chance to share the things in her heart.

The day her mother was shot would live forever in her memory. JoAnna had just stepped down off the bottom step of the church when their neighbor had come riding up, shouting at John Lund, and asking how he would like to lose his daughter as he had lost his son. Her mother had screamed and jumped in front of JoAnna knowing that she could not move fast enough to get out of the way, before JoAnna could understand what was happening. The bullet had slammed into her mother's chest. Rebecca had fallen backwards into JoAnna, taking them both to the ground. JoAnna remembered the horror of it seeing again her father bending over Rebecca, trying to stem the flow of blood. She had died within minutes of being shot.

Her father had almost gone berserk. His grief had taken a terrible toll on both of them. He could not face the congregation or his patients anymore. It had changed her father forever. He did not care what the people thought of him after that, his only desire was to leave Virginia far, far behind him. JoAnna had to admire him though, in all that, he had not blamed or questioned God, but it had definitely made him more somber.

She could not truthfully say she was totally happy here, or that she did not miss her friends and grandparents, but since meeting Notah and his sweet children, things had taken on a different outlook. Not that she saw him as husband material, of course not. But she was learning about a different culture and way of life and she was finding it fascinating, if not comforting.

JoAnna turned back into the house. Her father and Notah might come back to the house for a cup of coffee so she would start a fresh pot . . . just in case. It was one of the things Notah did seem to enjoy while visiting.

Out in the barn, Notah was questioning John about the incident.

"Did you sense anything different about it as it happened?" he asked.

"Now that you mention it, Notah, both JoAnna and I felt some trepidation or foreboding of ill will along with it. I thought it might have been an earth tremor, but it was there and gone before I registered just what it was."

This was confirmation to Notah that something bad had been loosed in Dinétah. But what could it be? It was like a premonition of a black cloud hovering over the land, waiting to be unleashed, but for what reason, and by whom? Was a war brewing? Were their enemies, the Piute, Apaches, or Comanche going to raid their lands to steal women and children and livestock? His sense of apprehension increased.

"I am glad we talked, John, but now I must get back to my people. I need to see what others might be thinking or what they saw or felt. I sense your spiritual intuitiveness and feel that if you felt it too, then I was not wrong to believe it is strong and has a bad intent."

"Won't you come into the house for a cup of

coffee before you go, Notah? By the way, did you ask JoAnna about the incident? She felt it, too."

"Yes, I did ask her before I came looking for you. She did say she had felt it, but I cannot stay any longer. If you could give me some coffee to take with me, I would be most grateful. I fear I have become accustomed to this bilagaana's drink."

Well, there is *one* thing good about us then, huh?" John said laughingly.

"*Aoo'*, yes," Notah agreed.

At the house, JoAnna was sorry to hear that Notah would not stay a little longer and share a meal with them. At her father's request, she put the coffee in a mason jar and wrapped it in a towel and gave it to Notah to take with him.

As he took it from her, their fingers brushed against one another. Immediately, little hot waves raced up her arm and she felt that strange warmth in her stomach again. Her eyes flew up to his and caught the flare of heat in them that she had glimpsed a few times before.

At her touch, Notah's heart sped up and heat raced to another part of his body. However, Notah swiftly controlled his features and the heat died as quickly as it came.

JoAnna thought that maybe she just imagined that he felt what she felt. And what had she felt? This was driving her crazy. Who could she ask about it? He caused such new feelings in her. Could she be falling in love with this Navajo or was it just the isolation of this place that was causing her to see him differently.

She'd heard enough talk to know that no decent white woman had any relations with an Indian, and she knew of no one who had ever married one. But more and more her thoughts had been turning in that direction. Mortified at the path her thoughts had taken, but helpless to stop them, she turned away from Notah and murmured a quick "Good-bye and God speed."

Chapter Nine

Navajoland
Early Fall 1862

Yes, the Hozho had shifted, and the evil it fore-shadowed was *war* coming to Dinétah.

After meeting with General Carleton back in the Spring, in two weeks Kit Carson was in the field. Start-ing at the northwest corner of the New Mexico terri-tory, he worked his way south. He tried to negotiate with the different clans, and to help them realize that to fight back would be futile. Carson planned to visit Chief Manuelito early on, as he knew the chief car-ried much influence among the other clans. He hoped to ask him to cooperate in helping him talk to the others; however, he did not expect a favorable outcome.

As the opposition increased as they headed south, Kit began to use what he called the "scorched earth policy." For the next six months, he and his men destroyed Diné fields, cut down their orchards, burned their hogans, and confiscated their live-stock. He hated it but he knew of no other way to earn their submission or to defeat them.

When he came to the area of the Turtle Clan, Chief Manuelito's camp, Kit's soldiers surrounded the camp. Colonel Carson held up a white flag and asked for permission to come in and parlay with the chief, instead of burning them out right away.

At first, the People could not understand what was happening. The chief had, of course, heard of the depredations being fostered on his people, and he was already wondering what kind of terms he could ask for. Since he had entertained Kit Carson in his home many times, he agreed to talk with the colonel.

Kit followed Manuelito and Notah to the largest hogan in the camp, knowing it to be the chief's.

As all of their dwellings did, this one faced east to greet the rising sun each morning. The floor was packed earth, covered with the beautiful woven blankets the Diné were noted for. A fire burned in the center of the room. The men circled to the right going clockwise around the fire, as was the custom; women sat on the left. However, there would be no women in on this meeting. They would come in only to serve food or drink. Several of the other sub-chiefs and elders had gathered with the chief and the holy man.

Kit waited patiently for Chief Manuelito to open the meeting. All Indians followed the custom of a time of silence before opening a conversation. It was considered extremely rude and bad manners to rush into a subject before opening remarks were made by the chief, and a pipe was smoked if the occasion called for it.

Finally, the chief said, "I see my friend in front of me, but I do not know whether he comes as my friend . . . or my enemy. I have heard the winds of war as you have made your way here. I fear I am not going to like what you have to say."

The others grunted in agreement, but no one else spoke.

The chief continued. "We have never harmed you, friend Carson, have we? You have had the freedom to come and go at all times. What have the Diné done to warrant this invasion of our homeland? I do not understand this action by my friend and your soldier-coats."

Kit knew he was on the spot and it was marked with a big "X." How was he to answer? He might not get out of here alive today when he told the chief what he wanted. Chagrined and feeling rotten, Kit took a deep breath, and answered. "I do come as a friend but if our differences cannot be resolved between us so that we can walk in *harmony,* then I will become your enemy as well. This is not my doing, nor is it anything personal between us; these are the orders of my commander-in-chief, the great White Father in the east. He has decreed that the Navajo people will be put on a reservation at Bosque Redondo. I have my orders and I cannot disobey them."

"If what I have heard of your treatment of my people so far is true, then it would seem we are already on the doorstep of *enemy,*" the chief answered. "Again, I ask, what have we done to deserve this?"

Kit flushed red, but could not appear weak in front of these men. He had to take the upper hand and yet, in his bones, he knew the outcome was not going to be good.

"True, your particular clan is not at war with anyone, but it has not been so on other parts of Diné-tah. Several bands have been raiding Mexican and white rancheros, stealing livestock and even killing the owners in some incidences. They have interfered with the copper mining being done by the Americans as well. And yes, I have met with some resistance as I made my way here, but I am hoping you will not resist me or what I have to say."

Alarm and concern showed on the old chief's lined face.

"Speak, then. I will listen. But I still say, what has that to do with us? If you bring these bad Diné to me, I will see that our Navajo laws punish them. There is no need to move a whole tribe of people for the misdeeds of a few." Manuelito tried to reason once more.

Again, Carson had the grace to look embarrassed. He felt like he was caught in a box canyon with no way out. He knew that the Americans and Mexicans were not entirely innocent in their dealings with the Indians, either. Atrocities were committed on both sides. But now enough of an uproar had been raised that nothing would suffice but to put the Navajos on a reservation so the Americans could move in and take the choice pieces of Navajo land for themselves.

Plus, the United States government wanted the mineral rights to the land as well. It was a no-win situation for the Diné no matter what he said to appease them.

Kit shifted his body as he sat on the floor. He leaned forward trying to show earnest empathy to the chief and those seated around him.

"I don't presume to understand all the reasons of those in charge above me. I am a soldier who must obey the orders given to him. And those orders are to round up your people and to march them south to Fort Sumner. It is the wish of the great White Father in Washington, that the Navajos stop their raiding of Mexican, Spanish, and white settlements now, and come together in one place where the United States Army can take care of you. You will be given food and shelter and taught new skills."

Indignation rose in the chief.

"We have no need for anyone to take care of us. We provide for ourselves, and our loved ones, sufficiently. We will not become wards of the white man's army. Why should we?" he asked furiously.

"Because the United States has bought up all the land west of the great Mississippi River and plans to settle it. Your people will have to adapt or be moved out of the way of this expansion."

"How can you own pieces of Mother Earth?" Manuelito asked incredulously. "The land was given to all peoples to live on and take from her what we need. We are taught to respect all living things, as we are all connected. How can you put a fence around a certain part and say it is yours?"

Kit knew the thought of private ownership of land was a foreign concept to the Indian. The various tribes had their territorial areas, of course, but no one claimed to own it.

He could see this was not going well. How did you explain the white man to the Navajo, who had a totally different concept of life and the things that were important in that life?

"I cannot answer that to your satisfaction, Manuelito, but you have a choice to make here and now. You can order your people to gather peaceably, or we can fight it out, but you will go one way or another, and you *will* go today."

Kit hardened his heart against the shock and disbelief that registered on the chief's face.

Manuelito sat in stunned silence for several minutes. Never had he heard such a harsh tone from his friend Carson. The chief glanced at his holy man, Notah, the Spirit Talker, and asked him with his eyes what he thought. He saw that he was in shock as well.

Notah knew his chief was looking to him for some kind of encouragement or explanation, but he had none. His main thought was that surely this land was big enough that the two races could manage to stay away from one another and live in harmony together. Colonel Carson must realize that the chief could not control all his people, all the time, but certainly something could be done to stop the raiding on Americans. At the very least, the chief could send out a call to his people to come in and talk to him and obey his orders not to raid.

The holy man took a moment to commune with the gods, to hear from them before he answered his chief. He withdrew inside himself, trying to find his balance and his Hozho.

The others sat in respectful silence waiting to see what more would be said. There was some shifting in their places, a cough or two here and there, but for the most part everyone stayed seated and still.

Kit had seen the exchange between the chief and his Hataalii and also waited in respectful silence to see what he might say and what would be done next.

Ten minutes passed, but nothing came to Notah. Nothing happened in the atmosphere around him, no sign that he was being heard by the spirits occurred. He opened his eyes and looked at the chief, and with a sorry shake of his head, indicated he had nothing to offer.

Manuelito's shoulders slumped in resignation and defeat. He could not fight the soldiers and see his people killed in cold blood, the old ones and children left homeless without someone to see to their needs. He thought that maybe if they went peaceably now, he could later reason with the white soldier chief in charge at the fort. Possibly he could explain his side, and maybe they could resolve any conflict, and hopefully the general would let his people return to Dinétah.

Finally, he looked over at Kit and answered the colonel.

"So be it. We will not fight you, but will go peaceably, as you have asked. Will you give us time to gather up a few things to take with us? It is a long trip and we have to think of the aged ones and the children."

Carson did not have the heart to say "no" to the chief's request, although the order was to destroy and burn everything left behind so they could not return.

"You can take only what you can carry. I have no wagons to transport goods for you," Kit replied. He realized how harsh and mean-spirited he sounded, but orders were orders.

He stood up and looking down at Manuelito, said, "You have one hour of the sun's passing to prepare your people to march."

With that said, he left the chief's hogan to round up his men. He gave the order that after the Navajos had gathered what they could carry, what was left behind was to be destroyed, but they were to take the livestock to feed the army on the way.

Chapter Ten

Chief Manuelito's Campground

After the colonel left, several elders who had sat in on the meeting, protested vehemently to their chief. Many said they would not go; they would fight to the death to keep their homes and families in place. Even Notah was not for the removal. The heated exchanges went on for several minutes before Manuelito stood and faced them down.

"No! Innocent women and children will be hurt, or worse, if we fight now. We will do as Carson says and maybe, some day, somewhere along the way, we will come up with a plan to come back to Dinétah. Now, go and make ready to leave. Already we have less time by our arguing."

Realizing they could not change the chief's mind and that time was rapidly slipping away, they hastened to obey and left the hogan.

As Notah prepared to leave, Manuelito laid a restraining hand on his arm and asked, "You received no message from the holy ones—no sign that this was coming. You had no prior warning for our people?"

Mortified, Notah replied, "No, my chief. The gods have shown me nothing. I am sorry I have no words for you."

The only forewarning he may have had was when he'd felt that shift in the balance of things the day he'd gone to see JoAnna and John Lund. Then stepping outside the door, he said, "Forgive me, but I must go and gather up my children and Old Woman."

The chief nodded. "Yes, go. Prepare yourself. I guess if the holy ones had told us this was coming, perhaps we would have fought, and maybe won. But who knows for sure."

Turning back into his own hogan, he said to his wife who had come inside, "You heard?"

"Yes, my husband. How much, and what do you want me to pack?"

She began gathering up their goods, as Manuelito gave her instruction.

Notah left to find his children. He called on Old Woman to help pack for the twins as he began to pack his medicine bundle and what herbs and unguents he thought might be needed on the trail.

His heart felt like a stone inside his chest. He thought of John Lund and JoAnna. An ache started in that area of his chest that he had once vowed would never feel love again. Notah realized he might never see JoAnna after today. There was no telling how long this journey would take, or if they would ever really come back. As much as he wanted to deny any feelings for the gentle white woman, he knew in his soul JoAnna had become more important in his life than he wanted to admit.

Putting his feelings aside, he went to gather his horse and pack it for the trip. He saw the soldiers rounding up most of the herd and shooing them away, keeping some of the best mounts for the army. Notah realized not everyone would have a horse to ride on this trip. Many would be walking. But surely, Kit Carson would not make the little ones and the aged walk. Would he?

Within the hour, Colonel Carson formed the Navajos into a double line with his men in front, beside, and behind them. Hating to do it as they left, he gave the order to torch the hogans, destroy their crops, and herd the animals in with the Navajos.

When the Diné saw what they were doing, a wail of protest rose from among them.

They watched in horror as their homes and livelihood vanished in the flames. The people raised dumbfound eyes to their leader, but he had no words of comfort or reasons to offer them.

The soldiers started prodding the Navajos to get moving. When some lagged behind or tried to look back, they were hit with a riding crop or pushed back in line. It was the beginning of a long, exacting, and terrifying walk.

Colonel Carson told his captain that he was

going to take a squad of men and ride on to the next village.

"You will be in charge of this group to see that they make it to our meeting place in a month around Canyon de Chelley."

Captain Bryce Cahill saluted and said, "Don't you worry, sir. I will get them there." *One way or another* was his thinking, but he didn't express that to the colonel. "We will meet you as requested."

Nodding and returning the salute, Carson rode off to gather the men he wanted to take with him. He had some misgivings about Cahill. At times he seemed to harbor a deep resentment toward the Indians and he could be combative with his men, but for the most part he was a good soldier and did as he was told. Carson silently hoped the Navajo would not give the captain any excuse to use force, for he felt Cahill would not hesitate to do so, and might even relish using it as well.

As Captain Cahill led his soldiers and the Navajos into the Lund's Trading Post yard, John Lund stepped out to see what was going on. He watched in shock as the army surrounded the group of Navajos as they streamed into his yard.

When the captain rode over to John, he introduced himself saying, "I'm John Lund, proprietor of this trading post. What's going on here, Captain? Has there been some trouble in the chief's village?"

Not bothering to dismount, the captain leaned down and said, "Colonel Kit Carson has orders from General James Carleton to move all Navajos south to Fort Sumner."

Stunned, John asked, "What on earth for? I've run this trading post for several years now. I've never had a minute's trouble from them. They come in and trade with me all the time."

"Not that's it any of your business, trader, but too much thievin' and killin' is being done by the Navajos. They've been raidin' ranches and stopping the copper and silver mines from operating. They've halted our people from homesteading and fight them off the good pieces of land."

"Well, of course they're going to fight to keep what is theirs," John answered. "But this clan has not been involved in any of that. They are industrious farmers and sheepherders. They weave beautiful blankets and I trade for them with the things they cannot make themselves. We get along well and have never had any trouble. Where is this Colonel Carson? I would like to speak with him myself?"

The captain didn't like the insistence of John Lund that the Navajos were no trouble.

"Well, you can't talk to him. He's gone on to the next encampment of Navajos to start them marching."

Just then, JoAnna came out to see the Navajos milling around and the soldiers with guns at the ready, surrounding them.

"What in heaven's name is going on here, Father?"

At the sound of her sweet, inquiring voice the captain's head swiveled around to stare at JoAnna. He felt an immediate tightening in his groin for the tiny,

but fully developed woman. Even in her homemade
cotton blouse, her full breasts were evident, and the
full skirt did nothing to hide a tiny waist and nicely
rounded hips. Something about her screamed innocence and purity. It sparked an immediate unholy,
consuming lust in the captain. What he wouldn't
give to be the one to break her in.

He moved his horse over to her and said, "Ma'am,
I'm Captain Bryce Cahill at your service. I'm with
the U.S. Cavalry as you can see, under the command
of Colonel Christopher Carson. We've been ordered
to take these Indians south to Fort Sumner to be put
on the Bosque Redondo reservation there."

JoAnna had to shield her eyes to look up at
Cahill. What she saw alarmed her. His leering look
sent a shiver of fear down her spine. She was more
afraid of this man than she had ever been of any
Navajo. She quickly looked away.

At that moment, the rest of the Navajos came
into view. Some leading horses carrying small children and what goods they had been allowed to take
with them. Pitifully little, from what she could see.
JoAnna noticed that some of the men's hands were
bound. None had any weapons on them and none
of this made any sense to her.

Turning to ask her father, she spied Notah with
a pack on his back with his hands tied in front of
him. A rope was even strung between his ankles,
giving him just enough length to walk but not run.
She didn't see the children and Old Woman and it
worried her even more.

JoAnna immediately ran over to him.

Notah saw her coming and tried to warn her away with a look, but she didn't heed him.

"Why have they done this to you?" she asked, noticing the bruise and raised welt on the side of his face—the size only a fist or rifle butt could make.

"Move away, JoAnna . . . please, for your own sake," Notah told her.

When the captain observed her concern for the holy man, he saw red. Riding over to them, he reached down and jerked JoAnna away from Notah.

"Get away from that filthy redskin, woman. You can't trust him. He's already caused trouble, that's why he's bound hand and foot."

When the captain grabbed JoAnna, something wild rose up in Notah and he finally acknowledged how he felt about her.

Mine! His heart and mind screamed.

She was his!

No one else had the right to touch her.

It took all of Notah's spiritual and warrior training not to reach up and drag the white dog off his horse and make him release her arm. But he knew it would only mean more trouble and hardship for his people should he interfere, although it galled him not to. This captain, he was learning, had a hatred for the Indian that was palpable. Any little indiscretion or misstep on the part of the Diné was quickly reprimanded or rewarded with the lash of his riding crop. He watched as JoAnna jerked out of the captain's hand.

Notah was beside himself. He pleaded with his eyes for John Lund to take control of JoAnna. He felt her anguish and concern wash over him and he feared it, even as he welcomed it.

John Lund had seen the exchange, as well as the plea in Notah's eyes, and walked into the fray.

"Come away now, JoAnna," John Lund said.

Then turning to the captain, he reiterated again his earlier comments.

"Nothing gives you the right to put your hands on my daughter, Captain. Your orders do not apply to us. Again, I say, we've never had any trouble with this band, and I still wish to speak to the colonel about this.

"And, furthermore, what has this man done to warrant tying him up? This is their holy man. A more peaceful man does not exist. You have no right to do this to him!" John exclaimed.

At the defense of the Navajo by John Lund and the obvious interest by the daughter in the man, the captain's anger increased.

Snarling his answer, he said, "I have every right, and my orders say to use whatever means I need to, to get them to Bosque Redondo."

"But they have done nothing to cause this kind of treatment," JoAnna protested, which only angered the captain even more.

By now everyone was within the post compound and were straining to hear what was going on in front of them. All were aware of the captain's dislike for them and feared what the outcome of this confrontation would be.

"Well, if you're so determined to see the colonel,

and you have such concern for these redskins, then you can just come along with them," answered Cahill.

Sputtering, John Lund said, "Now, see here. You cannot order us to go with you. I can't leave my trading post and the goods inside for any great length of time."

"Well, now, I just did order it . . . *sympathizing with the enemy* is what we'll call it. And don't worry about your goods, we can help you deplete your stock for now," he said chuckling.

"What do you think you're doing? We're not Navajo. You have no right to take my stuff or steal my cattle and horses. I'm a law-abiding citizen of the United States."

John drew his gun and pointed it at the captain. He was determined not to leave all that he had worked so hard to accumulate. Another soldier saw him draw and shot him in the shoulder.

JoAnna had spied Old Woman and the twins by that time and had gathered them to her side when she saw the soldier shoot her father.

"*My God, nooo!*" she screamed. It couldn't happen again. She couldn't lose another parent in the same brutal way. She ran over to him and knelt on the ground to lift his head.

"I'm okay," he told her. "It only grazed my shoulder. I'll live, JoAnna, honey. Don't fret now," he soothed, patting her and trying to calm her.

JoAnna was already tearing at her slip to make a binding. It looked like the bullet had passed through and wasn't lodged in his body.

Helping him to stand, she yelled at the men gathering in their yard.

"Murderers . . . robbers! Is this how the great United States Army conducts itself? Bullying harmless citizens."

"Listen, lady, we're just following orders. These Navajo haven't been all that peaceable lately, and since you seem to think they're so all-fired innocent and wonderful, you and your father can just go along with them and suffer their fate as well."

So saying, Cahill gave the order to torch their house and barn and take whatever they wanted from it first.

"You can't do this. I'll protest to your superiors," John exclaimed.

"We can, and we are doin' it," the captain answered.

"At least let us get some things out before you burn it," JoAnna pleaded. "You cannot be that cruel."

"All right, to show you my heart is in the right place, you may pack up what you think you'll need for yourselves and be ready to leave within the hour."

Then, turning to his second in command, he said, "Dismiss the men to grab a bite to eat and water their horses. I'm sure there's some food in the trading post that needs to be conscripted for the welfare of the army," he added, again chuckling to himself as he strolled away to take care of his own personal business.

His men hastened to obey, leaving some on duty to guard the Navajos while others watered the horses, and others ransacked the store. Since the captain had a thing for pretty little honey-blonde-haired girls, he thought that by appeasing her somewhat he might get a little reward for his benevolence, so he told the men to wait and let her go back into the house and get a few things to take with her.

John could see further protest would not get him anywhere and if he was going to salvage anything in his store for him and JoAnna, he'd better get inside and grab up what he would need.

Taking her gently by the arm, he said, "Come on, JoAnna. I don't see any way out of this for the moment. We'd better collect up what we can before the army cleans us out."

"But this is preposterous, Father. There must be something we can do."

Guiding her to the door, he replied, "Later, maybe, after I've talked with this Colonel Carson. Then I can write to our senator back in Washington and protest to Congress and to the president himself, if I have to. This whole thing is madness. I thought we had left prejudice behind us in Virginia, but apparently it knows no particular race or skin color, even out here. Now you gather some food, blankets, clothing, and whatever else you think we'll need. I'll go hitch up the wagon. I have a feeling it's going to be a long trip and you will not be able to walk it, let alone the little children."

He knew her damaged foot could not stand up to days of walking the rugged hills and valleys ahead of them.

With that, John headed to the barn.

JoAnna ran into the store, cutting around the

pillaging soldiers to get to her bedroom at the back of the building. She would not leave all her herbs and healing potions behind. They might need them on this crazy march.

The captain followed John. "What do you think you're doing?"

John answered, "I'm hitching up my wagon to carry our supplies and my daughter. She has a damaged foot and cannot walk for any great length of time on it. Surely, you cannot expect a white woman to walk all the way to Bosque Redondo. Also, I can carry some extra food and blankets on the trip for the Navajo children. I know you don't have enough food for all of them."

"As if I cared about that," Cahill answered. "They lived off the land before, let them do it now."

"You mean you have no provisions for them? How can they hunt and gather plants when you've taken away their weapons and confiscated their sheep? How do you expect them to make a trip of over four hundred miles on no food?"

"It's their problem," was his answer. "If they make it, they make it; if they don't keep up, they'll be shot."

John was horrified. He'd heard of some men who truly hated the Indians, but he had never met anyone as adamant as this captain, nor anyone so resistant to persuasion of any kind.

There was no appealing to his humanity or gentler side. John Lund felt he wouldn't have one. He felt the man was evil and knew it would do not good to cross him. He could tell the captain was just look-

ing for an excuse to do hurt, so John ignored him
and began hitching his team to their wagon.

Giving him a black-eyed glare, Captain Cahill
turned on his heel and left the barn. He headed to
the store to see how the little woman was coming
along. He thought he might have to change his tactics with her. Maybe show her his good side . . . make
her like him. He smiled a nasty smile. But no matter,
he had already determined he was going to have her,
one way or another.

Chapter Eleven

Notah saw the captain heading for the post door. His stomach clenched and he pulled against the ropes, although he knew he was helpless to interfere. He feared for JoAnna. He had seen the lust in the soldier's eyes when he spied her for the first time as she approached her father. The Apaches had a word for the "blood-lust-to-kill," *net-da-he;* and Notah felt it rise up within him like he had never felt anything before. He vowed to himself that if that man in particular, or any other man for that matter, ever laid a hand on JoAnna, he would not die an easy death. Notah would swear to his gods on it.

Oh, why hadn't she stayed away from him? Why had she come running over? He'd tried to warn her off. Yet, in his heart, he knew why.

She was falling in love with him.

He recognized all the signs, even if she did not realize it herself. Or maybe she did know it was happening, but chastised herself for falling in love with a man not of her race. After all, he was Navajo and she was a bilagaana and a love between them would be taboo in the white world.

But the signs were there. He'd have to be deaf and blind not to see how her eyes lit up at the sight of him. How her breath caught in her throat and then came out in a sigh as she breathed his name. If he was honest with himself, he knew the signs because they were the same ones he was having. He knew he was falling in love with her, as well, even though it went against his former vow to himself and his people.

He swore again, that if any harm came to her, he would kill whoever touched her, even if he died in the attempt. If he never could claim her for his own, he would make sure that she had the chance to make a free choice in picking the man she would marry.

And what a pain that caused in his heart. How, he now realized, he longed to be the one to teach her about the ways of a man with a woman. His woman.

He had to mentally and physically turn himself away from the goings on in front of him. The ability to Walk in Beauty and maintain his Hozho was leaving him by degrees. He needed to find a quiet place and center down on his teaching and seek his spirit guide. His people expected him to maintain balance for them. He had to guard himself, be strong and resolute, and plan ahead. He could not do anything foolish that would jeopardize JoAnna, or his people. They had to get to the Bosque Redondo and then, maybe, he and the chief could form a plan of escape for the Diné.

* * *

Inside the trading post, the soldiers were grabbing smoked hams, cans of coffee beans, and bags of flour, rice, guns, and ammunition.

JoAnna was appalled at their behavior. Where were the army's disciplined troops she'd heard so much about?

"You can't just take everything like this! Are you going to pay us back for what you're taking?" she asked over the clamor.

"We can, and we will," answered the captain as he came up behind her. "If you have a mind to take anything with you, you'd better hurry up and get it. We're leaving in twenty minutes."

Stunned, but spurred into action once more, JoAnna hurried to gather up flour, bacon, beans, and rice in a box for herself. She snatched the remaining blankets off the shelf, a tarpaulin to cover things, a pot to cook in, and a coffeepot. Then she headed for their living quarters once more, and rolled a frying pan, utensils, plates, and cups into her bedding. She pulled her trunk from under the bed and threw some of her and John's clothing in it. Spying her mother's silver comb and brush set and the flowered mirror, and her few remaining pieces of jewelry, she carefully placed them in the trunk under the clothes. She didn't have much left from her mother, and she wasn't about to let these thieving soldiers find what she did have, and take it.

And they called the Navajos thieves.

She also had a small pocket-size, two-shot derringer her father had allowed her to have. He was not in favor of a woman carrying a gun, but he had relented when they arrived in the west. Knowing there were snakes and animals out here that were dangerous, he'd taught her to shoot the shotgun and the derringer. She hid the small gun in her skirt pocket.

She took her father's shotgun and rifle from the gun case and put them in the bottom of the trunk, as well as bullets for each. JoAnna wasn't sure the captain would let them keep the guns if found, but maybe he would not look at her things too closely. She slammed the lid down on the trunk, locked it with a key, and put the key on a string around her neck.

Just as she finished, the captain appeared in her bedroom. He glanced over at her bed and an unholy gleam appeared in his eye. *Did he have time for a quick toss?* Guessing he did not, and it might be hard to explain her disheveled appearance afterward, he counseled himself to be patient a little longer.

Spying the trunk, he said, "You think you're going on some kind of holiday? This ain't no Sunday school picnic, lady. What all you got in there? I didn't say nothing about packing up your whole household," he added as he started toward her.

JoAnna panicked. She couldn't let him look inside, so she sat on it and looked up at him sweetly. "Nothing but clothes and linens. You can't expect me to go without a change of underthings and no nightgown to sleep in," she said demurely, batting her eyes at him even though it galled her.

She tried to appear at ease as she pretended to be a "lady" who could not do without some creature comforts along the way, no matter where they were headed.

Captain Cahill make a quick decision, smirking as he said, "Well now, little woman, I don't rightly care if you wear any underthings or not, in fact, I wish you wouldn't. Won't embarrass me none," and he laughed his sick laugh. But he decided to let her have her way, trying to score another point to show he had a better side. His next comment though belied that he did. "Where we're going the ladies I like don't wear none a'tall."

And he laughed at her shocked expression. Yes sir, she was going to be one little filly he was going to enjoy breaking in.

He turned and called a young private to come and get her trunk and load it with her other stuff on the wagon. When he saw her pick up her father's medical bag, and the box of jars with the herbs and salves in them, he asked what they were.

"My father was a preacher and a doctor in the town we lived in, in Virginia before we came out here. These are some potions that I have made to aid in healing cuts and different illnesses. I thought there may be accidents along the way and his doctoring skills and mine might be needed."

"Your skills?"

"Yes, I helped my father in his clinic, even with some of the operations. I guess you could say I am his nurse and assistant," JoAnna answered, telling this man more than she wanted to about herself and her father.

Before he could comment further, the newest

raw recruit, Private Toby Wiley entered the room. He was a big-boned, gangly boy, with a mop of red hair and freckles. It looked like he hadn't quite grown into his long arms and legs yet.

Toby smiled at JoAnna and then ducked his head in case the captain thought he was being too familiar. The captain scared him witless at times and caused him to become even clumsier than he normally was. Or he'd do some dumb thing and the captain would make an example of him, holding him up to ridicule, reprimanding him in front of the men, and even, on occasion, earning him a few slaps with the riding crop as well.

Again giving JoAnna a weak smile, he dragged her trunk outside.

JoAnna's heart turned over at the fear she saw in his eyes. What kind of monster was this captain? She had never been exposed to his ilk in her whole life. She vowed to stay close to her father at all times. The captain frightened her, too.

JoAnna called the twins and Old Woman to come with her. She told Old Woman to take the blankets. Then JoAnna put some extra shirts on Bacca, hiding a handgun and some bullets in the bulkiness of the too-big shirts. JoAnna didn't know if they would be searched, or be allowed to keep what little she had managed to salvage, but she prayed hard that God would let them keep it.

However the captain didn't make any further overtures to see what they had. He ordered the Lund wagon loaded and allowed JoAnna to put Old Woman and the twins in the back with their supplies. John had decided to walk with Notah and the Navajos for a while to see what he could learn. His arm was throbbing, but he had put some liniment on it in the barn, and rewrapped it tightly, so he felt it would be okay.

Dazed and shocked, JoAnna drove the wagon numbly, surrounded by soldiers. She glanced back to see how her father and Notah were faring; however, she could not tell as the soldiers riding behind her obscured her vision.

How was her father holding up? Was he losing much blood? She hadn't even had time to put anything on the open wound to cleanse it.

She could not believe this was happening to them. This was as bad as some of the stories they'd heard about the treatment of Southerners by the Union Army in the fighting going on in the east. How could this be? These were her countrymen. She and her father were not fugitives from justice or bad people, but apparently that meant nothing to this captain. She would just have to resign herself to going along with the Navajo for now and see what her father could do on their behalf once they reached the fort.

She said a silent prayer for all of them that they would have the strength to endure and make it to this place called *Bosque Redondo*.

Chapter Twelve

The Long Walk
Deep Winter 1862/1863

It had been a grueling three hundred miles so far. Many old people and young children had taken ill and died from dysentery, poor nutrition, two from snakebites, and others just plain exhaustion on the trail from walking so long in all kinds of weather. No shelter from the wind and rain, and even snow in the higher elevations, had been provided for them and many had developed pneumonia or lung problems, as well.

Captain Cahill had not brought enough food for all the Navajos under his control, nor did he let them hunt for food themselves. He had no qualms about letting them die along the way, either, as it meant less of the mangy dogs for him to have to worry about. Whether he would have to answer for such a number of lost lives when they reached the fort didn't even bother him. He would make up some plausible reason for their demise.

JoAnna, her father and Notah, with the help of Old Woman treated as many as they could with the pitiful few supplies they had brought with them. They were not allowed to leave the group to search for plants or bark they could use in healing the sick so they had to watch helplessly as many died in their arms. It was beginning to take a toll on JoAnna's sensibilities. She could not believe the heartlessness of Captain Cahill. She wondered if Kit Carson knew the real character of this man.

They had crisscrossed the Pecos River several times over the past week. It only added to the cold, damp camps, and illnesses. So far they had lost over one hundred men, women, and children.

Captain Cahill wasn't particularly bothered by the numbers, just less for him to have to play nurse-maid to, but as the numbers started adding up, he thought he'd better try a little harder to keep the rest alive.

Colonel Carson would meet up with them from time to time, and add more to Cahill's column of Navajos. It would not do to have him question what was happening to the Indians under his care.

On one such meeting with Kit Carson, John Lund had tried to get an opportunity to talk with him and register a complaint about his second-in-command's treatment of the Navajos, but Cahill got wind of it and blocked his attempt to see Carson.

In an effort to provide meat for the starving Navajos, and the short rations of his own men, Captain Cahill sent John Lund off with a squad of his men to hunt the countryside for any game they could bring in.

Frustrated, John vowed he would not be so vocal and let his feelings be known the next time and somehow he would sneak a meeting with Colonel Carson when next he came to the camp.

Along the way, when the army had used a local rancher's fields to camp in, Captain Cahill decided he would have to have another wagon whether he wanted to or not, for by now, he was losing too many people who could no longer walk. Approaching the rancher, he told him he was commandeering his hay wagon in the name of the U.S. Army and he could submit a bill for it at the headquarters in Santa Fe. Over the rancher's outrage and protests, Cahill seized it anyway, and let the men load the most ill into it with as many children as they could fit.

John Lund's wagon had long been depleted of the foodstuffs they'd brought along and now their wagon was filled with as many Navajos as they could carry as well. They had to exchange their beautiful horses for mules, asking the same rancher if he would care for Prince and Princess until such time as they could return for them. John even offered the use of his stallion for stud, should the rancher so desire. He was hoping it would not be for longer than a year, so the man agreed.

A week away from the ranch, on a cloudy day that threatened rain any moment, they came upon another stream to be crossed. The melting snow in the higher elevations was causing flooding in this section of the country.

When they reached the stream, they noted it was fairly wide, although not exceptionally deep. However, with the snow runoff, it was moving more swiftly than it looked underneath the surface. The Navajos picked up on this right away and worried about the crossing.

A few of the soldiers went across and waved that they'd had no trouble, so Captain Cahill motioned for John Lund to start his wagon over. Being solidly built and heavier than the other wagon, they made it across with just a few jerks and scary moments.

As the second wagon started in, a limb came racing downstream and lodged in one of the wheels, causing it to become unbalanced. It started to shift sideways, causing the horses to panic and strain in their traces because of the uneven pull. Seeing this, Captain Cahill immediately yelled for Private Toby Wiley to go to the head of the horses and calm them down, while two other men went in to try to pull the log out from the wheel.

Toby was frightened but he knew he could not afford to anger the captain any more than he always seemed to do, so he made his way into the water on the opposite side from where the branch was stuck. Before he could reach the horses and the front of the wagon, the current swirled the limb back out into the rushing water and swept it around the back end of the wagon and clipped Toby's horse in the leg as it whirled by.

The startled horse sidestepped and lost his foot-

ing on the uneven stones in the stream bed, causing
Toby to lose his seat and fall into the water.

Gasping for breath in the cold water and being
pulled under, Toby panicked. He was not a strong
swimmer, and he had no real strength in his body
from the lack of proper nourishment on this dread-
ful march.

The men gaping from the bank in horror waited
for an order from Cahill for someone to go in after
Toby, but the order was not forthcoming and no
one dared to defy him.

All except Notah. They had finally taken off his
leg chains but still kept his hands bound in front of
him. Seeing Toby's helpless struggles spurred him
into action.

No one deserved to die because of Cahill's callous-
ness. If Cahill killed him in the process of rescuing
the boy, or they both lost their lives in the water, so
be it; he could not stand by and let the boy drown.
The boy had formed an attachment to Notah and
his children, as well as Old Woman and JoAnna, and
watched out for them on the trail. He would steal
away when he could and talk to the holy man about
many things. He'd told Notah he'd never had a
father, but if he'd had one, he would have wanted
him to be just like the medicine man. High praise,
and Notah had taken on the responsibility of being
a worthy role model for the young man.

Toby valiantly tried using long, hard strokes as
the water tugged and pulled at him to drag him
under. He managed to snag an overhanging limb
and was holding on for dear life.

Notah sent a quick plea to his gods and the water people, asking for strength to help him save this young man. He ran and jumped into the water to the shock and surprise of all watching.

Notah found himself tumbling over and over but just when he thought he'd never reach Toby, he felt the brush of the boy's boot against his leg.

He acted on instinct, and with amazing superhuman strength, looped his tied hands over Toby's head and under his arms. Then, lying on his back, Notah kicked off toward the closest bank.

JoAnna and the others watched in morbid fascination at the unbelievable feat being performed in front of them.

When Notah made it to the other side, collapsing on the bank and gasping for air as he unhooked Toby from his arms, a collective sigh of relief went up from the onlookers. Then a mighty cheer and yell followed. The soldiers were jumping up and down and slapping each other on the back at the remarkable and dramatic rescue.

JoAnna's eyes teared and overflowed as conflicting emotions flooded her soul. She thanked God for sparing Toby and Notah. Her heart swelled with what she now acknowledged as love for this wonderful Navajo man.

She hugged Notah's children to her for she knew they had been as frightened as she. When they saw him crawl up on the bank, they cried and laughed together.

Old Woman visibly relaxed and in her anti-climatic

way, said, "Notah, Spirit Talker, not like mortal man, what else could you expect from him."

But JoAnna knew she had been just as scared as the rest of them.

A soldier within hearing distance of Old Woman's remark felt the medicine man was blessed by his gods as well, and his reputation increased among the troops.

At the incredible feat, Captain Cahill's blood began to boil. He had hoped to be free of the inept private and had been thinking that if the current took the redskin off, too, it wouldn't have bothered him none, either. It might also have paved the way for him to get closer to JoAnna Lund. He was not oblivious to her feelings for the Navajo holy man; and he felt he was better than any Indian any day. He felt that eventually she would come to see that, or he might just have to help her see it, he thought, chuckling to himself.

Splashing his way to the other side of the stream on his horse, Cahill called for five of his men to follow him.

JoAnna saw him coming and wanted to run to Notah's side, but her father held her back. She knew of his animosity toward Notah and feared what he would do to him because he never missed an opportunity to chastise Notah in some way if he could.

"This is army business, JoAnna," her father warned her. "You cannot interfere here." But it went against everything in him not to interfere, as well.

She strained to hear what Cahill was saying to the two nearly drowned men, but they had drifted quite a way down stream and though she could hear the sound of their voices, she could not make out any words.

If she had heard, it would only have been what she would have expected as Cahill berated poor Toby once again.

"What's the matter with you boy, that you can't carry out a simple order?"

Notwithstanding the fact that he didn't do anything to rescue the boy.

Then, turning to Notah in a scathing voice, he said, "Trying to be a hero now, are we? Trying to make me look bad in front of my men, were you?" He lashed out with his quirt at Notah, who ducked away.

"I do not have to *try* to make you look bad," Notah boldly answered him.

Cahill's eyes filled with fury and he drove his horse into Notah, making him fall backwards into the water. Then he sat on his horse at the water's edge just daring Notah to come out again.

JoAnna could not bear Cahill's injustice any longer. She jumped from the wagon and ran to where they were.

"What is wrong with you, Captain Cahill? Can't you see these men need to get dried off and into warm clothing? They need something hot to drink, too. Let Notah out of the water, please."

Her pleas on behalf of Notah only incensed him further and turning angry eyes on her, he said, "Woman, I've warned you before. I'm the law on this here hike. Now get back on your wagon and stay out of army business, and out of my sight."

She cast agonized eyes at Notah, but he just shook his head at her and floated away. Seeing him drift off in the current, JoAnna screamed, "Nooo. Notah, don't leave us." But before she could call out a second time, he disappeared under the water and was gone from their sight.

Crushed, she crumbled to the ground, her heart breaking in her chest.

Captain Cahill reached down and dragged JoAnna to her feet and said, "Get back in that wagon, woman, or I'll leave you where you lay."

She jerked her arm out of his hand and said, "Don't you *ever* touch me again, Captain Cahill. I am going to report your conduct the first thing when we get to the Bosque Redondo."

John had come up to them by then and put his arm around JoAnna to lead her away, glaring his own warning at Cahill.

"Why . . . Why, Father, would he leave us? Why would he leave his children? Do you suppose he was more hurt than we could see?"

She had more questions than answers.

Her father took her off to rejoin the children in the wagon, saying, "I don't know, JoAnna. He must have had a reason, though. Notah doesn't behave irrationally."

John was being cautious and trying to remain calm. He didn't want to say anything more in front of Cahill and the men who had come to help Toby.

As JoAnna and her father walked back to the wagon, John saw the tears she was fighting to hold back and patted her shoulder. When she was finally seated again, he put his arm around her and said, "Don't grieve too much, sweetheart. You know Notah well enough by now to know he's not a coward and he just wouldn't give in to a bully like Cahill. I don't think he was hurt, so let's wait and see what happens before we believe the worst. Okay, gal?"

She leaned into his comforting arms and tried to get ahold on her own emotions before she faced the children and Old Woman, mindful that they had witnessed the whole thing, too.

JoAnna turned around in her seat and lifted Bella onto her lap as John started the wagon rolling again.

Bella sat wide-eyed and stiff in her arms until JoAnna wrapped her arms around her and pulled her close, saying, "Bella, do not fear. Your father is a holy man. The gods will not let anything happen to him until they decide it. We will trust that your father has a plan. We will keep believing in him and look forward to seeing him again soon."

She prayed her words would come true.

"You truly believe this?" Bella asked.

"Yes, and you must believe it, too," JoAnna answered.

Bella, feeling her love and seeing the assurance in JoAnna's eyes, finally relaxed back against her and fell into an exhausted sleep.

Notah floating away saw Cahill reach for JoAnna and pull her roughly to her feet. He almost turned back, but he knew his time to deal with this vile man was not yet. While he hung suspended in the water watching Cahill watch him, a plan had begun to form in his mind—a plan of survival, and of help for his people. Notah sank farther into the water and just let it carry him downstream. He knew he could not stay in it much longer; already the cold was sapping what little strength he had left, but he knew he was not alone. His spirit guides were with him. He would live and he would rejoin his people soon.

It was five days later in the evening when Notah appeared at his clan's campfire. At first sight of him, many thought they were seeing his *chindi,* his ghost, and cried out in alarm. When they started to back away, he hastened to reassure them.

"No. I am not chindi. Touch me . . . feel me . . . I am flesh and bone."

Even then, some were not convinced. But not Bella and Bacca. Realizing it was their father, they jumped up and ran to him crying out, "*Shizhee, Father!*"

He gathered them close in a big bear hug.

Seeing that display, the others relaxed and came to him as well, slapping him on the back or just touching him in awe, to let him know they were equally glad to see him. His people had sorely missed his calming influence and had felt his loss keenly.

After the greetings were over, everyone sat down around the fire again. They wanted to ask him what had happened and where he'd been. How had he survived the cold water with no food or dry clothing to put on?

Seated in front of them with his children in his lap, he described the last five days to them.

"I drifted downstream a short way, then got out. With two sticks I made a fire after laying a snare for a rabbit or other small game. When I had dried off a little, I checked the snare and found a hare in it and cooked it over the fire. I traveled parallel to you all the way. I met up with a Navajo family, who are in hiding from the army and they provided me with clean, dry clothes and this sarape. In exchange, I gave them my silver belt for a day's rations and a knife."

Bacca looked up adoringly into his father's face and said, "I knew these soldier-coats could not kill you. I knew you would come back for us."

"You were right to believe that, son. I will never leave you again, I promise."

When everyone's questions had been answered, the people asked him if he would conduct a sing, and pray for traveling mercies from their gods, and for health to be restored as they were still losing the very young and the old ones.

He told them that he did not have all the proper ingredients to do a real sing, but he would say a prayer and ask the gods for their favor. They all sat quietly and reverently while he chanted a song for them in his powerful voice.

This covers it all, the Earth and the Most High Power,
Whose ways are Beautiful.
All is beautiful before me,
All is beautiful behind me,

All is beautiful above me,
All is beautiful around me.
We Walk in Beauty.

As the song ended, the people all breathed a grateful sigh of relief. Harmony was being restored unto them. Their Hataalii had returned and they could Walk in Beauty once more. Everyone fell asleep easier in spirit that night because Notah had returned.

The next morning as the Navajo were being herded into line, Notah fell into line with them.

When Cahill saw him, he could not believe his eyes. *How had the man survived?*

He certainly didn't look the worse for his sojourn in the water. His clothes were new and he had cleaned himself up.

Cahill ground his teeth together. He'd thought he was rid of the Navajo dog once and for all without having to actually kill him. But he knew one day, it just might come to that.

When Cahill caught Notah's eye, something in the Navajo's stare warned him to stay away from him. He did not order Notah tied up again.

Well, Cahill reasoned, they were still a hundred miles from the fort. Anything could happen. He'd just double the guard around Notah from here on out, and he would sleep with one eye open.

Chapter Thirteen

Fort Sumner
Bosque Redondo
Early Summer 1863

The last one hundred miles had nearly done them all in. Even the trained troops were beginning to sag in their saddles because of the bad weather, bad food, and long hours. They had been marching since last summer through wind, rain, snow, and heat. The winter had been terrible and had taken a great toll on the peoples reserve and spirit.

As other bands of Navajos were brought up to join with their numbers, JoAnna and John were told the story of the siege on Canyon de Chelley and of the destruction there. How the army had literally cut down the Navajos' peach orchards and burned their crops of corn and squash. Their sheep, cattle, and horses were either seized or slaughtered. Some Navajo men and women had even jumped from the cliffs, killing themselves, rather than leave their homeland.

Both father and daughter were numbed by the revelations. What was their government thinking? How was this ever going to help settle the west? Destroying a whole people's way of life couldn't be the answer. What would make the Navajo want to live like a white man after this?

The captain had informed the Lunds that the government's plan was to turn the Apache and Navajo into farmers on the Bosque Redondo with irrigation from the Pecos River. They were to be "civilized" by going to school and practicing Christianity.

When they finally arrived at the fort, they learned that four hundred Mescalero Apaches, the hated and dreaded enemies of the Navajos, were already there. It seemed that before Colonel Carson had rounded up the Navajo, he had been sent to bring in the Mescaleros, as well. After the same policy of starvation and burned crops, the Apaches had been herded to Fort Sumner earlier in the year. This could only add to an already bad situation, Notah informed John Lund.

As they approached the fort that was called Sumner, the Lunds could not believe their eyes. A few scattered buildings and a half-built adobe wall surrounded the acre of land on which it sat. Barren land—inhospitable land. The brackish Pecos River ran below it. They learned the reservation was comprised of forty square miles of land. At this point in time, General James Henry Carleton was the fort commander.

He came out to meet the cavalry and the prisoners, for this was what it was going to be, a virtual prison camp for the Navajos. Seeing the white man and woman on a wagon, he turned to Captain Cahill.

"What is the meaning of this? No white people were to be rounded up," he said.

Having saluted the general and having his salute returned, Cahill answered. "Well, sir, these folks, John Lund and his daughter, ran a trading post outside of Chief Manuelito's campgrounds. When we passed through their compound, they protested our rounding up the Navajos. Mr. Lund, there, drew a gun on me to try to stop me from carrying out my orders as Colonel Carson commissioned me to do. So, since they were so sympathetic to the Navajos and their cause, I thought I would just bring them along. As it turns out, he is a doctor and I thought it might be good to have him along to help with any illnesses that developed along the way."

Stunned, General Carleton said, "This will be looked into, Captain. Bring them to me immediately. Then show the Navajos where they can bed down. There should be enough room for everyone. They can pick their own space, but once chosen, they must abide in it."

Captain Cahill knew a moment of panic. What would the Lunds say in their defense and what would they say about his treatment of the Indians on the way here?

As he walked toward them, Cahill motioned for John to get down from the wagon. After John was down, he turned and helped JoAnna. They waited in tense anticipation for Cahill to reach them.

They were both surprised when he said, "General Carleton would like to speak to you. Remember there are always two sides to every story."

John wondered what that meant. Was it a veiled warning from Cahill?

Taking JoAnna by the arm, he led her over to the general. He could not tell by the expression on his face if he was pleased or angry.

John spoke first. "I'm Dr. John Lund, sir, originally from Virginia. A few years ago my daughter and I came west and settled on the edge of Navajo land. This is my daughter, JoAnna."

The general acknowledged them and said, "I'm General James Henry Carleton, commander of this fort. Will you please follow me into my office? I would like to know why you are traveling with the Navajos. There were no orders to take any white people into custody."

Well, then, John thought, it had to have been the lone decision of Captain Cahill to bring them along for his own perverse reasons. One of those reasons, he felt sure, was JoAnna. John had not been oblivious to the lecherous looks the captain cast her way. For that reason he had always tried to be with her or have Old Woman by her side if she went for water, or to perform some personal chore.

They entered a rough, adobe building with a plank floor, to pass through a gated area to a door in the back of the 12 by 12 foot room. The front half was partitioned off as a waiting or reception hall with a desk and chair, and a file cabinet behind the railed-off section. The general's adjutant sat there at the desk when they walked in, but immediately jumped to his feet and saluted the general.

"At ease," said the general. "I do not want to be disturbed for a while by anyone," he added as he motioned for the Lunds to follow him into his office.

"Yes, sir." The adjutant saluted again, and closed the door after the general and his visitors were inside.

General Carleton pointed to the two chairs facing his desk and proceeded to sit behind it.

"Please, have a seat. I am anxious to know how this situation came about. I take it Colonel Carson was not the one to bring in this particular band of Navajos. And, yet, I know he planned to talk with Chief Manuelito personally and this is his clan, is it not?"

"Yes, this is Manuelito's band and Colonel Carson did talk with the chief and explained the situation to him. He told him they had to report to this fort by July 1863. But he left to gather up other bands and put this group under the command of Captain Cahill. It was Cahill that came through our trading post and compound. I admit I protested heartily to these Navajo being taken from their homeland as we had lived there two years and never had a moment's trouble with them. When my protest became too much for Captain Cahill, and I demanded to talk to this Colonel Carson, he declared that since I was so sympathetic to the Indians, I could just share their fate, come with them to this fort, and then try to talk to the colonel in person."

"I see. Well, you do not need to talk to the colonel.

I am the one who issued those orders, so I am the only one you need to talk to," replied the general. "Did you also draw your gun on Captain Cahill?"

Flushing a little, John answered truthfully.

"Yes, sir, I did. However, I was doing it in self-defense. He was threatening to burn my trading post. I was not going to leave my home and store to be destroyed or looted after I left. We had worked too hard to just up and leave it."

"Are you aware it is a federal offense to draw a weapon on a United States Army officer or to inter-fere with his duties? Was there no other recourse you could have taken?" asked the general.

"Well, possibly, but Captain Cahill was not open to hearing anything else, I can tell you that."

"That is unfortunate. I will have to discuss this with my superiors and Captain Cahill. For now, you will have to stay within the fort. We don't have much yet in the way of accommodations, but there is an old sutler store you may be able to use for now. We will have to conscript the Navajos into molding adobe bricks and have them help in building the rest of the fort and necessary out-buildings. Unfortunately, this has not turned out to be the wisest choice of a place to build a fort. The water is poor and there is a min-imal provision of wood in the area. But I am not the one who makes the decisions, I just follow orders as do Colonel Carson and Captain Cahill."

So saying, he stood up and called his adjutant to come in.

When he came through the door, the general

told him to take the Lunds to the sutler's store to settle in there for the time being.

John held out his hand to the general, who after a moment's hesitation took it.

"Thank you, General Carleton. I'm grateful to you. It has been a long and horrific journey and it will be good to have a roof over our heads once more. I am a doctor and my daughter is a capable nurse. She has assisted me in healing the sick and in many operations. Should you have need of my services while we are here, please feel free to call upon us."

"Thank you, that is good to know. We do have our own staff doctor but with the number of Indians being brought in every day, it will be more work than one man can handle."

John wanted to ask more questions, but he knew they were being dismissed. However, he wondered how much doctoring their doctor actually did among the Indians. He'd bet it wasn't much.

As they left the commander's office, JoAnna turned to her father and said, "Why didn't you speak up and tell him how atrocious the treatment of the Navajos was on the way here by that Captain Cahill? We should report his mistreatment of them to somebody."

"I plan on it, JoAnna, but first I want to get the lay of the land, so to speak, and feel this general out a little more. Maybe he condones such treatment of them. He seems a man to look down his nose on anyone he considers beneath him. We'll just have to observe him for a while and see what his true feelings are."

Chapter Fourteen

JoAnna walked through the late afternoon gloom toward their home within the fort complex. There were no real walls around the fort. The buildings sat in a rectangle with the parade ground in the center, atop an open plateau that was Bosque Redondo, which meant "round grove of trees" in Spanish.

Their home was an adobe two room, flat-roofed affair, with two windows and two doors, front and back set in wooden frames that John had helped build. As wood was scarce or almost nonexistent, only the commander's house had more wood in it. Their casa had a thatched roof over the front portion of the house that acted like a porch, if you considered a dirt floor a porch. They were living little better than the people they had come west to serve. She'd been given a small ration of coal to heat and cook with from the fort's store because of the shortage of wood.

She was cold and miserable but not as cold as the Navajo were. They were being deprived of coal and huddled together for warmth in their makeshift shelters. They preferred to live in their hogans, if they could find enough material to make them. The army was cutting down on their food, too, and JoAnna wondered if the army was trying to kill them off rather than provide for them or make them wards of the government.

She still couldn't understand why the red man and white man couldn't live together in harmony. Surely, this country was big enough for both races. It had taken her and her father months to cross it to reach New Mexico. But she knew what had happened to the tribes in the east and the terrible *Trail of Tears* that the Cherokee had been forced to make, so she guessed a reservation was inevitable for the Navajo, as well.

If they lived that long!

So far Chief Manuelito was not giving in and signing any peace treaty with the United States government. Notah was doing all he could to keep Hozho going among the people, conducting sings when he could, even though the army had forbidden it, encouraging the Diné not to give up hope in the Blessing Way of living in beauty and harmony. But the long march, bad weather, lack of food, and horrible living conditions were taking their toll on the people. They had lost so many on the march and now more to dysentery, pneumonia, and disease, that JoAnna wondered who would be left to put on a reservation.

JoAnna ducked into their shelter and went over to check on her father. She was afraid the hostile environment, unsanitary living conditions, poor food and bad water were taking their toll on his health, as well as that of the Navajos. He had a recurring bout of bronchitis that even all the poultices that Old Woman had devised, and what little medicine JoAnna could beg from the fort doctor, was not curing him. When she went in, she found him propped up against the wall on a mattress and springs someone had scrounged up for them.

"How are you feeling, Father?"

"About the same, dear. No worse. I still have an intermittent cough, but the poultice has helped me breathe a little easier. You must thank Old Woman for me. We've learned so much from her about the healing properties of the plants out here. It's a shame we can't go out and gather the ones in this area that may help the Navajos and the Apaches."

"Well, little luck with that. That horrible Captain Cahill watches everyone like a hawk, me as well. He won't let me near the Navajo camp or let them go far from the fort to gather what wood may be about, let alone hunt game or gather plants that might be useful."

"Has he made any improper advances toward you, JoAnna? We can report that to the general if we need to."

"No. So far he has just made snide remarks about my caring more about the Indians than my own 'white' people."

"He is a small-minded man," John remarked. "I

know many of the soldiers don't like Indians, but he seems to have a special hatred for them. Almost like a personal vendetta against them."

"Well, we both know that when Notah saved young Private Wiley from the floodwaters in front of his men, while he sat on the bank and did nothing, didn't help much. To think he would have just let the boy be swept away rather than order someone to go in after him. Yet, Notah, even with his hands bound, dove in the water and somehow got his arms under the young man, and managed to swim them to shore."

"Yes, that showed up Cahill for sure. His men lost respect for him after that and talked about him behind his back. That new recruit was well liked by the older soldiers and they had sort of taken him under their wings. They were shocked, too, when Captain Cahill didn't make any attempt to save him. It just goes to show you the deficiencies in the character of the man."

Unwrapping a parcel JoAnna had carried in, she smiled at her father saying, "The post's store clerk gave me a piece of ham hock today. I traded my cameo earrings for it, but I can at least make us some beans, ham, and rice for a nice change."

"Oh, my dear daughter, I'm so sorry. I've regretted bringing you out here so many times. I should have left you with your grandparents in Richmond. You deserve so much more than this. A chance to meet decent young men, marry, and have your own family. I have failed you, and your mother, in this regard."

JoAnna went over and knelt beside him, taking his hands in hers, and looked into his face.

"No, Father. You did not do anything wrong. I could not have stood it if you had gone off without me. Just think of all the wonderful things we saw on our way out here, the things I've learned about healing from new plants, and survival, in general. It has been worth it. I love the Navajo people, especially Old Woman and the twins. They have added so much to my life. I only wish I could help them more."

"And, Notah, JoAnna? What are your real feelings for him? I'm not so old that I do not see the light that comes into your eyes whenever you look at him."

"Oh, Father. I don't know how to answer that. Yes, I admire him. There are so many strong and good qualities about the man and he is so dedicated to his people. But you know any relationship between an American woman and a Navajo Indian would be decried by our people as tainted and improper, to say the least. Besides, the children tell me he has vowed never to marry again. His only desire is to devote himself to being the best holy man and spiritual leader of his people that he can be. It must have something to do with the way his wife died, but the twins and Old Woman will not talk to me about it."

"I see. Yes, I agree, the wife's death is a mystery and must play a part. He has not shared anything about it with me, either, other than that it was a female illness."

"Do you suppose he might have done a *sing* for

her and it failed to heal her, and he somehow feels responsible for her death?"

"You know, you might have guessed it, JoAnna. That would account for him studying so hard at the sixty or so rituals for blessings, healings or curses, which he is constantly rehearsing. Why, he said in just one Blessing Way alone, there were as many as ninety stanzas, and all must be done in just the right order, with no words misused or left out, and all completed in a certain amount of time. Their sand paintings, too, need to be done exactly right. If he felt he missed one verse, or left something out of the sand painting in which they lay the patient, it might be enough to cause him untold guilt."

"Well, I guess we'll never know. It is not something he would ever discuss with me. In fact, he seems to be withdrawing from any overtures from me to help him anymore. He used to talk to me and try to explain his ways, his thinking about things, showing me plants to use for healing, but I can see the hope dying in his, and all their faces, now. It is like he is ashamed to face me for some reason. But I don't see him any differently, Father."

"He comes from a proud people, dear. This has to be a very humbling time for him. Where he used to roam free and provide well for his family and Old Woman, he is now confined to a few square yards of space within shouting distance of army guards. He can no longer hunt and must accept what handouts the army gives. Certainly, he feels he has lost face and it must be an embarrassment to him. Maybe that is why he turns away from your offer of friendship. He cannot stand to be an object of pity."

"But he should know I'd never pity him. I stand up to Cahill on his, and the rest of the Navajo's behalf, whenever I can."

"Yes, but there again, how humiliating is that for him? The strong warrior and spiritual leader of his people, dependent upon the goodness of a small white woman. Might make his pride smart terribly, don't you think?"

JoAnna looked up from the pot she was stirring their little bit of rice into.

"Of course, you are right, Father," she said, the truth of his statement dawning in her eyes. "I never thought of it like that. I only know they don't deserve such harsh treatment by Cahill. Especially Notah. He has done nothing wrong. Oh, this whole situation just stinks!"

"I agree, JoAnna. I have asked for an audience with Colonel Carson when he returns from his latest scouting expedition, even though the general is not pleased by my request. He needs to be made aware of how badly the Navajos are being treated, especially by Cahill, who reports to him. It is rumored that Colonel Carson was once a good friend to the Diné. I wonder what changed his mind about them, or maybe he's just caught between a rock and hard place, having to obey the orders of the men in charge above him."

"You may be right again, Father. For I do remember Notah saying that he had been friends with Kit Carson in the past, and they had camped and hunted together. If you can get his ear, possibly you could get him to show the Navajos better treatment."

"Well, I will do my best . . . *if* they let me have a word with him when he returns, that is."

Dishing up a bowl of the simmering rice and beans, JoAnna handed it to her father.

"Well, that is all we can hope for, I guess," she said.

He nodded as he accepted the food and waited until she had her own bowl in hand before bowing his head. Then he said grace, and asked God to have mercy on them and the Navajos and their plight.

Later that evening, JoAnna managed a furtive visit into the Navajo camp. She wanted to report to Old Woman on her father's progress and see how Bella and Bacca were faring.

Notah came upon her as she was getting ready to leave.

"JoAnna, it is not good for you to come here. You know what will happen if you are caught here after dark by the army. Come, I will escort you to the edge of the fort."

Saying her good-byes to his children, she willingly turned to walk back with Notah. For if truth were told, she had hoped desperately that she would have just such a chance to be alone with him for a few minutes.

Taking her elbow, Notah helped her keep her balance over the uneven ground. Although his touch was light and proper, his fingers left heated imprints on her skin, even through her threadbare cloak. Her heart sang inside her breast.

Oh, how much she was coming to care for him.

Right or wrong.

Couldn't he see it . . . couldn't he feel it? There were times when he looked at her that she felt he must have some affection for her. His eyes would heat up and she would melt at the look he gave her. Then, as quickly as the look came, he would erase it and his eyes would go cold and flat again. She decided to confront him once and for all about it. She may ruin any chance she had with him afterward, but she had a desperate need to know exactly how he felt.

She knew eventually she and her father would be let go. No charges would be filed against them. Apparently, General Carleton was satisfied with Cahill's and her father's answers, and since medical help was scarce at the fort, let alone in the whole area, he had kept them on under his watchful eye.

As they neared the forts outbuildings, JoAnna turned and faced Notah. With her hand on his chest, she stopped him from going any farther. His sudden intake of breath let her know that her touch affected him and that he was not indifferent to her, but how much, she wondered.

"Notah, I have a question to ask you. We've known each other for almost three years now and in all that time, you have not mentioned your wife or whether you ever intend to take another. May I ask why not?"

Notah was taken aback. Where had this question come from, and why now?

"JoAnna, I am surprised. Why should you want to know this thing?"

Taking a deep breath and gathering her courage, she answered, "Because I am falling in love with you, and I want to know if you could love me back?"

It was like an arrow shot right into his heart. How did he answer that?

He took so long to answer that JoAnna began to feel like a fool and her eyes filled with tears of humiliation and heartbreak.

The Navajo believe that tears have words, and her tears were speaking loudly to him right now. They spoke of hurt, pain, injustice, compassion, and of her love for him and his people.

"JoAnna you cannot mean this. I am Navajo. You are bilagaana. This is forbidden among your people."

JoAnna asked him, "Does love have a culture or color, Notah? Everyone laughs and cries in the same language, is it any different with love?"

For all her casualness in their friendship, JoAnna doubted she had concealed her true feelings from him. She knew she loved him with all her heart. If he could not love her back, perhaps she could convince him to just let her stay near him and his family and she would be content with that.

Notah felt a surge of joy within his heart. Her declaration of love left him breathless and cracked open his hardened heart a little bit wider. He could barely stand the hurt in JoAnna's eyes. She had no idea how easy it would be for him to love her—indeed, already did love her. But it went against everything he had vowed. Besides that, he had nothing to offer her even if he did declare his love.

"You should stay with your own people, JoAnna. Find a man among them who will love you and give you children."

"Your people have become my people. I cannot go back to the greedy men and narrow-minded, bigoted women of my race who cannot see beyond the color of a person's skin in order to judge their worth.

"All I'm asking is that you just let me stay near you and help with the children and old ones. You have given my life purpose and direction. I've learned so much from the Diné. The will to Walk in Beauty; the grace to accept things that cannot be changed and still go on . . . to strive to bring Harmony out of this hell-hole here.

"Anyway, I'm considered an old maid now by my people because I have not married before this."

Then sighing audibly, she added, "No one would have me anyway with my deformed foot."

Notah's heart turned over in his chest. She thought she would be rejected because of a foot turned inward; that no one would see the beauty of her spirit, her face, her skin, her hair, and her tender sweet ways.

"Ah, JoAnna, a scar of the body cannot wholly destroy beauty. Only a scar on the spirit can do that. You are lovely by anyone's standards. And you are still young; you have plenty of time to meet someone."

He could see her trying to stem her tears, while at the same time remaining calm enough to discuss the situation without emotions becoming any more involved.

Notah felt her love reaching out to him, but what could he offer her? Years of living in squalor, no decent hogan to house them, and no way to feed her or any children they might have.

He ached to take her into his arms and hold her close and whisper the words of love he knew she longed to hear—promise her a tomorrow, but he could not. Nor would he.

He had cared once. Very deeply, but all his caring and prayers, the conducting of the ceremonial sing, hadn't saved his wife or secured a future together for them.

The agony of his failure to save Squash Blossom washed over him once more. He still questioned his skill at drawing the sand painting he had laid her down on. Had he become tired toward daylight of the fourth day and left out some words of the healing song. He had racked his brain trying to remember every detail of those four days and nights, to no avail. She had died in agony and pain, calling out to him to help her. And he hadn't been able to . . . not as her husband, or as the healer of his clan.

No, he couldn't . . . he wouldn't encourage Jo-Anna; nor would he love like that again.

But, oh, something in her trusting blue eyes and gentle manner reached down into that cold implacable chamber of his dead heart, to stir it every now and then as if to bring it back to life.

Notah saw the longing in her eyes and steeled himself against it.

"No, JoAnna, this is no place for you, especially should your father die. You cannot help us—you only bring the chastisement of your people down on your own head. I cannot give you what you want and I will not watch you waste away like the Diné are doing."

She held back the sob that rose up in her throat. Why couldn't she make him see that she loved him and just needed to be near him, to be able to see him, and hear his voice, if nothing else.

JoAnna didn't care what the soldiers at this ridiculous excuse for a fort thought of her. She just wanted to throw herself into his arms, hold him close, and declare her love for him once more.

He read the desire in her eyes, and took a step back fearing he could not resist her should she choose to close the distance between them. Even so she swayed toward him, unconsciously, and when she tried to catch herself, her lame foot turned on a stone and twisted her ankle causing her to fall into him anyway, as she cried out in pain.

Immediately, he reached out with both hands to grasp her shoulders and steady her.

She raised her face to his and realized they were only a breath away from each other. She turned her head up a little to touch his lips with her own.

She had to kiss him . . . had to. Just once! And if he never touched her, or kissed her again, somehow she would learn to be content with that.

Notah saw the desire in her eyes and knew his own reflected the same emotion. Feelings and desires too long denied erupted in him as he bent his head and took her mouth, not in a sweet, first lover's kiss that he meant it to be, but with the heated desire of love mingled with lust.

JoAnna had never been kissed like that before but she gave herself up to it without any hesitation. She answered it with all the pent up longing in her own heart. When he pushed against her lips to open them, she did so willingly. When he thrust his tongue inside to taste her, she moaned in pleasure. This was not at all what she expected his kiss to be like, but she gloried in it, and the fact that he was holding her close.

Notah felt her response and clasped her tighter to him. Her little moan stirred him deeply. Every curve of her seemed to fit exactly into a curve of his. He cupped her bottom against him and felt desire pulsate in his manhood.

Unconsciously, JoAnna pressed herself against him, not completely understanding what she wanted, except that she wanted to be closer still.

Notah knew this was madness. He told himself that he must regain his control and stop before this went any further.

She trusted him! And in these heated moments, it was the man's responsibility to control how far things went. Their first joining, if they could ever have one, should be on a bed of soft furs under a nighttime sky. He could not take her in the dirt outside this fort and shame her.

Mustering all his Navajo training and control, he dropped his arms from around her and stepped back, holding her at arms length but not letting go of her completely.

"JoAnna, forgive me. That was not supposed to happen. You see what our life is like. I cannot . . . and will not . . . take you in conditions like this. I will admit to having strong feelings for you and a desire to mate with you, but it would be against my beliefs and yours to take you outside of marriage. Again, I say, you must find someone of your own race to marry and have a family with."

"No, Notah. I cannot, because my heart already belongs to you whether you want it to or not. I love you; that's all I know. I will wait for you forever if I have to."

He couldn't fight her or himself any longer.

Taking her back into his arms, he kissed her on the forehead, and said, "So be it for now, JoAnna, but I don't see things changing for either of us."

Then remembering her turned ankle, he bent down to look at it.

"Is your ankle badly twisted, JoAnna? Let me see."

As Notah leaned down to raise the hem of her skirt to check her ankle, while keeping one hand on her waist to steady her, Captain Cahill came around the corner and saw what he thought was a compromising situation. All his rage and hatred for this particular Indian came to the forefront. His blood boiled to see Notah's dark head bent too close to JoAnna and his hands on her. He was also instantly insane with jealousy.

"Hey, Redskin, what is the meaning of this? Get

your filthy hands off Miss Lund." He drew his pistol and yelled out, "Guards, come here this instant."

When several soldiers arrived in answer to his call, he said to them, "Arrest this man and lock him up. I caught him manhandling and threatening Miss Lund."

Captain Cahill knew a moment of intense satisfaction. He'd been aching for a chance to punish this uppity Injun ever since that day at the river, and he seized this opportunity with glee.

Startled apart, Notah stood up and looked impassively at Cahill.

JoAnna protested his wrong assumption.

"Captain Cahill, you have completely misjudged the situation, as usual. Nothing happened here. I twisted my ankle on a rock that rolled under my foot and Notah Begay simply reached out and kept me from falling."

"So you say. But I know what I saw. He had his dirty hands under your skirt on your person."

Outraged, JoAnna couldn't believe her ears. "That is not the way it was at all!" She screamed at him.

As he spoke, the troopers who had been summoned surrounded Notah and pulled his hands behind his back and tied them together, although they wished they had not been the ones called on for the job.

Most of the men in the command had watched how the Navajos had conducted themselves in the midst of overwhelming and horrible circumstances, and especially Notah. He was a never-flagging source of encouragement and hope for his people. *And he had saved young and inexperienced Private Wiley.*

Notah did not struggle, merely looked each one in the eye as they jostled him into a better position. He would not give them the satisfaction of a fight for he knew Captain Cahill longed to do more than just tie him up. He vowed to give them no excuse to do anything else in front of JoAnna.

However, his cold stare and the contempt in his look was enough to give them pause for a moment. The soldiers knew he was considered a holy man with strange powers, and even in his weakened condition from the poor food and hard living, he was still someone to be reckoned with.

They tried to drag him away, but Notah shrugged off their hands and walked off with his head high as they marched away with him in the middle.

Cahill called out after them.

"Lock him in the hole. Let's see how long his cockiness lasts then."

"Captain, you can't do that!" JoAnna cried. "He has done nothing wrong. You're just being pigheaded about this."

"I'm sorry, ma'am, if I seem to care more about your reputation than you do. He must be taught a lesson and made an example to the others; fraternizing with a white woman will not be tolerated."

"Fraternizing!" JoAnna sputtered. "Admit it, Captain, you have been itching for a chance to get back at Notah ever since he showed you up by rescuing Private Wiley."

"Woman, you would be wise to watch your tongue.

I am just about to lose my good opinion of you as a *lady.*" As if her being a lady mattered to him at all. *When he got through with her she wouldn't be a lady anymore, anyway.*

"After a couple of days in the hole, we'll see how smug he is," he continued. Then he turned and walked away, leaving a worried and fuming JoAnna behind.

He smiled to himself. That wasn't all he had planned for the red bastard, either. A whipping at the stake would seem to be in order as well.

Chapter Fifteen

Oh, what should I do? JoAnna wondered.

The hole was literally just that, a pit dug into the hard ground with a grate put over the top that locked down. It would be roasting in there in summer and freezing in winter. Thirst would become unbearable. She'd heard some men even lost their sanity after being left in there too long. Although, she was very sure *that* would not happen to Notah. If anyone could control his mind and his body, it would be him.

She rushed back to the cabin she shared with her father and related the incident to him railing at the injustice of the whole thing.

John was not surprised. He had known a show-down would come eventually between the captain and Notah. But what chance of winning would the medicine man have surrounded by the U.S. Cavalry.

JoAnna realized there was nothing she could do tonight. However, she was sick with worry about Notah being cold in the hole. Did it get cold in a hole in the earth? At least he wouldn't have to worry about the wind.

But, what about thirst? She worried he might become dehydrated and yet she knew she couldn't risk sneaking out to the hole tonight. He would be too heavily guarded. Maybe tomorrow night she and Toby Wiley, the young private he had saved, could bring him something to eat and drink.

Private Wiley had developed a sort of hero-worship of Notah since his rescue and would try to visit with him at the Navajo camp every chance he got. JoAnna could see the difference in him through his association with the medicine man. He was becoming a more mature and confident young man. But who wouldn't benefit from Notah's wisdom and instruction? Look what he had taught her.

She tossed and turned on her bed, torn between remembering the wonder of Notah's kiss, and his harsh treatment by Cahill. It was not until the wee hours of the morning that JoAnna finally fell into a restless sleep.

When she awoke, she realized it was much later than she normally arose. She was still feeling the effects of the loss of a sound sleep. Sitting up and rubbing her eyes, she tried to identify the sound that had awakened her. Then she heard the shouts of men coming from the middle of the compound, and the snap, snap of leather.

What was that?

Something was fearfully wrong.

She could feel the tension in the air.

Hurriedly, JoAnna dragged her dress on over her

nightgown and pulled on her shoes. Her father would know what was going on. As soon as she was dressed, she went to find him, but he was not in the other room.

Swirling her cloak around her, she pulled open the door to go search for him.

However, when she stepped out the door, she didn't need her father to tell her what was happening, for she could see for herself.

Notah, stripped naked to the waist, was strung up between two poles. His back was bleeding from the stripes already laid on him by Captain Cahill. That had been the thwack, thwack, she'd heard; the unholy smack of leather on a flesh and blood body. It made her sick to her stomach and she smothered a scream with her fist in her mouth.

It seemed like the whole army post had turned out to watch the whipping. Half were cheering Cahill on. The other half were booing or standing silently, watching in awe, when Notah never cried out or uttered a sound but managed to stand there stoically and take the beating.

Where was the general? Surely, he would not let this go on if she could just explain to him what really happened. He would stop this travesty of justice, wouldn't he?

She turned and saw her father coming to her with a furious expression on his face.

She ran to him and said, "Father, where is the general? This is insane. Why is Notah being beaten? He did nothing to me last night but escort me back from the Navajo camp and kept me from falling when I turned my ankle on a rock. Can't we stop this madness?"

He took her by the arm and led her back to their front porch.

"Ah, JoAnna, I warned you about going to the camp. Please, don't watch any more of this. And, no, the general is not here. I just came from his office and his adjutant told me he had to go up to Santa Fe to the Army Headquarters there to report on how many Navajos and Apaches are now confined at Bosque Redondo. It is one reason Cahill is getting away with this. Colonel Carson is with General Carleton, too, so there is no one to override Cahill's actions for the moment. But you can bet, when they do return, I will make a complaint this time, loud and clear."

"But that will be too late to help Notah now, won't it?"

He could only nod in agreement. Putting his arm around her, he held her as she faced the parade ground once more.

Some Navajos had gathered to watch; however, JoAnna was relieved to see that neither the twins nor Old Woman had come onto the post grounds. Her heart ached for the children. They would never understand this treatment of their father—the Hataalii of the tribe—whose only desire was to help and heal people. She could never explain it to them, for she couldn't even explain it to herself, except that Cahill hated Notah, and the grudge he had against him would not die.

She didn't know how many more stripes Notah

bore before Cahill, sweating profusely, stopped. She was numb and knew she was in a state of shock. Her hands were like ice cubes, but it was the cold that went all the way to her soul that froze her to the spot.

John turned her away and said, "He's one amazing man, JoAnna. He never did cry out, not once, and never even sagged between the ropes. If he called upon his gods to help him, they must have. I called on Jesus, too, to have mercy on him and to remember how those stripes he bore for our sakes felt."

JoAnna looked up then to see Notah walking upright, although not as steadily as he usually walked, shaking off the help of the soldiers as they escorted him back to the hole.

"Oh, no!" JoAnna cried out. "Not the hole, Father. They can't put him back in the hole without any medical attention and some warm food and drink in him!"

"I guess they can. I'll go by the army doctor's office and see if he is going to be allowed to look at Notah. If not, maybe we can think of something. You need to go see the children and Old Woman. I'm sure she knows what has just happened, knowing the Navajo telegraph, but you might be needed to comfort Bella and Bacca."

Squaring her shoulders, JoAnna, answered, "Yes, Father, that is a good idea. But how in the world can I explain something like this to those darling children who have known only love and care from their father. It just isn't conscionable."

"I agree, sweetheart. It has certainly turned my stomach today to think our army could be so heartless. You'd better change your clothes and get something to eat before you venture down to Notah's camp. Maybe you can take them some of the ham and rice from last night's supper. I'd rather see them have a decent meal than eat what's left myself."

"Yes, Father, I'll do that. Please try to persuade the fort doctor to see to Notah's back. He will be subject to terrible infection without proper treatment."

"You bet I will, darlin' . . . and if he won't, we will!"

So saying he turned away, and JoAnna went back in the house to prepare for her visit to Old Woman and the children. She dreaded the visit but ached to comfort them and be with them at the same time. They were all becoming so very precious to her.

Chapter Sixteen

The soldiers taking the medicine man back to the hole had the grace to be embarrassed by his proud carriage and the unbelievable courage he had displayed. It must be true, they thought, that Notah had supernatural powers, for who else could have born twelve lashes and never even utter a grunt.

And just look at him now. Still holding his head high. The only sign Notah gave that he was in any pain was an involuntary shudder when they lifted the grate covering the hole. One of the soldiers dropped a rope ladder into the hole to let Notah climb down. When he was on the floor of the hole, the soldier quickly pulled it back up in case Notah made a grab for it.

Nothing was further from Notah's mind. He had only one wish right now, and that was for oblivion. His body was racked by pain so intense he felt faint. A scream was just waiting to be released from his mouth in the wild Apache yell of his enemies, but he knew if he did, he would lose *all* control and he vowed he would not give the army the satisfaction of seeing that.

His back was on fire. He knew he'd lost a lot of blood and had no way of replacing it. His throat was raw and he craved a drink of water.

Navajos were trained to run for miles on just a mouthful of water in the high desert country where water was scarce, so he could endure a little while, but what he wouldn't give for a mouthful of it right now.

He'd known that Captain Cahill was planning some sort of revenge—possibly hoping Notah would try to escape, then he could say he shot him as he tried to elude recapture.

But Notah had no idea he would be whipped. Humiliation and shame burned within him. To slap a Navajo in the face was one of the highest insults one could give to another, but flogging was unheard of. It was something the Mexicans were fond of doing to their slaves. He didn't know the army used this method also.

His shirt had been cut down the back and hung at his waist. He needed to take it off and turn it around so it opened in the front. He needed to cover his back again. However, each movement brought excruciating pain and he shook from the effort it took to quell it. Taking a deep breath and holding it, he pulled the shirt off his arms and then put them through it once more, the back now becoming the front.

He had to sit down before his knees buckled and he fell on his face. He pulled his legs up to his chest and crossed his arms over his legs. Then he laid his head down on top of his arms, pulling the sarape over him like a tent.

He closed his mind to his surroundings and withdrew into a secret place within himself. He started one of the healing chants in his head for his teeth were chattering so badly he could not form the words out loud.

As the calming words filtered through his mind, he was able to relax the tense muscles as he called on the holy people to help him bear this pain and shame.

Slowly he withdrew deeper and deeper into himself until anyone looking at him would have thought he was dead sitting there.

In this trancelike state, his breathing slowed to almost nothing. His body temperature dropped and his spirit seemed to float just above his body. In this place of being, with his spirit flying free, he could no longer feel any pain.

He let his sprit rise up through the grate and fly over the fort to where Old Woman and his children sat under a cottonwood tree. JoAnna was there. He could tell she was trying to comfort and reassure them that their father would be all right. Old Woman might suspect otherwise and see through JoAnna's false cheerfulness, but she would not discount what JoAnna told the little ones.

Notah then turned his eyes back to where their homeland was. Dinétah beckoned him to return to what he'd left behind. He could see the burned out hogans, the destroyed peach orchards and corn crops trampled by the army's horses. What possessed the American army to be so wasteful and cruel, to treat another human being in such a manner? Although he had heard the soldiers refer to them as "savage animals" it was far from the truth. The Diné were not rabid wolves to be shot down. Yes, they knew how to kill; but mostly they were honor-bound to Walk in Beauty and treat all life as sacred.

Didn't even the white man's god, Jesus, say all men were brothers and created by their Father-God? He could not believe Captain Cahill or his men knew about this Jesus if they acted as they did.

He was skilled in the arts of war, too, but he preferred to live a life of peaceful coexistence with all things. *Yes,* he thought, *and look where that philosophy got me.* However, he could not change what the gods had called him to be.

As he flew over another area dear to him, a vision of Squash Blossom rose up before him, appearing like she had looked on the day they married. She had been a tiny woman—just like JoAnna—tiny hands and tiny feet. Her laugh tinkled like a brook tumbling over stones. Her smile lit up her whole face and her eyes glowed with her love for him.

He felt acute pain in the region of his heart and he tried to reach her. He felt her fingers touch his face as she shook her head.

"Don't grieve anymore for me," Squash Blossom seemed to be saying. "I am free from that horrible pain and I am happy here."

Then she kissed him and said, "You must go on with your life, and love again. Give Bella and Bacca brothers and sisters to play with, and when your time here is over, I'll be waiting for you on the

Hanging Road in the Sky," their word for the Milky Way constellation.

When she started to fade away, Notah cried out, "No . . . stay, Squash Blossom. I have missed you so."

She stopped a moment more and said, "I cannot stay; and you have someone in your life now who wants to love you very much. Let her. You need each other. And always remember, you have my heart." And then she was gone.

He wanted to protest her leaving again, but instead new warmth stole into the empty chambers of his heart and brought him peace.

Notah came awake then. He didn't know if he had actually traveled out of his body like some holy men claimed to do, or if it had all been just a vision. Seeing Squash Blossom though had freed something inside him. He suddenly realized he knew a peace about her passing into the afterlife that he had not had before this. And, the amazing thing was, she knew about JoAnna, which in itself was not terribly surprising as the spirits knew all things, but that she had given her blessing on a love between him and the bilagaana woman was the surprising part.

But he would have to think long and hard about that before he acted on it.

Now that he was conscious again, the pain slammed though him once more. He would have been better off if he had stayed in the trance, yet he knew he could not recapture that state again right now.

Looking up at the sky, he realized he must have been out for several hours as it was late afternoon.

Although the pain was not gone, those hours in the trance had dulled the worst of it and the pain had been reduced to a dull throb that he could bear providing he did not move a muscle.

Just then he heard some scuffling above him, and an, "*Oomph.*"

"Just don't stand there like a nit-wit," he heard JoAnna saying to one of his guards.

Oh, what was she up to now? She was determined to bring Cahill's wrath down upon her head, and Notah loved her for it.

"Listen, Miss JoAnna, you know we can't be coddling a prisoner," one of the men was saying.

"Coddling?" Her voice raised an octave. "The man had his back beaten raw . . . he's lost a lot of blood; he needs a drink of water. He may even be dying down there. Can you not spare a drop of human kindness and give the man a drink?"

Private McGillicutty was having a hard time with the situation as it was. She could get them both in hot water if they were caught even talking. Everyone in the fort was aware that JoAnna Lund had strong feelings for Notah and his family. He admired Notah as many of his fellow soldiers did. If the truth were known, most of the men felt the beating had been way out of line and spiteful on the captain's part, but orders were orders.

He tried to reason with her once more. "You're taking a serious risk of punishment if Captain Cahill walks out and finds you here. We'll both be in the brig, for sure."

"I know that. But you're wasting precious time with

all this talking. Just drop this bottle of water down to him on a rope, and no one will know but you and I. Quickly now, before your partner returns."

McGillicutty took the jar and told her, "I'll give it to him. Now git before someone sees us and reports it to Cahill."

JoAnna flashed him her best smile and hurried away.

Notah had listened in amazement. The audacity of this bilagaana woman surprised him at times. What wouldn't she dare to help someone she cared about?

After several moments passed, he heard a "Pssst" from above. Looking up, he saw the soldier leaning over the grate.

"Are you alive down there?" he asked.

Notah had trouble getting his mouth to work, it was so dry, but he managed to croak out a "Yes."

"Okay, then, I'm sending down a jar of water from Miss JoAnna. Untie it and I'll pull the rope back up."

"Thank you," Notah managed to get out, and greedily reached for the jar as it came down through the slits in the grate that were just wide enough to let it pass through.

Notah quickly untied the bottle and tugged on the rope to let the soldier know it was loosed.

It was quickly pulled up out of sight.

At first Notah was unfamiliar with the screw cap on the neck of the bottle but he soon figured it out. Most bottles used corks. This must be some new invention of the bilagaanas, he thought. He had to admit, they did create some wonderful things. They just didn't know how to live together in harmony it seemed.

Cautioning himself to go slowly and not gulp it all down at one time, he took a small sip and let it sit in his mouth a minute. Drinking it all, or too much too fast, would only make him sick.

Cooling, healing water! The beginning of all life! Nothing had ever tasted so good, except, something said, *JoAnna's kiss.*

Yes, he remembered, that had been life giving, too. He'd felt her surprise at the intensity of the kiss as it had deepened, and then she had returned it with an intensity of her own that, even now, had the power to arouse him.

He took another swallow and then another before he put the lid back on. Who knew how long he would be in this hole or how much longer it would be before he got any more water. He could not count on JoAnna getting away with this a second time.

Both JoAnna and the soldier had taken a great risk to do this act of kindness and he would not forget it.

He wished he dared to use the water to cool the fire in his back, but he was afraid to use it up. He could go without food for days, but no one went very long without water, even with all his Navajo warrior and Hataalii training.

He sat down in the same position again—oddly feeling much better and let the serenity he believed in steal into his soul.

Notah vowed he would make a bigger fool of this Captain Cahill. He would endure this hole; and he would come out of it a better man than when he went into it, and certainly a better man than Cahill.

In his spirit, he knew it was only a matter of time before he and Cahill met on a battlefield. Oh, not a literal battlefield maybe, but they were definitely headed for a fight, and only one of them would come out of it alive.

Notah was determined it would not be Cahill.

Chapter Seventeen

A couple of days passed before JoAnna could find a way to help Notah again. Captain Cahill must have suspected that she would try to help him because he'd doubled the guards at night, and although the men assigned to follow her had tried to be inconspicuous, she knew she was being watched.

Her break came when every man in the squad had been rotated once and Private McGillicutty was back on duty and had been paired up with Toby Wiley. Praise God, JoAnna thought; she knew Toby held Notah in high esteem, and McGillicutty had helped her once, maybe he would again.

She waited until the middle watch of the night. She drew on her father's long, black broadcloth coat and his slouch hat, and slipped out of the house. Old Woman had managed to get some unguents to her to put on the cuts from the lash, providing they hadn't gotten terribly infected already, and she'd made a healing tea that JoAnna kept warm wrapped in a hot towel. Now her only problem was getting down into the hole to see how Notah really was.

Her father heard her moving around and saw her reach behind his bedroom door and take his coat, yet he felt the less he knew the better, but he had a pretty good idea what she was planning and where she was going. He didn't have to be a medicine man to figure that out. Well, he would follow her to make sure she didn't run into any trouble, and he'd see how far she could get with this scheme. He felt she'd be fairly safe, for most of the soldiers respected and liked her; plus she had treated a lot of them for one thing or another over the course of the Long Walk, as the Navajos were beginning to call it.

The only one who might do her harm was Captain Cahill; however, everyone knew what he did with his nights. With both General Carleton and Colonel Carson away, he was either drinking and playing cards, or sneaking onto the reservation and abusing the young Indian girls.

John was sickened by his conduct and vowed he would not be put off any longer in talking to the general about Cahill's behavior. The captain had gotten away with too much, for too long.

JoAnna kept to the shadows and crept from building to building. The real problem lay in the fact that the hole was right in the middle of the compound and could be seen from everywhere. However, there was only a sliver of a moon tonight. If she was lucky, in her father's hat and coat, with her hair tucked up inside it, she may reach the guards before they realized who was approaching them.

Private Toby Wiley and Private McGillicutty sat on campstools on either side of the hole, their pistols in their laps at the ready. By this time of night, hardly anyone was still awake; most were sleeping soundly.

"Damn sorry business this," McGillicutty said. "Bad enough putting the medicine man in there, let alone whipping him, too. Sometimes I hate this man's army."

'No. I don't hate the army . . . just Captain Cahill," Toby answered. "There weren't no call for him to do what he did. If Miss JoAnna says Mr. Begay was just helping her because she twisted her ankle, then that's what happened."

"Yeah," McGillicutty answered. "He's just been looking for a chance to get back at the medicine man 'cause he couldn't break him on the trail here, let alone get him to bend. You could see it tore Cahill up that he couldn't rile that Navajo."

Just then, both men jumped to their feet when they heard someone stepping cautiously in their direction.

"Halt! Who goes there?" McGillicutty called out.

"Hush, Private," JoAnna answered. "It's me, JoAnna Lund."

Both men were shocked to see her.

"What in the Sam Hill are you doing out here at this hour, ma'am? Trying to get yourself shot, and us in trouble . . . again?" McGillicutty asked.

Private Wiley came up on the other side of her and asked the same question, "Miss JoAnna, what are you doing here?"

Neither one could believe her daring and lack of common sense.

"Please, gentlemen, I have brought some ointment for Notah's back and some hot tea. He must be freezing cold in the hole, and his cuts could well be badly infected by now."

"Well, that may be, but Miss JoAnna, we can't go down in the hole and give them to him. You know better than that," Toby told her.

"No, *you* couldn't. Of course not, but *I* could."

"You!" both men exclaimed at the same time.

"Have you lost your mind, ma'am? How are you going to get down in there? The man might be out of his head by now. You don't know what he might do to you," McGillicutty said.

"Notah would never hurt me," JoAnna answered in complete confidence, "no matter how much pain he may be in."

Both men felt that might be true. Everyone had observed the familiarity between the two, but that didn't mean he still couldn't hurt her.

"Well, maybe. I reckon he might not," Toby agreed. "But what you're asking is just plain foolishness."

"I know that, Toby, but I've got to see him. I'm going crazy not knowing how he is." JoAnna was afraid she was admitting too much in front of these men about her feelings for the Navajo, but it couldn't be helped. She *had* to know how he was faring.

"Can't you open the grate and let me climb down the rope ladder by myself. I'll be quick, I promise. I won't stay any longer than necessary. I just need to see that he isn't dying," she pleaded.

"Well, he ain't dead yet. We heard him down there chanting a little while ago," McGillicutty told her.

"Then, please," she begged them, "let me go down and see him."

Looking around the compound and not seeing any lights anywhere, McGillicutty considered whether they should chance it or not. Anyway you looked at it, it was a great risk and they could all end up in big trouble. Finally he came to a decision.

"Okay, but be mighty quick about it. How are you going to see his back in the dark anyhow?"

"I've brought a candle and some matches," JoAnna answered.

"We can't have a light out here," Wiley answered.

"Just for a second and if you can see it from up here, I'll put it out right away," JoAnna told him.

Acquiescing, McGillicutty said, "All right. I guess we can let you see how it looks. Let's get it over with before the captain finds out what we're up to."

He turned around, bent down and unlocked the padlock on the grate and Toby reached down to raise it. Thank God they kept it well greased because of the terrible weather conditions. Toby let the rope ladder down and whispered loudly into the void, "Mr. Begay . . . Mr. Begay, can you hear me?"

They heard some shuffling and then a muffled, "Yes, I hear you."

"It's me, Toby. Miss JoAnna is here, and wants to tend to your back."

Notah knew a moment of panic.

"No!" he said. "She should not be here, send her away."

Before he could finish the sentence, he saw a darker shadow coming into the opening above him. By all that was holy, she wasn't going to listen to him.

He didn't want her to see his back and witness his humiliation. It was infected, he knew, as he'd been in and out of fever for the last two days. He'd used the last of the precious water earlier in the evening because of it.

Just then he heard a thump on the ground and realized they'd let a basket down by another rope. He prayed it was more water even as he wished she hadn't come.

Reaching up for her as she neared the bottom of the ladder, he turned her to face him and held her close, even though he knew he should not.

"Ah, JoAnna, why won't you listen to me when I tell you something for your own good?"

"Because I love you," she answered, as she wrapped her arms carefully around his waist. Even so, she felt him flinch.

"That is not a good enough answer, JoAnna."

"Well, it's the only one I have, Notah. Now, we only have a few minutes so let me see your back. I've brought you some water, an herbal tea, and a little food. Old Woman has prepared a salve for your back. Is it infected?"

Letting her go and reaching for the basket, he felt for the water first and gratefully took a long swallow. Oh, what blessed relief to his burning throat.

"I must light a candle to see your back and it can only stay on for a few minutes, so get ready. Take your shirt off and turn your back to me. I will only get one chance to see it and then I'll have to work by feel when I spread the ointment on it."

Notah didn't want her to see his back like this. He knew what it looked like and was mortified that she would see his shame. He was glad it was dark and she would not be able to see his face, as he was afraid to read the expression on hers.

Undoing the shirt was agony. The blood had dried and the shirt stuck to his back. He could not repress a groan when the shirt came away with more skin and his blood started oozing once more.

JoAnna lit the candle when she felt he was ready, and held it up to see his back.

God in heaven, how had he stood it!

It looked like it had been caught in a meat grinder. An involuntary gasp escaped her lips although she tried not to react or let him know had bad it was.

He started to turn around, saying, "JoAnna you don't have to do this."

Stopping him from turning, she said, "No, Notah, stay still. I think I'll use some of the warm herbal tea as an astringent on your back before I put the salve on it. I would have brought you a clean shirt but there would have been no way to explain that."

"Light out, down there," McGillicutty whispered urgently. He'd heard a noise and hoped it wasn't Cahill returning from one of his excursions into the Indian camp. He started to sweat.

JoAnna doused the candle quickly, waving it a little to dispel the smoke and smell of it.

Glancing around all the guard saw was a soldier returning from the latrine and he let out the breath he'd been holding.

"It's okay, but hurry it up now," McGillicutty called down.

Notah gritted his teeth and waited for JoAnna's touch on his raw back. It would hurt no matter how careful she was. He leaned his head against the side of the hole with his arms outstretched to brace himself.

JoAnna poured some of the tea onto the towel she'd wrapped around it to keep it warm, and tried to remember from her quick survey where the worst cuts were. That wasn't even the question though because they were all bad.

When she touched his back, he only flinched once, and then, oddly enough, her touch didn't hurt like he'd expected. Instead, warmth and healing and love followed each swipe of the towel as she gently drew it across his flayed back.

His breath came out in a sigh. "You do have the hands of a healer, JoAnna. Your touch is very sooth-ing. I have seen this many times on our trip here when you ministered to the sick and the dying. I appreciate what you did for my people."

"I was only sorry I could not do more."

Then, strictly going by feel, she spread the salve over the ridges made by the lash.

"Oh, that Cahill," she muttered. "He should be horsewhipped himself. If I were bigger, I'd take one to him myself."

"Oh, my little warrior woman," Notah said. The image of JoAnna wielding a whip on Cahill made him smile. Her fury at the captain on his behalf warmed his heart. She had the heart of a mother lion protecting her cubs in that little body of hers.

Still, not turning around to face her, he said, "JoAnna, I am grateful for this help, but you must promise me you will stay away from me the rest of the time I am in here. I could not bear the thought of the captain taking out his spite on you if he finds this out. The holy ones have not deserted me. I *will* make it through this; the more so now, because of your care, but I will be the one to take revenge on Cahill. *I* will do it, not you."

Then turning around, he felt for her face and took it between his hands and in that moment he could see her as plain as day in his mind's eye.

Looking into her face, he said, "Promise me, JoAnna, you *will* stay away. I will have your word on this."

Grudgingly, she answered, "Oh, all right, but you still need more water and salve and food."

"I am not a Hataalii for nothing, JoAnna."

"I know, but you can't make food out of dirt," she

couldn't help answering. It would kill her to stay away and not know if he was thirsty or hurting.

He touched his forehead to hers and said, "You would be surprised what I can do."

Then he kissed her tenderly on the mouth. For in truth he could not hold back any longer. He needed to taste her as much as he had needed the taste of water.

It was a gentle kiss, full of promises that he wasn't ready to share with her yet. He felt Squash Blossom's smiling approval.

"Now, go, JoAnna. Please . . . for my sake, get out of here." He turned her toward the ladder just as it started to come down. More time had gone by than they realized and the men above were getting anxious.

Toby's ghostly face appeared above the hole.

"Come on now, Miss JoAnna. It's about time for the watch to change again. You've been down there much too long."

"I'm coming," she replied.

Notah tied the basket back onto the rope they dropped, and then helped JoAnna reach the first rung of the ladder.

She didn't want to leave him, but he was pushing on her bottom to move on up.

Just that light touch on her bottom made her want to stay and she hesitated on the next rung.

As if sensing her feelings, Notah said, "No, JoAnna, go!"

But he couldn't resist giving her a love swat on her perfect little backside.

She gasped, and then smiled. He'd never done anything like that before. He used to be so careful not to touch her in any familiar way. Something had changed between them since their first kiss. She could only hope that it meant he was beginning to feel something *more* for her.

JoAnna reached the top and McGillicutty helped her out and Toby handed her the basket he had hauled up.

"Now, git, girl," McGillicutty said. "But know this, we will not take this chance again, ye hear?"

"Yes, Private, I hear you. I am sorry to have pushed you into it, but I am also very grateful. Thank you from the bottom of my heart." Then she leaned up and kissed each one on the cheek.

Now that it was almost safely over, Toby couldn't help asking, "Well, how bad was it—his back, I mean."

"Bad, Toby. It made me sick to my stomach but he'll make it, he told me so," JoAnna replied; and for the first time since she'd seen his back, she firmly believed it.

"Well, then, he will; after all he is a holy man," Toby agreed. He had the utmost confidence in Notah's abilities and believed he did have supernatural powers. Look how he had saved him with all the odds against them. Yes, sir, if Notah said he'd make it, then he will!

McGillicutty patted her shoulder and said, "Git on with you. Hurry home now. Go back the way you came but please be careful. We can't leave our post to walk you back."

JoAnna knew she had to go. She pulled the hat down tighter on her head, and the collar up on her coat, and hurried into the shadows once again.

Notah had been listening intently to everything being said above him. He let out a sigh of relief when he finally heard her leave. Again, he had the thought that for such a tiny thing, she had the fearlessness of a mother mountain lion. What was he going to do with her?

"Love her," came a faint voice in his head that sounded like Squash Blossom's.

He smiled, "Thank you, Squash Blossom. You were my first love, and the love of my youth. I will not forget you and I will not let our children forget you, either."

He felt a cool breeze touch his cheek and then she was gone. And this time he knew she was truly gone. She'd come to him when he needed her and she had set him free to love again, to move on with his life, and leave his grief behind.

The holy people had truly blessed him. It humbled him to think he'd been allowed to know the love of two such women. He would not take lightly their beautiful gift.

Taking another swallow of water, he decided not to put the shirt back on for now. He sat down as he had been sitting—knees drawn up, arms crossed over the top of his legs, head bent down on his arms, pulling the shirt over top of his head.

He was in harmony with all things again. Surpris-

ingly, he found his back wasn't hurting like it had
been earlier. He was sure it was a combination of
the tea, the salve, and JoAnna's touch on his
scarred back that had worked their magic. He fell
into a peaceful slumber with a smile in his heart for
a feisty, little bilagaana woman.

JoAnna reached the house without any mishaps
and breathed her own sigh of relief. When she went
to hang up her father's coat on his door, his voice
reached out to her in the pre-dawn darkness.

"It went well, JoAnna?"

So, he had heard me leave, JoAnna thought.

"Yes, Father, forgive me for not telling you, but I
was afraid you would not let me go, and I just had
to know how he was doing. I needed to see his
back."

"How was it?"

So for the second time, she explained what she
had seen.

"Very bad. Old Woman gave me some salve for
him, and I used some of the herbal tea to wash his
back. I confess I thought I might throw up when I
first saw it. I tried not to let on to Notah how terrible it looked."

"I'm sure he knew how terrible, by the way it felt!
There was infection, I presume?"

"Yes, hopefully the tea and salve will help as he
has forbidden me to come back." A little sob of
anger came through her voice at his order not to
return.

"As was his right to do, JoAnna. I'm sure it galled him to have you see him thus. I would not have let you go a second time, anyway."

"Oh, I know, Father," she said as she lit the kerosene lantern so she could see him as she talked with him. He was sitting in his rocking chair, fully clothed.

Apparently he had been waiting up for her ever since she'd left.

"You heard me leave, didn't you?"

When he nodded, she asked, "Why, then, didn't you stop me?"

He managed a small laugh. "Could I stop the wind from blowing? You were going, come hell or high water, so I followed you to make sure you made it there safely. I saw who was on guard duty and trusted them to take care of it from there, but I admit I have been a nervous wreck for the past two hours.

"But Notah was right, JoAnna. No more chances. You've satisfied your need to know. I'm not so blind that I can't see that you've fallen in love with him, and like I said before, you would have my blessing should he ask you to marry him, but have faith now in the man he is, and let him deal with his captivity in his own way. Don't let him think that you feel he can't make it without your help."

"I see what you're saying, Father. Of course, I believe in him, and the man he is. I will not embarrass him any further or cause him to lose face among his people. But, oh, when I saw his back, I felt like I wanted to take a whip to Captain Cahill myself."

John chuckled at that. "And, did you say that to Notah?"

"Well, yes," she admitted.

"And?"

"Well, he said not to, that he'd take care of it."

She didn't tell him that he'd called her his *little warrior woman*" but the memory of it brought a dreamy expression to her face, by which John could only surmise there was definitely more to the story. He smiled at that.

"Okay, darlin', then leave it to him, and now get yourself to bed. It's almost time to get up again."

"Yes, Father," she replied, and leaned down to kiss him on the cheek. "Sleep well," she called back as she exited the room.

"You, too, daughter."

JoAnna knew she would sleep better than she had for the past three nights now that she had seen Notah and knew he would be all right.

She went into her bedroom, undressed, and pulled on her nightgown. Crawling into bed, she fell into a deep, much needed sleep.

Chapter Eighteen

After a week had passed, Captain Cahill ordered Notah to be brought up out of the hole, fully expecting either a blithering idiot or a man half dead. To his shock and chagrin, he found neither. Although Notah certainly looked the worse for his treatment, he climbed out of the hole on his own and stood before the captain as composed as ever.

Cahill couldn't believe it. He had commissioned several soldiers to spy on the hole to make sure Notah received no help from anyone and they had not reported anything amiss to him. He didn't know which infuriated him more—Notah's being alive or the look of contempt on his face, as if Cahill were some insignificant bug he need take no notice of.

It was all he could do not to order Notah back into the hole, but he knew the general would not stand for it a second time. He'd had a hard time convincing General Carleton and Colonel Carson that Notah deserved the punishment he'd given him while they were in Santa Fe. He had made it sound like Notah was practically raping JoAnna Lund when he came upon them, and that he felt he could not let this pass. He'd told them he did not *"want any other redskin to think he could take liberties with white women."*

Although not convinced as to the veracity of Cahill's statements, it was already too late to change the punishment by the time the officers returned late the night before. Today both men planned to talk to JoAnna and her father to get at the truth, for both Carleton and Carson knew enough about the Navajo's regard for the Lunds to believe that there was more to this story than they had heard so far. They were present when Notah came up from the hole, as were JoAnna and her father.

General Carleton noted that neither of the Lunds looked angry or fearful of Notah's release. Rather they looked sad and upset.

Looking at Notah, Colonel Carson said, "With your permission, sir, I would like to talk with Notah privately about this incident. Something just doesn't ring true to me about it."

"Yes, I agree," answered Carleton. "Just look at him standing there . . . it must be true what they say about him being a medicine man with supernatural powers. He certainly doesn't look as bad as I expected. What do your suppose accounts for that, Colonel?"

"I don't know. I certainly expected him to be in pain and agony and much thinner. At the least, thirst should have gotten to him by now. But I can tell you, I have witnessed some strange things in his presence."

"Like what?"

"Well, one time he called down lightning to strike near a man who had stolen another man's wife and sheep. It didn't kill him, but it scared him half to death, and he returned both sheep and wife. Another time, he took a child's broken arm in his hands, held the bones together for a minute and then released the arm; the boy scampered off to play as if nothing had been broken at all."

"Amazing," said the general. "I think, while you're talking to Notah, I will speak with the Lunds."

So saying, he turned and walked to his office. When he got there, he ordered his aide-de-camp to bring the Lunds to him.

Watching the two officers converse, Cahill knew a moment of panic. What were they talking about? However, when he saw the general head back to his office, he breathed a sigh of relief. He noted, though, that Carson stayed nearby.

The captain knew he had to release Notah now and send him back to the Navajo camp.

Gritting his teeth and in a low voice only Notah heard, he said, "You may have won this time around, redskin, but the year is not over yet. Watch your back!"

"Watch yours, also," Notah answered without any change of expression.

Cahill wanted to slap the Navajo's face or call him out for insulting an officer, but instead, through sheer grit he refrained, and said, "You're dismissed. Get back to your camp and never let me see you in this fort again after today."

Notah didn't bother to acknowledge his dismissal,

just turned on his heel and walked through the fort's entrance, and left. He'd seen JoAnna on the fringe of the crowd and he prayed she would not try to follow him from the compound. In fact, he willed her not to with everything in him.

As if she heard him, JoAnna hesitated after taking a step in his direction, then stopped when she felt her father's restraining hand on her arm.

"No, JoAnna, let him return to his family first. Later I'll go see him and see how he is doing. You need to stay away from him right now."

"Oh, Father, how can I bear to do that?"

She would have said more, but at that moment the general's adjutant approached them and asked that they follow him to the commander's office.

John was more than happy to go with him. He turned to JoAnna and said, "Come, daughter. This may be our only chance to set the record straight with the general. We've wanted an audience with him for some time. Let's take advantage of this unexpected meeting."

"Yes, of course. You're right. We do need to talk to him."

Turning to the adjutant, John said, "We're ready to see the general. Please, take us to him."

Nodding, he led them off.

Cahill had hung around in the background after everyone left the field and saw the general's aide come for the Lunds. He could only surmise what it was about and he just hoped he could undo whatever damage they did by their testimony.

He'd also seen Carson head off to the Indian encampment. *Now what did that mean?* Cahill became uneasy again. What would happen if Carleton and Carson compared notes? It did not bode well for the thinking. He'd have to come up with something to countermand whatever the Lunds and Notah told his commanding officers.

Notah reached his camp and was immediately surrounded by his clansmen and his children. His back still hurt, but he had to pick Bella up in his arms and hold her close while Bacca clung to his leg as he stroked his head.

He told his people he would talk to them later in the evening but for now he wanted time with his children and needed Old Woman to tend to his back.

They understood and reiterated how glad they were to have him back with them. They planned for everyone to contribute to the evening meal since it was hard enough to feed one family let alone all the others. And that galled everyone, for cooking pots were always filled and left cooking over the fire. Hospitality was always practiced so that if someone stopped by they could eat, or not eat, any time of the day or night.

After they left, Notah went into their brush and adobe shelter. How pitiful it was but so much better than being in the hole. He had feared that if he had had to stay another few hours, he might not have been able to stand it. Never had he valued freedom more.

Sitting down inside, he took off the remains of his shirt and asked Old Woman to look at his back.

Bella climbed into his lap and he let her, but cautioned her about touching him.

"Can I hug your neck?" she asked in a small, frightened voice.

"Yes," he answered, and bent down so she could more easily reach him. Tears filled his eyes as Bella hugged him, then patted his face.

He looked at Old Woman and she nodded and went behind him to look at his back.

Even knowing what to expect, Old Woman was shocked. Some cuts had headed over but would always be raised up as scar tissue, but some lash marks were still oozing pus from an infection. She was amazed that gangrene hadn't set in.

Anticipating his release, she had set about making a poultice to draw out the poison and some of the tea that JoAnna had used as an astringent to once again bathe the stripes on his back.

"Truly, the gods were with you, Notah," she said. "You will bear these marks the rest of your life. This should not have happened."

While she was speaking, Bacca scampered behind his father to take a look before Notah could stop him. He couldn't stop the cry of horror that escaped his lips at the mangled mess of his father's once smooth back.

"Oh, Father, why would they do this to you?"

"Bacca, come here," commanded Notah, holding onto Bella as she struggled to get down and go see for herself what had happened. He did not want her to look upon his shame.

When Bacca sat down in front of him with fear in his eyes, Notah reached out and touched his shoulder and said, "It is very hard to understand the bilagaana soldiers right now, and to understand why they do what they do. There was a misunderstanding when JoAnna visited us last. You remember I was walking her back to the fort, right?"

"Yes," Bacca answered. "But she loves you; she wouldn't do anything like this to you?"

So, Notah thought, even his children and Old Woman thought they knew of her feelings for him. His suspicions were confirmed when he turned and saw the woman nodding, *yes*, confirming Bacca's statement.

"No, of course, JoAnna wouldn't order or do such a thing. You know she has a crippled foot . . ."

Bella chimed in then and asked, "Yes, Father, we know about her crooked foot. Why haven't you been able to lay hands on it and straighten it out for her? I think she would let you, if you asked her," she said with confidence.

He smiled at the innocence of the young.

"Well, little one, we've never discussed it, but some things that happen in birth cannot be reversed. But someday, if she will let me have a really good look at it, I will see if something can be done for her."

Satisfied with his answer, Bella said, "That is good."

But Bacca would not be put off. "Why did the soldiercoats do this to your back, Father? I will never like these bilagaanas and when I am grown up, I will fight them to the death."

Another smile crossed Notah's face at the fierceness of Bacca's declaration; however, he could not stop the shudder when Old Woman touched a particularly tender spot.

"All right, Bacca, I will tell you what happened. JoAnna stumbled on the rough ground and her bad foot gave way beneath her, I reached out to stop her from falling. Just then the captain who led us here, came around the back of a building and saw me holding JoAnna and he thought I should not be touching her in any way. So he called his guards."

Old Woman snorted her opinion of such an action.

His son cried out, "How stupid of the soldiercoat not to see what you were doing. The Bluecoat Cahill does not like you, Father. He has wanted to get back at you for a long time for saving one of his soldiers."

Notah was surprised at the maturity and understanding of the situation Bacca showed. He had not thought he would know what was happening.

"Yes, son, it was Captain Cahill. He came just as I was looking at JoAnna's ankle to see if she had sprained it and he thought I meant to harm her and that's when he called his guards to arrest me."

"You would never hurt JoAnna," Bella cried. "You love her back."

Her statement startled Notah. Had his children seen his love growing for JoAnna all along, when he had failed to acknowledge any feelings for her, let alone call it *love*? It was a wonder to him that they accepted it so easily and he had struggled so hard with it himself.

Old Woman could not keep still any longer. "Didn't JoAnna give an explanation to the captain? Would they not believe the word of the holy man? How ignorant are these Bluecoats?"

"I cannot explain them," Notah answered. "As Bacca said, Captain Cahill was out for revenge. I believe his heart is only evil and full of bitterness, there is no harmony in him."

"I knew it," Bacca exclaimed. "He treated you mean the whole way here. That is why he whipped you. When I grow up, I will take vengeance on him for you."

"Yes, son, I'm afraid it is. But, Bacca, it is done. I do not want you to carry vengeance in your heart over this. It will only upset your Hozho and keep you from Walking in Beauty. If there is vengeance to be done, it is mine to repay, but for now we will do nothing."

Notah continued, "I think it is time to teach you about the two wolves."

Bacca's ears perked up. "What is it about two wolves, Father?"

"Son, it is like this. There is a battle between two wolves that live inside all of us. One is Evil. *It is anger, envy, jealousy, sorrow, regret, greed, self-pity, lies, guilt, and the like. The other is* Good. *It is joy, peace, love, hope, harmony, humility, kindness, truth, compassion, and faith."*

Bacca thought for a moment, and then said, "Which wolf wins?"

"The one you feed," answered Notah.

"So," Bacca replied, "you are telling me if I

continue to hate this Bluecoat, I am only hurting myself?"

Again, Notah was amazed at how astute Bacca was becoming. Maybe he had the makings of a holy man one day.

"Yes, son. We will leave his punishment to the gods."

And to me, he thought, ignoring what he had just taught the children.

Bella's eyes filled with tears and she patted her father's face.

"He is a bad man and the gods should not be nice to him," she said.

Notah had to squeeze his own eyes shut not to shed tears at his daughter's tenderness.

"It is over now, and we will not dwell anymore on it. We will just stay away from the fort and I have to ask you to stay away from JoAnna as well, for a while. Although she will probably try to come to see you, for her own safety, I do not wish her to visit our camp. She did come and bring me water, and Old Woman's healing unguents for my back while I was imprisoned though, and I am grateful for the risk she took to help me."

"I'm glad she did. It is most likely what kept you from having a worse infection," Old Woman said as she finished wrapping his back in clean cloths.

"I'm sure of it. Thank you Old Woman, for everything. My back feels better already. I am grateful for your skills and I know they are what saved me."

Chapter Nineteen

Just as Old Woman was finishing up her ministrations to Notah, and he started to rise to put on a clean tunic, a cough with a hesitant knocking sounded on the outside of the hogan's wooden doorframe.

"*Ho-ta-hey,*" Notah answered the knock.

"It's Colonel Carson," came the answer. "I'd like to talk with you for a moment, Notah, if you have the time?"

Realizing he didn't want the children in on their conversation, he asked Old Woman to take the children out for a while.

Seeing the look on their father's face and knowing this was serious grown-up business, they left with Old Woman but not before Bella grabbed her Raggedy Ann doll that JoAnna had given her. It had become a sort of security for her.

Notah patted her and assured her things would be fine as she left reluctantly.

He then bade Carson to enter his home.

"Please sit, friend Carson," Notah told him,

although he was not sure about the friend part anymore.

Carson glanced around the meagerly furnished hogan, so much different from the wealth the medicine man had left behind. He knew a moment of regret to think that he had had a hand in reducing this proud man to such humble leavings.

He sat down cross-legged across from Notah and realized that this was the first time he had been inside a Navajo dwelling since they'd arrived here many months ago. He was surprised at how bad off they were. He'd thought the army had been supplying them with food, clothing, blankets, and other necessities. It appeared the army had not followed through on its promises. How galling this must be to Notah and the others. He wondered how the chief had fared.

Carson felt Notah's eyes on him and he squirmed a little under his scrutiny. Well, he figured there was no use in beating around the bush, or holding to polite talk and ceremony now before getting down to business.

Notah determined that he was not going to be the one to open the conversation. He waited patiently so see how Carson was going to handle this meeting. He could sense the officer's unease.

When Carson looked at Notah, he saw him looking back at him squarely, with a question in his eyes.

Kit knew a moment of misgiving—he wasn't afraid of Notah, but he did not underestimate him, either. This was his home territory, not Carson's. Finally, he knew he had to begin.

"Notah, I'm here to get to the bottom of what happened while the general and I were away. I assure you, we had no knowledge of Captain Cahill's treatment of you until we returned last night and attended your release this morning."

When Notah didn't say anything, Carson continued.

"I was not aware of any discord between you and Captain Cahill but some of the soldiers have reported things to me recently concerning his actions toward you and your people, both on the trail here and since your confinement on the reservation."

"What exactly have you heard?" Notah was not gong to tell the colonel anything yet.

"While I'm not at liberty to discuss the actions of the army with you, I was told of your rescue of Private Wiley and how that made Captain Cahill look bad in front of his men."

"He made himself look bad," Notah replied, "by not sending someone in after the young man. The current was too strong for him."

"Yes, I was told that, and I want to have a talk with the captain about it. Is there anything else I should know about before I talk with him? Like why you were whipped and put in the hole?"

Rather than give him an answer, Notah said, "Walk with me through our camp and see how we are living and tell me what you see."

As they made their way from campsite to campsite, Carson was appalled at their living conditions. Their clothing, such as it was, hung on their emaciated frames like rags. Their makeshift hogans were poorly constructed due to the lack of wood and bear grass. Water was scarce and had to be hauled a good distance from the Pecos River and was known not to be the best water around. The cooking pots that were over the fires were mostly empty. Carson again wondered at the army's promise to supply the Navajo with food, farming equipment, and housing once they were settled on the reservation.

He was embarrassed for the army and ashamed before these previously industrious people.

Finally, they came to Chief Manuelito's dwelling and Notah announced them.

The chief stuck his head out of his door and seeing who it was, invited them in. Turning to Notah, he spoke rapidly in Navajo to him.

"Hataalii, I am grieved that such a thing should befall our holy man. It was all I could do to restrain myself and our people to keep them from storming the fort and coming after you."

Notah took the chief's forearm and clasped it.

"It would have done no good and only brought harm to the Diné. I am glad you did not come or let them come, either."

Carson had followed most of the conversation, but he knew there was a lot more going on behind the scenes here than either he or General Carleton were aware of.

Then, as if remembering his manners, Manuelito turned to Kit Carson and bade him sit down opposite him.

Carson seated himself after Notah did, and then the chief sat down as well.

Not waiting the respectful amount of time before beginning a conversation, Manuelito went directly to the point.

"Why are you here, Kit Carson? Have you come to gloat over us, to see if we are being *good* Indians?" he asked with scorn in his voice.

Carson had the grace to flush and squirmed in his place; however, he could not show any weakness in front of these two men. So, looking directly into the chief's eyes, he answered him sincerely.

"No, Chief Manuelito, I am not here to gloat. I am here to find out what is going on with you and your people. I want you to know the general and I had no idea that Notah was being punished or imprisoned as we were away on army business in Santa Fe."

"Yes, we know you were gone, but what we do not know, is whether you would have stopped his punishment or not, had you been here," answered the chief.

"Well, that is exactly why I am here, and what I hope to find out. But I won't know unless someone tells me what has been going on, and what led to Notah's arrest, and why things are so bad in your camps."

"Ah, so you acknowledge that our camps do not look like the ones we lived in back in Dinétah."

"Yes, of course, I can see a drastic change in your status of living," Carson answered the chief. "I would have to be blind not to notice. It was my understanding that the army would be supplying you with food, shelter, and tools to farm and work with."

"Ha!" exclaimed both Notah and the chief at the same time.

"What housing or tools do you see? What meat do you see in our stew pots? Where are our sheep herds?" the chief asked.

Then, before Carson could answer, he said, "There are none!"

"I can see that, Chief, and I will look into it when I return to the fort. It is not only the army's word that is being besmirched here by failing to keep its promise, it is mine, as well. And, you know me from the past, I was true to any word I ever gave to you."

The chief nodded in agreement to that.

"So, what do you think you can do?" Notah asked.

"I don't know truthfully," Carson replied. "But I do promise to speak to the general on your behalf. However, you still haven't told me about the march here, and what caused you to be locked up?" He directed his question back to Notah.

Manuelito said to Notah, "Go ahead and tell him. Tell him about the old men, women, and children we lost on the Long Walk. Tell him of the lack of food and heat on cold nights. Tell him of this Captain Cahill's hatred for the Navajo!" he exclaimed, his anger mounting with every sentence.

Carson became alarmed. Apparently a lot more had gone on than he had ever imagined. Hearing the vehemence in the chief's voice as he mentioned Cahill's name spoke of more than just privation on the trail. Had his misgivings about trusting Cahill with the responsibility to bring the Navajos in proved right?

"All right, Notah, what is it about Captain Cahill that I don't know?" Carson asked.

Notah thought about it for another minute. Maybe if Carson knew the true character of the captain, some justice might be forthcoming for the Navajos. So he began from the beginning after Carson had left the chief's clan in the care of Cahill, through the raiding of the Lund's trading post and ordering them to come along with the Diné because they had protested the Navajo's treatment . . . to commandeering a farmer's wagon along the way, the dysentery, the lung fever and illnesses that plagued the weaker ones, and how they had no blankets against the cold. That they were not allowed to hunt for food on their own as their weapons had all been confiscated. He told of his rescue of Toby, and, lastly, why Cahill had imprisoned him.

Shocked, Carson did not know what to say, or how to answer all these accusations. He vaguely knew Cahill hated Indians for some personal reason, but he had trusted him to do his duty as an officer of the U.S. cavalry with a better performance than this.

And to command the Lunds to forsake their homestead and force them to come along was certainly against army policy.

Finally, when he had digested what had been told to him, he said, "I am appalled by the actions of Captain Cahill and I intend to look into the matter immediately. I trusted him to do his duty as an officer and carry out his orders in a timely manner. He was not instructed to use brutality after you had surrendered yourselves into his care."

Then Carson realized how that sounded as the

chief picked up on it right away. The chief shook his head as if to say, *I knew it.*

"So, you are saying brute force would have been used had we not submitted? I thought as much; so that is why I counseled my warriors not to put up a fight. Innocent women and children would have died had we fought you."

Carson knew then that Manuelito's band did not want to give in but would have fought him had the chief said to. He was relieved they had not.

Turning back to Notah, Carson said, "So you feel that Captain Cahill has some personal grudge against you, and that he has singled you out for harsher treatment than the others."

Notah was not going to tell this officer the real reason that Cahill hated him, Cahill's lustful interest in JoAnna, but the chief had no qualms about it. He himself answered the colonel.

"It has been observed by many that the captain has an interest in the bilagaana woman, JoAnna Lund; and we all know that this woman has an interest in us as a people, and in Notah and his family, specifically. Cahill does not like her interest in us, or him. He takes offense in us having anything to do with the bilagaana woman."

Carson was stunned again by these further revelations about Cahill.

"Is this true, Notah? Has Cahill behaved badly toward Miss Lund?"

Notah wanted to choke his chief at the moment for revealing something so personal, especially since he had only recently admitted to himself that there were feelings between he and JoAnna. But he knew Carson was waiting for some kind of an answer from him.

"It is an observation by many that Captain Cahill would like to pursue JoAnna Lund. She has befriended me and my children for over three years now, and we are all good friends, her father included. If the captain has misinterpreted her friendship with us for something more, he is wrong."

Notah was not about to let anyone know of her declaration of love for him, nor of his real feelings for her.

"I see," Carson said. "Has Miss Lund ever said the captain has acted improperly toward her, for indeed, that will not be tolerated by the army."

Again, Notah did not want to answer with specifics.

"I think you will have to ask Miss JoAnna about that," Notah replied. "She does not confide such things to me."

"Yes, I suppose you're right. Why would she discuss that with you," Carson surmised.

Why, indeed? thought Notah, but of course, he knew why. She had told him of her fear of Cahill's advances, but it was for Carson to get those answers directly from her.

Getting to his feet, Carson said, "Thank you, Chief Manuelito and Notah. I will be going back now and I promise you, I *will* look into this whole situation. I intend to tell the general what I've seen and what I've been told. I would like an explanation for the way things are myself."

The chief and Notah had risen with him.

Notah said, "I will walk you back through the camp to the edge of the fort."

Carson knew he could find his way back, but surmised he might be safer with Notah. Maybe there was more hostility toward him in the camp than he knew.

"That would be fine," he answered and left the hogan with Notah leading the way.

As promised, at the edge of the fort grounds, Notah left Carson with a nod. Carson knew there was nothing more to say, so he just turned and continued into the fort.

Arriving back at the fort, he made a beeline for the general's headquarters, and told his adjutant that he needed a meeting with Carleton as soon as possible. He was told the general was at dinner, but he would give him the colonel's message as soon as he was through eating. He could see that Carson was upset, but he still hesitated to interrupt the general during mealtime.

The colonel could do nothing else but acquiesce and wait for a summons later. He turned and left for the officer's mess hall, thinking he might as well eat, too. Then he felt guilty remembering the empty stew pots of the Navajos.

He wondered again what had gone wrong with the plans the army had for feeding the Navajos.

Oh, well, he knew he couldn't change things and he wasn't all too sure the general could either.

Chapter Twenty

While Kit Carson was busy in the Navajo camp, General Carleton was seated with the Lunds. He did not liking what he was hearing.

"So, you're telling me that on this 'Long Walk' as the Navajos are calling it, Captain Cahill did not seem to care for the overall welfare of those he was assigned to bring in?"

"Yes, sir, I am," John Lund answered. "He would not let them bring enough provisions to begin with, killing most of their sheep, not providing clothing or warm blankets, or enough firewood to keep warm. They were not allowed to hunt along the way. There was dysentery, lung fever, fatigue, and any number of illnesses that JoAnna and I could not treat for lack of medicine or good food."

"I see, but you can also see the necessity of taking their weapons from them in case they rebelled and tried to go back home. I recall now, Captain Cahill said you were a doctor and that your daughter helped you in caring for the sick. I do appreciate that."

"Yes, JoAnna is a skilled nurse. She is good in the use of plants and herbs in healing wounds and fevers. But we quickly ran out of what little we could bring with us as well."

"Were your observations prejudiced in any way, because the captain forced you to come along with the Navajos?" the general asked.

"No," JoAnna answered this time. "Of course we didn't like being uprooted and leaving our home, which Captain Cahill torched, but the Navajos are our friends, and in the end, we felt that we might be of help to them on the way here. As it was, we were there because of them, and without them, we really had little reason to remain behind."

"All right then. Did you observe any special hostility developing between Captain Cahill and this holy man he imprisoned?" he asked.

Again JoAnna answered. "Yes, very much so. Especially after Hataalii Notah saved young Private Wiley from drowning. Even with his hands tied, he jumped into the water and brought him to the other shore. It made the captain look bad in front of his men, I'm sure, but it was his own fault for not sending someone in to rescue Private Wiley."

The general's eyebrows rose on that bit of information. He would like to have seen that feat performed by this Notah, himself.

"Oh? Explain that in more detail for me, if you would, please," the general asked.

John took up the story again and explained in detail everything that had led up to that water rescue, and how the captain had not ordered anyone to go in after young Toby Wiley. He fully described Notah's remarkable rescue and how Cahill would not let Notah out of the water. Then about Notah's subsequent drifting away downstream, not to be seen again for five days.

"Are you insinuating that you think Captain Cahill meant for something bad to happen to Notah?"

"Yes," JoAnna quickly stepped in and answered. "He *wished* him to die as we saw it. The weather was cold and the water had to be freezing—no one thought he could make it."

"But, apparently, he did. Amazing. And where was he for the five days that he went missing?"

"He never told us," John answered. "But we assumed he found help somewhere, for when he rejoined us, he looked fine and even had a change of dry clothing."

"Again, amazing," said the general. "You know these are very serious charges you are bringing against a military officer?"

"Yes, sir, we do," replied John, "and we will swear that everything we have told you is true in a court of law, if need be."

"Father," JoAnna spoke up, "that is not the worst of it. What about the captain's treatment of the Indian girls?"

"I don't like the sound of that, young lady; nor do I think I want to hear about it," said the general.

JoAnna bristled and said, "Well, maybe you should care. He's been harassing the young girls and maybe he even goes further than that."

The general leaned forward in his chair and stared hard at JoAnna.

"Do you have proof of this, Miss Lund?" The frostiness in his tone, did not bode well for JoAnna, but she persisted.

"No, I have no actual proof but there have been rumors abounding around the Navajo and Apache camps."

"Did any one of the girls come to you personally and tell you she had been mistreated?" the general asked JoAnna in an even harsher tone.

JoAnna hated to admit that no one had ever come forward to her and told her anything. They had gone to Old Woman though. However, JoAnna knew the general would not take the word of an old Navajo woman against the word of a captain in the U.S. Cavalry.

As the general was waiting for her answer, she had to reply.

"No, I have no actual proof from anyone."

"Then we will not address this issue any further at this time," the general said in dismissal.

The Lunds groaned inside. This General Carleton did not have a heart for the plight of the *People*. What the soldiers said about him having some grandiose idea of making *Christians* out of them, *civilizing* them to turn them into farmers and upstanding citizens in a society totally unprepared to accept them, and one that the Diné were not prepared for at all, must be true.

The general stood and said, "Thank you for coming in Dr. Lund, and Miss Lund. I will look into all this, and I will also see to releasing you from staying here at the fort any longer. You are free to leave and return to your home as soon as you want to. I will see if there can even be some sort of restitution made for your losses."

JoAnna knew a moment of panic—*no*, they could not leave yet! There was too much unfinished business concerning the Navajos, and between her and Notah. She knew, though, it wouldn't do any good to say anything further in front of the general.

John had risen, too, and held out his hand to the general.

"Thank you, General, for hearing us out. I know this puts you in a delicate position with the army officials and your troops, but justice must be done for these Navajos."

The general did not like to be told what to do, especially by a civilian, but he hid his feelings and shook John's hand, saying, "You have my word, Dr. Lund. I am going to look into it. Good day to both of you . . . and, again, thank you for coming in and making your feelings known to me."

John and JoAnna knew when they were being dismissed and turned and walked out into the outer office and waiting room. The aide-de-camp bid them good-bye as well and then rushed back into the general's office to see if he had any further instructions for him.

Taking JoAnna's arm to cross the compound, John remarked, "Well, I'm not sure we accomplished much after all, my dear. The general doesn't seem to like criticism about army policy."

"That was obvious. I hope we haven't made things worse for the Navajos by speaking up in their behalf, and against Cahill."

"Well, only time will tell, I guess. What do you make of his telling us we're free to leave and go back to our property?"

JoAnna stopped dead in her tracks and faced her father.

"We can't leave yet! I can't . . . I mean, I don't want to leave now. I would die not knowing what was happening with the Navajo."

"What you really mean is, JoAnna, you will die not knowing what is happening to Notah and his children, isn't that so?" asked her father.

Seeing her crestfallen look, he pulled her into his arms and asked, "What has happened between you two, daughter? Why can't you leave him now?"

"You're right, Father, something did change recently between Notah and I, but I can't tell you what exactly. He promised me nothing and said nothing, it was sorta' *just there* after I visited him in the hole. But I want to *see* where it could lead, although it is not likely to lead anywhere with them penned up on this horrible reservation."

They continued on toward their home, and John remarked, "So Notah did not ask you to become his wife?"

"No, Father . . . well, not in so many words. Actually, he said he was not the man for me and that

I should look for a man among my own people to marry."

"I see, and what was your answer?" he asked.

"I told him that I loved him and there would be no one else for me, and that I would wait for him forever if I had to."

"Well, well, well, that declaration must have shocked him. How did he answer you?"

"Yes, I think it did shock him. His answer was, 'so be it for now.' He made no commitment or promises about tomorrow, but there was definitely some feeling on his part."

Yes, there had definitely been a new and different feeling emanating from him while she was ministering to him in the hole—a sort of acceptance, maybe, of a time when he could welcome her love. Again, it wasn't anything that had been spoken; it was just a quiet feeling that it would somehow work itself out and she had felt encouraged when she left.

"Be that as it may, JoAnna, I don't think we'll be able to stay indefinitely, and it does not look like the Navajos will be leaving anytime soon. I get the feeling the general would be happy to see us out of here as soon as possible."

"Yes, I got that feeling, too."

Then she wailed, "Oh, Father, I can't leave him right now, I just can't!" And her tears started to flow.

Stopping for the second time to hold her, he said, "JoAnna, let's try to be objective about this. When we started on this journey, we had no idea we'd even make it this far, let alone live on the army post; but we've been here almost six months now. Things are not good for them or us. From what I can gather, Chief Manuelito is hoping that eventually they will be allowed to go back to their homeland, if they behave in their captivity. But that may be a long time in coming, and I don't believe the general will let us stay that long."

"Yes, I know," she admitted. "Could we, maybe, just go to some nearby town and live for a while and wait and see what happens?" she asked hopefully.

"Well, we can think about it. If the general compensates us for the things the captain burned and looted we may be able to, but it's a long shot, JoAnna. He didn't guarantee anything."

"Couldn't we go over his head?" JoAnna persisted.

"I know he's the one over the whole New Mexico Territory at this time, but maybe we can write to the senator from here or the war department's head, Stanton, I think his name is. But without a whole lot of proof or documentation to show someone, I don't think we'd get very far," John answered.

"Oh, Father, there *must* be something we can do!" JoAnna insisted.

"All right, daughter. I'll think on it some more. Now, let's get a bite to eat and go to bed. This has been an exhausting day."

JoAnna had to let it go for now, and then felt badly. Her father was still not back to his usual

robust self and it had been a very strenuous day—
for both of them.

   She quickly agreed, and told him to get comfortable while she whipped up some scrambled eggs
and bacon, all the while thinking ahead to what
they might be able to do to stay in the area.

Chapter Twenty-One

Later that same evening, Colonel Carson sat in the general's office to report on his meeting with Chief Manuelito and Notah Begay.

"General, have you been over to the reservation at all? Have you seen the squalor the Navajo and the Mescalero Apaches are living in? Did you realize that the Apaches and the Navajos were bitter enemies when you tried to put them on the same reservation?"

"If I remember correctly, it was you who brought the Mescaleros in Colonel Carson," the general answered. "And you think to bring this question up, now? I had my orders, and I gave you yours," he said tersely.

Kit knew he was hitting a sore spot, and pulled back somewhat.

"Yes, yes, I know that, General, however, there weren't any Navajos on the reservation at that time. It's beside the point now anyway. What is important, is that you also promised the Navajos if they came in without a fight, you'd see that they were housed, fed, clothed, and taught to grow crops to feed themselves—which I might say, they were already doing judging by the number of crops and peach orchards we burned."

Bristling at the implied criticism, the general said, "I don't have to explain myself to you, Colonel. However, I am interested in your opinion and still want to get to the bottom of Captain Cahill's treatment of their medicine man. While you were with him, I had a talk with the Lunds. When I first saw them with the captain, I was shocked. And I did reprimand him for bringing them along, as we're not waging war on our own people. His reason for doing so, he said, was that John Lund pulled a gun on him and tried to interfere with the assignment you gave him to bring the Navajos to Canyon de Chelley to meet up with you there."

"Yes, those were my orders to Captain Cahill, but not to use excessive force or inhumane treatment in order to get the job done. It seems that the captain used both. And, from what Notah says, Cahill was abusive and rough in handling even the women and children on the march here, as well as harassing Miss Lund. They told you, I'm sure, that his soldiers stripped their trading post of most all they had and then torched it. Then, to top it off, Captain Cahill refused to send someone into a raging creek to save a private whom he'd ordered into the stream to calm horses who had gotten spooked trying to cross the swollen stream," Kit explained.

"I had not heard this story until the Lunds told me

of it today. An amazing story, what? The medicine man, apparently even bound, jumped into the water and got the boy safely to the other side. Remarkable."

"That's the way I heard it," Carson agreed.

"That would cause bad blood between the captain and the Navajo for sure, plus his hatred for all Indians already," remarked the general.

"Why does he harbor such bitterness toward the red man?" Carson asked. "I've always felt he was a little imbalanced in his feelings about them, but he was good about doing his duty, so I overlooked his quirks. Maybe I shouldn't have."

The general had asked around and he had an answer.

"From what one of the staff sergeants told me, when Cahill was a boy he was traveling west with his family on a wagon train headed through Texas, when they were attacked by Comanches. It was a fierce fight, and when it was over all the men were dead, the women raped and left for dead or captured, the children stolen and not much left of the wagon train. Apparently, Cahill's mother had hid him in a false bottom of their wagon and told him not to move or make a sound until all was silent again. He was about eight years old, or close to it. Well, when smoke started to seep through the wagon floor, he dropped to the ground through a trapdoor, just in time to see the Indians riding off with their captives, yelling and screaming in victory."

"Did they look back and see him?" Carson asked.

"No, apparently not, they were too busy whooping

and hollering and driving off the stock and horses they captured."

"Well, that would explain a lot about his attitude toward the Indians. How did he survive?"

"Fortunately, another wagon train was a day behind them and Cahill started walking back in that direction. He had the presence of mind to take with him some water and he found some biscuits his mom had made that morning, finally meeting up with that next train. He went a little crazy when he saw them, wanted a gun to go after the Comanches to kill the bastards who had raped his mother and taken his little sister. When they told him nothing could be done for the women and children, that there was no way to find them at that point, he withdrew and clammed up and never said another word the whole trip to the next town. He decided to stay behind in the town when the wagon train pulled out and he apprenticed himself to a blacksmith there. When he was old enough to leave, he told the man good-bye and he joined the army with the idea that he would fight Indians and maybe get into their camps and try to find his baby sister. He swore he would kill every Indian he came across until the day he died."

"Whew!" Kit exclaimed, "and I let him join my cavalry unit and gave him charge of this march. It's a wonder any of the Navajos made it, if that was Cahill's attitude. I'm not real keen on keeping him in my outfit, General. What are you going to do about him?"

"What would you suggest, Kit, off the record, of course. Has he ever disobeyed a direct order or treated his fellow soldiers harshly, gone AWOL, or failed to salute an officer?"

"No, can't say that he has. What he has done is shown he can be a model soldier when it suits him."

"All right then, another reprimand may be in order, and a possible lowering of his rank. There isn't much else I can do besides have him transferred to another unit," the general said. "Plus, get the Lunds off the fort, as soon as possible. With Miss Lund out of the picture, maybe he'll find some other diversion."

"Well, sir, there is another rumor that's floating around, that he has found diversion among the young Apache and Navajo maidens."

This really hit too close to home for the second time today and the general did not want to hear it.

"Here now, that is a very serious charge, Colonel Carson. Do you have proof of that?"

Carson noted that the general had gone from calling him "Kit" in a confidential manner back to Colonel Carson. He sighed; he knew the general did not like to be crossed or talked back to, so he answered truthfully.

"If you mean, have I observed it myself, or has someone come forward to tell me of any such incidences, no . . . but where there's smoke there's usually a fire, as they say. It appears to be general knowledge among the men, but I don't know if anyone would be willing to point the finger at him. Even Chief Manuelito hinted that it had been going on for a while."

"Okay, that does it," the general said. He would

have to, at the very least, look into it now. "I'll bring Captain Cahill in for questioning. We'll confront him together. Possibly I can arrange for an immediate transfer out of here; but with no actual proof of this accusation, it is just his word against whose?"

Getting up and walking around his desk, he went to his office door and opened it, calling his adjutant to come in.

After salutes were exchanged, General Carleton said, "I want you to find Captain Cahill and tell him I wish to see him, tonight, in my office as soon as he can make it. Don't make it sound dire, just that I have something I need to discuss with him."

"Yes, sir," the young aide saluted, then he added, "It may take me a little while to find him."

"Why is that, it's almost light's out, where do you think he is?"

"Sir, I truly don't know. I've heard rumors of card games that go on into the wee hours of the morning, but I will get right on it, sir," and saluting again, he left posthaste. If he didn't find him playing poker in one of the barracks, then he hoped the rumors would not prove true about his nocturnal visits to the Indian camps.

Luckily, though, he found him in a reasonable amount of time as he was washing up for bed. Saluting, he gave Cahill the general's message.

"What's it about, boy?" Cahill asked him.

Resenting being called "boy," but knowing this was not the time to object, he answered, "The general is not in the habit of discussing such things with me.

He just requested that I find you and bring you to his office as soon as you could make it."

"All right then, lead on, my boy," he said with false bravado for the benefit of the other troopers in the room. Inside though he was feeling a bit queasy in his gut. His spies had reported Carson's visit to the Navajo chief and he knew the general had talked to John Lund and his daughter this afternoon. Had the two officers compared notes and put two and two together?

Cahill's mind began working on a good story to tell them. After all, he'd gotten this far by using his wits and he wasn't about to go down yet, especially not over some red Injun bastard.

When he was ushered into the general's office, he noted Colonel Carson standing by the window and Carleton seated behind his desk.

After returning the captain's salute, General Carleton told him, "Have a seat, Captain Cahill. The colonel and I have a few questions we'd like to ask you, so just relax. This won't take long."

Even though the general said *relax,* Cahill found he couldn't. He started to sweat. His gut feeling was that this was not going to be an informal discussion. However, he knew he'd been ordered to sit, so he sat. When he glanced at Carson, he could not tell anything from his stance or the look on his face. Deciding the take the initiative, Cahill asked the general a question.

"Sir, do we have a problem here I'm not aware of? Why is Colonel Carson here? Did I fail in some order he gave me?" Cahill asked, trying to appear humble and inquiring at the same time.

The general snapped back, "*I* ask the questions, Captain."

Cahill flushed a dull red and said, "Yes, sir. Your pardon, sir."

The general then said, "It has come to my attention that you may have used undo force in bringing the Navajo in, and that maybe your pride was involved in the punishment of the Navajo medicine man."

Cahill knew a moment of panic but tried to appear calm on the outside.

"I was just following my orders to deliver them to the fort, sir. As for the so-called 'holy man' he was nothing but trouble on the march . . . rebellious . . . couldn't trust him. I had to keep him bound and watched at all times."

"I see, then you were pleased when, with hands bound, he dove into the water to save Private Wiley?"

A trickle of sweat ran down the captain's back. He sat up straighter in the chair to appear confident, even though he was feeling less and less so.

"Now, sir, I was going to give the order for one of the men to go in after him, but it happened so fast, and then that Navajo tried to be a hero in front of everyone and dove in before anyone else could," he lied.

"So there was no time in between when Private Wiley got in trouble and when Notah dove in? You didn't even have time to issue an order?"

"Yes, sir, that's how it was."

The general looked him in the eye and could see that the captain was uncomfortable with the questioning, and he pressed in with his next remark.

"From what the Lunds say, you did not give an order to save young Wiley, and you did keep the medicine man from getting out of the water after he saved him, and just let him drift away in the current."

"Well, that's their version. They're in love with the Navajos, especially Miss Lund. She practically drools over them. I wasn't about to risk any more men to save one Indian man . . . holy man or not," he almost snarled, but checked himself just in time.

Colonel Carson couldn't stand still another moment.

"Isn't it true, that from that point on, you did everything you could to see that Notah Begay was watched and treated more harshly than anyone else?" Carson asked.

Turing to face Carson when he strode over to stand by the general's desk, Cahill answered him.

"Like I told you, sir, he incited the people to revolt. He had to be taught a lesson. Then, when I found him man-handling Miss Lund, I knew he had to be made an example of."

"Rumor has it, you haven't protected the other women you were escorting here quite as well," Kit Carson stated.

"But they're Injun women, they don't have any virtue to protect," Cahill answered hotly.

Cahill knew immediately that he had probably damned himself in his superior's eyes with his outburst, but he was tired of pussy-footing around, and nursing a bunch of dirty thievin' redskins.

The general waited a moment for the tensions in the room to die down and then he said, "All right, Captain. I think we understand where your sympathies lie. Why did you join the army?"

Cahill's anger was beginning to take over. He became reckless and said, "What kind of a question is that, General? I joined to fight our enemies and to help settle this country for the white race."

"And to kill Indians?" the general prodded.

"Yes, sir. To kill Indians, too! They don't deserve to live alongside decent white people. They live to rape white women, take captive innocent children, murder and steal." He began to shake in his rage remembering his own escape from the Comanches and the loss of his own family. Killing them outright was too quick, a long slow torturous death was what they deserved.

By the time Cahill finished his tirade, sweat was beading on his forehead and his fists were clenched on the arms of the chair.

Colonel Carson and General Carleton exchanged telling glances. They knew they had no real proof of any disobedience on Cahill's part but he needed to be taught a lesson as well.

"Very good, Captain. I can't agree with your tactics, but I can take away any leave or privileges for the next month. You will not leave this fort for any reason. You will be confined to quarters when you are not on duty and you will stay away from John Lund and his daughter," said the general.

"What has she got to do with this?" Cahill wanted to know.

"Have you forgotten what I said, Captain, *I* ask the questions and you are being insubordinate at the moment. Suffice it to say, she feels threatened by your presence, and that is all you need to know. You will stay away from her until such time as she leaves this fort. And, for everyone's sake, I will be requesting a transfer for you within the month out of Colonel Carson's cavalry unit."

Shock and fury burned within Cahill. He would be the laughingstock of his squad when this got out, and he knew it would. Nothing was kept secret very long on an army post. He also knew he had some enemies on the post who would be very happy to see him gone.

His attention was caught once more, when the general said in a warning voice, "You do understand me, Captain Cahill? All my orders?"

Cahill knew he was defeated at that point and answered in the affirmative.

"Very well, you are dismissed to head straight to your quarters and you are to stay there except for trips to the mess hall or when on duty. This is in effect until such time as I release you."

"Yes, sir." Cahill saluted as he stood, then turned stiffly and walked from the room, out into the dark night.

After he left, the general turned to Kit and asked, "Well, what do you think?"

"I know he lied, General. I only wish we could have

done more to him, but like you said, we have no real proof, and his men won't speak against him."

"Afraid of him, do you think?"

"Possibly, General. We've just observed a sample of his temper, and I have seen him in action and he is a mean one when riled."

"All right, we will watch him. I will fill out the transfer request and we will work on getting the Lund's off the post."

"Yes, sir," Kit answered. "And I ask your permission to see about purchasing some cattle and sheep from the local ranches around here. Maybe we could even have them supply meat for the Indians on a regular basis. They *are* starving, General, I do have proof of that."

"So be it. I will authorize you to buy on behalf of the U.S. Army what stock you can, and I will petition Washington for better provisions to build shelters and for clothing. I had hoped for a better response from the Navajo . . . that if they saw how becoming civilized would be a better way of life for them, they would conform more."

Carson declined to answer that, but shook his head on the inside. He knew the Navajos were more civilized in their dealings with one another than the general realized. They had already been farmers and sheepherders, weavers of beautiful blankets. They had a way of living in beauty and harmony that the white man would never comprehend.

As he left the general's office, he wondered at the definition of the word "*civilized.*"

Chapter Twenty-Two

JoAnna spent the next three weeks alternating between fretting and fuming. Fretting over Notah's healing, and fuming that she was not allowed to travel to the Navajo part of the reservation.

They'd been told that they needed to leave within the next sixty days and that General Carleton would have their wagon repaired and put in shape to travel. They would be given two horses to pull it to replace the ones they'd left behind, and a lump sum to compensate for their lost merchandise. But what was there to go back to if the Navajo weren't there?

She was more determined than ever, that some how . . . some way . . . she was going to stay in the area to see what became of the Diné. JoAnna was longing to see Notah and know if his back was healing. She sorely missed the children and Old Woman. JoAnna spent a lot of her time just looking out over the reservation, hoping to catch a glimpse of one of them.

Her problem was solved at the end of the fourth

week when Notah appeared at the fort's entrance carrying Bacca in his arms.

John and JoAnna were in the infirmary helping the post doctor when they heard the shouts of alarm and commotion coming from the front of the fort. They rushed outside as others did from various parts of the grounds, only to see Captain Cahill pointing a gun at Notah and saying, "You're not allowed on these grounds anymore. Turn around and go back before I have you arrested again for trespassing."

Notah stood his ground and looked Cahill directly in the eye.

"I will not go back until I have seen Dr. John Lund. My boy has been struck with an illness I cannot cure."

"What? The great medicine man of the Navajo cannot heal his own kid?" Cahill asked sarcastically, gloating all the while.

"Take care, Captain. I will not be mocked in this. You will let me pass or you will end up dead by morning."

Infuriated because he could not intimidate Notah, Cahill said, "You dare to threaten me?"

"I don't dare, I promise it. If not by my hand, someone else will do it, but you won't live to see the sun rise tomorrow."

By now a crowd had gathered, John and JoAnna among them. Fearing for the boy's welfare, they elbowed their way to get closer to Notah.

When Notah saw them approaching, he breathed a sigh of relief. Truly, he had not known if he could get past the captain or not.

Ignoring the sputtering Cahill, Notah said, "I need your help, Dr. Lund. Bacca is ill with the same sickness that took my wife."

John, knowing that Notah would never come here if it wasn't very serious, turned to the captain and said, "Let them pass, Cahill, or I swear by God, I'll kill you myself. This is a child we're talking about here. Forget your personal feelings for once and act like a decent human being."

Cahill was livid. He was just about ready to charge John Lund with insulting and threatening an officer, when the general's aide-de-camp appeared and wanted to know what was going on.

"Please, ask the general if I may have permission to take Notah Begay's very ill son to the infirmary where I can examine him properly. Quickly, the child has a high fever as it is."

The aide turned on his heel and immediately went to tell the general, sensing the seriousness of the situation.

A hush fell over those who had gathered and they all waited in tense silence for the aide to return.

In the meantime, John turned to Notah, hating to ask any questions in front of the captain, but he needed to have all the facts as fast as possible.

"When did Bacca become ill, and what were his symptoms?" John asked Notah who had shifted the boy in his arms. Bacca lay like a rag doll, head lolled to one side.

"Yesterday at sunrise a pain started in the belly area and he could not keep down any food and very little water or tea. Then, this sunrise when he stood up, he doubled over in much pain and clutched his right side. This is how Squash Blossom acted, too, and I knew if he had the same thing, my medicine might not be able to save him, either, so I want to see if your bilagaana medicine can do it."

John turning to JoAnna said, "It sounds like a ruptured appendix to me and we have no time to waste before the poison spreads to the other organs. Run and ask Dr. Benson if we can use the other operating table as he is in the process of taking off a man's leg because of snakebite and the gangrene that has set in. We need sanitary conditions to perform an operation on Bacca. If not, we'll have to use our dining room table."

JoAnna rushed off to seek the post doctor's aid. Surely, he wouldn't turn away a little boy in distress.

As she ran off, the general himself appeared and walked over to John and Notah and the sizeable crowd that now had gathered around the Navajo and his son.

Speaking to the captain, he said, "Captain Cahill, let this man and his son pass. Dr. Lund, you have my permission to use whatever means we have available to try to save this boy's life."

The general wouldn't admit it to anyone, but he was becoming a secret admirer of this particular Navajo.

Grateful, John said, "Thank you, General. This will go far to help improve relations and understanding between the army and the Navajos if we can save him."

"Follow me, Notah," John said over his shoulder as he headed in the direction of the infirmary.

When they reached the operating room, JoAnna had cleaned off the table and laid out the instruments her father would need. She borrowed a few drops of laudanum from the post doctor who could not stop what he was doing to assist them.

"You're on your own," Dr. Benson said. "Good luck!"

Notah laid Bacca down and carefully stripped him of his breechclout, tunic, and moccasins.

John moved up beside him and noticed the swelling on the right side. Bacca moaned when John touched the area and he opened his eyes and saw his father, JoAnna, and John Lund standing over him.

"Am I going to die, Father?" he asked.

"Not if we can help it, son," John told him, "but I must put you to sleep for a little while so I can relieve you of your pain."

"Sí," Bacca answered, as he reached for his father's hand and held on tight.

A lump formed in Notah's throat and he could not stop the tears that formed in his eyes. All his Hataalii training seemed to be for naught right now, and he vowed he would never try to heal anyone again if Bacca died. He silently called out to the holy ones to assist John Lund and JoAnna in whatever they were gong to do. He felt so weak and helpless he couldn't even say the Blessing Way prayers.

JoAnna tried to give Notah a reassuring smile, for she could see the tension radiating throughout his body. She touched his arm and squeezed it to let him know he was not alone.

He placed his hand over hers for a moment and tried to smile back.

JoAnna poured several drops of laudanum onto a cloth and told Bacca, "Be calm, little one. This is just going to make you go to sleep. Don't fight it. We will all be right here and we won't let anything happen to you," her own throat constricting as she spoke.

She then placed it over his nose and mouth and waited for it to take effect, all the while praying to Jesus to help them, and to guide her father's hands in this delicate operation. She knew she would be just as devastated as Notah should they lose this precious little boy.

For a second Bacca's eyes opened wide in alarm, but JoAnna soothed him saying, "It's all right, Bacca. This will make you dream for a little while and when you wake up, it will be all over."

They all watched in silence as it took hold and he drifted down into oblivion. Notah sighed audibly. It was like putting someone into a trance when he had to set a bone, so he tried to relax and just concentrate on goodness, beauty, and harmony for Bacca.

John taking advantage of his unconscious state scrubbed the area with alcohol and poured it over the scalpel he would use to open the abdomen.

With JoAnna attending, ready to staunch the blood flow, John made a clean cut in the cleansed area. As soon as the cut was made, a foul smell assaulted their nostrils and pus and blood flowed out of the incision.

"It has already begun to putrefy, JoAnna, suction as much of the poison out as you can while I cut off the appendix."

Notah watched in grim fascination, realizing as he did so that he would never have known how to do such a thing.

Father and daughter worked deftly and swiftly together, doing what was necessary, but never getting in each other's way. It was a miracle to watch and it humbled Notah as nothing else had ever done. He was glad he had come to them for help.

He felt his own stomach roil, but he would not leave his son. Notah also realized, to his sorrow, that he could not have saved Squash Blossom if an *operation* was what was needed for this *appendix* thing. And, even as it brought him pain, it also liberated him from the guilt that he had carried these past years over her death. That was why she had come to him in the hole, too, to set him free from the guilt that had bound him and his heart from ever seeking to love again.

In that moment of clarity, Notah knew he was now free to really and truly love JoAnna, and if there was a way they could be together, he would love and cherish her for the rest of his life.

After thirty minutes, John declared they'd done all they could and partially closed the wound, leaving a drain in it. He lightly covered it with a soft bandage while JoAnna cleaned up.

Turning to Notah, he said, "I've done what I could, Notah. Even though some of the poison has spread, the young recover more rapidly than adults.

We will pray to our Father and his son, Jesus, and you pray to your holy people and ask them to finish the healing. It's in their hands now."

"I am grateful to you, John Lund. I know now that I could not have saved Squash Blossom or Bacca without your bilagaana doctor's skills, if this is what was required. I thank you with my whole being. How long will he have to remain here?" Notah asked.

"He should stay here at least seven suns, Notah. We must guard against infection spreading to the other organs and fever setting in," answered John truthfully. There was still a chance Bacca might die, but John didn't want to mention that right now.

"Will I be allowed to stay with him?"

"I'll see what I can do, Notah. They should let you stay for this night at least, as the next twenty-four hours are the most critical."

"My heart would be grateful for that much, John Lund. You have my undying friendship and gratitude for saving Bacca's life."

JoAnna could not stand by and be left out of the conversation any longer. She reached over and hugged Notah. He hesitated for just a second in front of her father, but he found he needed her touch and her comfort at that moment, and he held her close for a second. Then he set her away and thanked her, too.

"I told you, you have healing in your hands, JoAnna. You are a blessing to those who know you . . . *and to me,*" he whispered only for her to hear.

They both remembered when he had first told her about her *healing hands*; it was in the hole when she had spread the salve on his back. She smiled at him and nodded her head as a lovely blush crept up her face.

Dr. Benson came in just then, interrupting the tableau, and asked, "Is everything all right, Dr. Lund? I see you have closed up the incision. May I just take a look at it?"

"Certainly, doctor. Please do. It was a ruptured appendix as we thought. I believe we've done all we can do. Now it is up to the Good Lord and Bacca's strong constitution to do the rest."

Dr. Benson, after examining the drain in the wound, proclaimed it nicely done and complimented John and JoAnna, saying, "Barring complications, the little guy should make it. I envy you such competent help in your lovely assistant, Dr. Lund. Any time she wants to join the army and become my nurse, I'd be happy to let her, even though women aren't allowed in the services."

Turning to Notah, Dr. Benson held out his hand, and said, "Be assured, we will all keep an eye on your son and will make sure he comes to no harm while in my hospital."

Notah took the extended hand and clasped it as he had seen the bilagaanas do. He was too choked up to do more than just nod at Dr. Benson to convey his gratitude. Notah had not thought that he would ever take comfort from a bluecoat soldier's words, but he found the white doctor reassuring.

Dr. Benson smiled once more at them, and then excused himself to go to the room he used as an office to write up the day's events. The man whose leg he had to amputate and Bacca's operation would need to be documented for future reference, for sure.

Going over to stand by Bacca once more, Notah asked John, "How much longer will he sleep this sleep you put on him?"

"Oh, he should be waking up soon, and when he does, I want to give him a little morphine for the pain," John answered.

"What is this *morphine*?" Notah asked. His people had peyote that induced dreamlike trances, and plants they used to dull pain, but he was still apprehensive about the white man's medicines.

"It is a drug for killing the pain from the operation. We will not give him much, but he will need something for a couple of days."

"I think I would rather use my own remedies for pain. If I am allowed to come back, I will bring them," he told John.

"That's fine. I know you have things that work just as well. Old Woman has been sharing some of them with JoAnna, but we haven't had any chance to look for those plants around here, yet."

John turned to JoAnna and said, "Honey, will you go make us some strong coffee while we wait here. I think I could use a cup and I'm sure Notah could, too. If you have anything left from dinner tonight that would be a blessing, too."

"Yes, Father, I'll go do that right away." She started to leave the hospital just as the general's aide came through the door.

"The general wanted to know how the operation

went, and he has given permission for Mr. Begay to stay through this night and tomorrow night, but then he must return to the Navajo camp."

John said, "Tell the general that we think it went well. The next twenty-four hours are the most critical, but he is young, and we're believing for the best. Thank the general for his kindness to Notah, here. He would very much like to stay with his son tonight, and I plan to stay with him as well, in case the general should feel he needs to be guarded," he said, smiling over at Notah.

Notah ducked his head lest he show his vexation. No one need guard him tonight. He would not leave his son for any reason.

The aide saluted and then said he would convey John's message of thanks and the good news to the general. Then he bid them good night and left.

JoAnna left then, too, to go make the coffee and fix them all some dinner. She wanted to get back as fast as she could and stay with them in the infirmary tonight, as well. Who knew how many more chances she would have in Notah's company.

She wondered what he'd been thinking as they operated on his son. She had glanced over at him every now and then to gauge his reaction. He had seemed more awed than worried or upset. Thank heavens.

Now Dear Lord, she prayed, *please let Bacca make a speedy recovery,* that's all she would ask.

Well, maybe one more prayer, *that someday she might share her love with the boy's wonderful father.*

Chapter Twenty-Three

Notah could not believe the kindness of General Carleton in letting him come and go from the fort after the first twenty-four hours. He would go back to his camp and check on Bella and Old Woman every other day and then spend the night in the infirmary with Bacca.

The general had even come by in person to check on Bacca's progress. He also gave Notah a side of beef to share with his clan. It was too little, too late to do much good, but Notah was impressed with the general's goodwill and his apparent desire to make amends for Notah's treatment by Cahill.

In fact, Notah had never expected to feel gratitude toward the bluecoat general or have kind thoughts about one of them, but for some reason he sensed the general had taken a liking, or at least a sincere interest in him personally.

At the end of the seventh day, Dr. Lund pronounced Bacca free from any further risk and told Notah he could take him home. Both father and son were ready to leave. Bacca did not like the infirmary although the bed was comfortable, and he had never been this clean since leaving Dinétah, but he had never been separated from his sister before, and, as all twins do, they shared a special bond. He had missed her very much, but Notah would not bring her to the fort to see him.

JoAnna helped Bacca get ready to leave. She had cut down a flannel shirt of her father's, and found a pair of pants in the stuff she had brought from their trading post. They were a size too big, but he would grow into them. She was glad he was well enough to leave, but she knew it meant the end of Notah's visits as well.

She had gotten used to his presence in the afternoons and knew she would miss him terribly when he left for good. She couldn't help fantasizing that it was almost like being a real family. Did Notah feel that way, too, she wondered. Every now and then, she would look up and find his warm, onyx eyes on her and she would think he felt a oneness with her. Other times she couldn't be sure.

In the afternoons, she'd taught Bacca a card game for children, and read to him on the days that Notah could not be there. She thought he was beginning to be more open with her and to converse more easily in English. He had picked up the language quickly, as the young do, and he had even asked Dr. Benson questions when he came in to check on him.

Dr. Benson thought he had a fine mind and was very intelligent. He admitted to JoAnna, not to his credit, that he had not thought of Indians as being *that smart.* She could have hit him on the head at that remark. Why did everyone think that all Indians were stupid, primitive, and unable to have an intelligent thought? Well, she guessed it wasn't too surprising; that's how they viewed the negroes in the South, and some said that's what the war was all about. However, it seemed very far away from them here.

Bacca was especially pleased when she presented him with a sketch pad with pencils and showed him how to use it to draw on.

She was amazed one day when she picked up the pad and saw the likenesses of her father and her on a couple of the pages. There was also a sketch of Dr. Benson in his lab coat, and one of the room in which Bacca stayed. She had no idea he could draw and thought he was quite good.

When Notah came again, she showed the drawings to him.

"Did you know he could draw so well?" she asked.

"No, we do not have anything to draw with except for our sand paintings. Many of us are skilled in the working of silver, decorating pottery, and weaving blankets, so I can see where it would come out in drawing, too. This is a very good likeness of you, JoAnna. May I keep it?"

For a moment she wanted to say, *No*, for she wanted it for herself, but then she said, "It is Bacca who drew it, so it is his to keep or give away, but as you are his father, I don't think he'll refuse you," she answered with a conspiratorial wink. "He can take the pad and pencils as well. Someday, I'll give him pencils with colors in them when next we find a town with a mercantile store in it."

She didn't know when or where she'd find them, but she was determined to stay in touch with Notah and his family. She wanted to make sure his children kept up with their English lessons and learning the American's ways. Who knew what the future would hold for them. She felt a need to prepare Bella and Bacca for whatever happened, if only she could.

Bacca was getting impatient to leave. He felt he'd been ready days ago, but Dr. Lund would not release him. He was not a baby anymore and he didn't like lying in bed all day, no matter how comfortable they tried to make him.

His face lit up like a hundred candles on a birthday cake when he saw his father come through the door to get him.

"I am ready to go, Father."

Turning to JoAnna who could not help the tears that misted her eyes, he said, "Thank you, JoAnna, for your good care of me." Then spying Dr. Lund in the background, he added "And you, too, Dr. Lund. I am glad the bilagaana medicine is strong like my father's."

"Yes, my powers are good, but I could not do what Dr. Lund did for you, so I, too, am glad for the white man's skills," Notah told him.

John said, "I'm just glad you got him here when you did. I am happy it turned out so well. Bacca is a fine lad; you have reason to be proud of him."

"Yes, I am proud of him, and my precious Bella.

I do not think I would have survived without them after their mother died. They kept me going."

Gosh, JoAnna thought, *that is the most he had ever said about that period of his life.* She wished she could make up for all those years he'd lost. Well, she knew she'd never give up trying. Even if they never married, she was determined to remain in their lives somehow, and lately, she'd had the feeling that Notah might let her.

Something had changed between them since his time in the hole and this scare with Bacca. There was new warmth in his glances now, and he always managed to touch her hand, or arm, or her face before he left her. Not obvious caresses to anyone watching, but they made her heart sing.

Father and daughter walked them to the edge of the fort. JoAnna couldn't hold back her tears as they slipped from the corner of her eyes. She was happy, of course she was, but she would miss them so much. The eventual parting was becoming a constant ache inside her. She so wanted to be part of Notah's life—to be his woman, no matter how they had to live or where. She'd be content in his mud hut if he would let her stay. But she knew the army would not allow it, either.

Seeing her tears and sensing her sadness, Notah reached up with his finger, and took one away. He ached to hold her in his arms, but as usual, there was an audience watching them, so he did not dare.

She could not help it. When he touched the side of her face, she placed her hand over his to hold it there, pressing it against her cheek.

John looked the other way.

"Ah, JoAnna, we must talk soon. Please don't cry. It hurts my heart to see you sad. I must go back to our camp for now. All is not lost, I'll see you again."

It was the closest Notah had ever come to hinting that there was the possibility of a future for them, and JoAnna grabbed onto it with her whole heart.

She smiled then, and said, "Yes. Soon."

Then she waved them good-bye saying, "Give my love to Bella and Old Woman and let them know I miss them."

Notah nodded and carried Bacca through the gate.

JoAnna watched until they were out of sight. When she went back to their house, John told her the general had sent his aide-de-camp by to check on Bacca to make sure he was ready to be released.

"Isn't that amazing! Who would have thought the general would take such an interest in Notah and his son. Do you think his conscience began to bother him about Cahill's treatment of the Navajos?" she asked.

"I would hope so. Well, girl, it's time we started our packing and decided what we're going to do. The general's aide also said he had all the paperwork done for us to officially be compensated for our losses, and that we should plan to leave as soon as possible. We can go to the town nearest here, Sumner City, for a while and stay until we figure out where we want to end up. If they have a store there, maybe I can buy into it, or work out some arrangement with the owner to help him in it. There isn't much sense in going back to Dinétah without the Navajos being there."

JoAnna started to cry again.

"I want to end up here, Father!" she exclaimed through her tears. "I want to stay near Notah and his family. They've come to mean so much to me. Dear Lord, I don't want to leave them," and she cried harder.

Walking over to her, John took her in his arms and spoke soothingly to her as he had when she was a little girl.

"Now, JoAnna, we knew this was coming. It only got delayed because of Bacca's appendicitis. I promise we will stay near here as long as we can, and somehow, we'll stay in touch with Notah. I do believe he has come to care for you very much, but sees that he cannot offer you anything at this time."

"I don't need anything but his love," she sniffed into her handkerchief. "I would be content with that. I'd live anywhere with him."

"Yes, I believe you would, but his pride as head of his household, and your provider, would be sorely tested, knowing he could not give you the basic things you need, let alone what you've been used to. He would be ashamed that he might not be able to provide for you and his children. You see that, don't you, JoAnna?"

"Yes, I suppose so. Oh, men and their silly pride!"

She stamped her foot in exasperation. "If they only knew what was important to a woman and what she really wanted . . ."

Before she could finish her remark, John laughed

out loud and said, "The man who figures that out will have the world at his feet."

She had to smile at him then. "All right, Father, you win. I'll start getting things together tomorrow so we can leave by the end of the week," hoping against hope that she would get to see Notah one more time before they left. After all, he had promised they would have a talk.

"Good girl, and I will find out more about the town across the Pecos and get directions for getting there," John said.

While Bacca recovered and Notah came and went from the fort, Captain Cahill was fanning the flames of his hatred for the medicine man. He burned with lust for JoAnna and a desire for revenge on her father for bringing him down in the eyes of his commanding officers.

Confined to quarters when not on duty, he still had a good view of what was happening in the fort, for his window faced the infirmary. He watched as JoAnna, her father, and Notah took turns coming and going in and out of the clinic.

Even from afar, Cahill could see a glow about JoAnna and a new spring in her step. He knew it was because of Notah and he hated the man even more. *What made her think the Navajo was better than her own kind?*

The more he dwelt on it, the hotter his desire grew and it became mixed with the need to teach her a lesson for rejecting him for a dirty redskin.

He plotted and schemed for a way to catch her alone. It would have to be at night, he reasoned, as there was too much going on during the day. Because Carleton and Carson were still not sure about his nighttime activities, he was not given night duty, so he would have to think of a way to bribe one of the soldiers into letting him take his shift. He knew the officers had no convincing proof against him or he would be in the stockade instead of confined to quarters.

Cahill was glad when Notah took his son and left the fort. He knew he didn't have much time to get JoAnna alone when he heard of the general's plans for them to leave the fort later this week or the first of next. He would have to get busy to work out the details of his assault on the lovely JoAnna.

Chapter Twenty-Four

After returning to the camp and the happy reunion between brother and sister with everyone else dropping by, Notah was alerted to the rumor that JoAnna and her father were being forced to leave the fort by the general's orders at the end of the week.

Alarmed, he wondered where they would go. There wasn't anything to go back to at the trading post and it was a long, dangerous journey for the two of them alone. But then he remembered them telling him how they had crossed half of America to reach his homeland on their own. Yet, he knew he could not let her go before he had a chance to talk with her and tell her he loved her. She said she would wait for him forever. He had to know if she really meant it and if she would be willing to wait for a time when they could be together.

Notah sent JoAnna a message by Old Woman the next day. They had not confined her to the reservation because everyone knew she and JoAnna exchanged remedies and worked together to make salves and herbal teas. In fact, several of the soldiers had benefited from her treatments on the march.

When JoAnna saw Old Woman coming in the gates, she ran to her and hugged her close.

"Oh, I am so glad to see you, dear one. I've missed you and Bella so much. How is Bacca doing? Can he move around fairly well now? How did Bella take their being apart for so long?"

She had a hundred questions to ask, the most important one being, how was Notah.

Her father had had a chance to take a look at his back while he was visiting Bacca and proclaimed that he was healing well. His back bore terrible scars that he would carry the rest of his life, but there was no longer any sign of infection. They all credited Old Woman's cures for that. But even John, hated to see that beautiful, sculpted back of Notah's marred by the whip.

Old Woman answered her, "Everyone is fine. Bella is relieved to have Bacca home and won't leave his side. She is acting like a mother prairie hen clucking over her chick."

That made JoAnna smile. She knew Bella would be protective of him when he returned home. He was the other half of her life.

"And, as to your other question, Notah is fine, too. He has heard about you having to leave this place and he wanted to know where you planned to go since the bluecoats burned your casa. He wishes to meet with you and talk to you. He asks if you can slip away tonight and come to the edge of the fort grounds near the stables and he will meet you there at moonrise."

"Of course, I will. I'll do my best to be there. How will I find him?"

"He will find *you*," Old Woman assured her. "Now let us make a batch of the tea that has become better for healing wounds than for drinking, and you can tell me what you and your father will do when you leave here."

They spent the rest of the day working together in JoAnna's kitchen. When Old Woman was ready to return to the reservation, she took JoAnna's hand in hers and looked deeply into her eyes, tears misting in her own as she said, "I never expected to like a bilagaana before I met you, but I have come to think of you like the daughter I never had. I am glad the holy people led you to Dinétah. Do not worry, our paths will cross again."

"Oh, I hope so," JoAnna said, her own tears streaming down her face. She hugged the elderly Navajo to her and said, "I miss you already. You filled the empty place that was left when my mother died, and kept me from losing my mind. I am so glad we became friends and I am honored that you would consider me a daughter."

Old Woman pulled away first; then patting JoAnna's arm, she turned and walked out of the fort. She wondered how beauty and harmony would ever be restored in the world of change and challenge they were living in now. Her heart ached for JoAnna and Notah and his family. She was getting older and slowing down herself now. Who would take care of them if something happened to her? She would have to get Notah to do a sing to restore her own Hozho.

JoAnna watched her go and wondered if she would ever see her again. She felt like running after her and going back to Notah's camp to say good-bye to the children but she knew she could not. The army was not letting any civilians onto the reservation for any reason.

Oh, the heartache of not being able to hold Bella in her arms one more time and sing her to sleep.

The pain of separation was tearing her apart.

Later that night as the moon was making its climb into the night sky, JoAnna once again dressed in her father's coat and hat and made ready to go to meet Notah. She had been on pins and needles all evening, alternating between the thrill of seeing him again and the despair of leaving him.

Her father met her at the door. "Should I go with you, daughter?"

"No, Father, I need to see him alone. Maybe you could follow me, though, to make sure I get there safely, then leave when you see him come?"

"Yes, I can do that. I had planned to follow you anyway, so if you're ready, let's go. Where are you supposed to meet him?"

"At the back of the fort near the stables, other than that, I do not know. Old Woman said Notah would find me."

"I'm sure he will," John agreed.

They made their way past the darkened buildings, clinging to shadows, placing their feet carefully to minimize the noise of their footsteps.

As they neared the stables, all seemed quiet except for the occasional shuffling around in the stalls, and the snuffling noises of the horses. A guard usually stood on duty at the front of the building, but he was out of sight at the moment.

One moment they were alone and the next moment Notah appeared in front of them.

JoAnna let out a gasp that Notah quickly stifled by placing his hand lightly over her mouth.

"Hush, little one, it is I," he whispered.

He nodded to John, who bent his head in acknowledgment and then turned to walk out of earshot, but he did not intend to leave completely. Maybe he would find the guard on duty and engage him in conversation, saying he couldn't sleep and thought a walk around the grounds might help. It would distract him from checking in the back of the stables at the same time.

As soon as her father was out of sight, JoAnna could not restrain herself any longer. She literally leaped into Notah's arms and he swung her around in the joy of holding her once again.

Yes, she thought, *something has definitely changed between us.*

"Ah, my little warrior woman, I have missed you in the few days we've been apart. I've wanted to hold you . . . to kiss you . . ."

"Then do it," JoAnna pleaded. "Every day when you came to the infirmary, I longed to reach out and touch you and to kiss you. I could hardly keep my hands off you."

He didn't hesitate then, but took her lips in a kiss filled with desire and possession.

"You are mine, JoAnna," he said when they finally broke apart breathless. "I do not know how we will do this, but you will be my woman. I love you with my whole heart now."

JoAnna told him, "I knew your feelings had changed after your imprisonment, but I couldn't figure out why. It was as if you finally felt it was all right to let me love you and for you to love me in return. What happened to make you change your mind?" She gloried in the words he had spoken, *I love you.*

"I can tell you now." And he proceeded to tell her about his vision of Squash Blossom and how she had given him her blessing to love JoAnna. That she knew of JoAnna's love for him and their children.

"And, then, when you and your father performed that operation on Bacca, I knew I could not have saved Squash Blossom and the pain and guilt over her death finally left me, and I felt free to love again."

"How beautiful—how wonderful that she came to you. I am so very glad she did." JoAnna had heard that some people said they'd seen a loved one who had died, and she believed it was possible in rare circumstances, so she believed Notah.

"She also told me you loved me and I should love you, that we needed each other," he continued.

"She knew that?"

"Yes, in the spirit world, things are much clearer

and you can travel from place to place and see what is happening; so she had seen you and observed you with me, with Old Woman, and with the children, and she approved of you."

"That is absolutely amazing," JoAnna said. "A little scary . . . but amazing! I'm glad she approved of me. I hate to think of what would have happened, if she had not."

"If she had not approved, she would have let me go on in my grief and not set me free; but Squash Blossom is much like you, tenderhearted, loving, and kind."

Reaching up to put her arms around his neck, standing on tiptoe she gave him a quick kiss and said, "Oh, Notah, I do love your children. They have become so dear to me. I know I can never take Squash Blossom's place, but I will love them as if they were my own. I already do."

"I know that, woman of mine, and you are the only mother they would have. They were too young to remember Squash Blossom. So you are their mother in that sense."

Then he nestled her against him, holding her close, just breathing in her fragrance, and loving the feel of her arms wrapped around his waist.

She melted against him, reveling in the hard strength of his body, unable to get close enough.

Notah's hands stroked her back and for just a moment cupped her buttocks and rocked her against his hardness. When he heard her moan, he quickly removed his hands and put them somewhere safer.

"Ah, JoAnna, I waited too long—denied myself, and you too long. We could have married back in Dinétah had I not been so blind. I have desired you from the moment I first saw you."

"Well, you certainly hid it well. I fell in love you at first sight, too. I know that now, but as I had never had these feelings before, I did not know what to call them."

Finally, after another mind-drugging, breath-stealing kiss, he said, "JoAnna, it is not right that I ask you to wait for me, but I cannot take you to wife under the conditions in which we are living. Chief Manuelito is hoping that in time the army will see what a bad plan this reservation thing is, and will eventually let us go back to our homeland. Will you be there waiting for us to return?"

"I don't know yet if we'll go back. For now, we are going to the closet town near the fort and staying there awhile. Father is thinking maybe he could start up another trading post. He says he'll find a way for us to stay in touch, although he doesn't know how at the moment."

"That is good. There are some Apaches and some Navajos who slip on and off the reservation that the bluecoats do not know about. Maybe when I learn how, and where they are doing it, I will be able to slip away, too."

"Oh, Notah, I hate all this stupidity of my government. Why couldn't they have left you where you were?"

"You are asking *me* to explain your government to you? I cannot. I only know I want you more than

I ever thought possible. I want to be with you and make you mine in every way, but I will not take you outside of a marriage vow. It would shame me to break my vows as a holy man and I think your God Jesus would not be happy with me, either, if I did that."

"No. He would not, Notah, but now I know why some women give in to what we call *friendly persuasion*. I fear you could persuade me very easily to lay aside my virtue if you tried."

"I will not try, beloved, for I will not bring shame on you that way, but you will be mine one day, I promise."

Then tilting her face up to his, and pulling her closer once again, he took her mouth in a long, slow, deep kiss, pouring all his love and desire into it, until JoAnna went weak in the knees and would have fallen had he not been holding her up.

"You taste like wild honey," he told her after slipping his tongue from her mouth.

JoAnna could not answer except to moan deep in her throat again. Truly, she never knew kisses could affect one so. Her need for him was overwhelming.

She wanted to be wed to him tonight, not in some distant future.

"JoAnna, I must leave now. It is not safe for you out here this late at night. Besides, if we keep touching and kissing, I cannot trust myself not to take you right here, and I would hate myself later for it."

Still dazed, she said, "Yes, I know. I never dreamed feelings could be this powerful. Go, before I beg you to stay. It is not safe for you, either. I'm glad you came and told me you love me, though. It will help in the days ahead. Notah, I will wait . . . a lifetime . . . if I have to, as I told you before."

"My sweet little one, this is not good-bye just *adios.*" And with that he was gone, a shadow among shadows.

She stood there, not knowing for how long, savoring the memory of his holding her, his kissing her, and his declaration of love.

So this is what love is all about, she thought, *this wanting to be one with someone and never wanting to let him go.*

Fleetingly, she wondered if this is what her father and mother had shared and that was why he had been so devastated by her death. She realized it must have been so. She thought she understood his grief better now, for she was loath to leave Notah and could not bear the thought of his dying.

She was touched by his story of Squash Blossom appearing to him and giving her blessing for him to love again. Anguish tore through her once more over their parting.

Oh, why, couldn't things be different?

Just as she was turning to go back home, another shadow loomed out of the darkness. JoAnna knew real fear when the shadow spoke.

"Well . . . well . . . well, if it isn't Miss JoAnna. Pray tell me, little lady, what are you doing out here at this time of night. Waiting to meet an Injun lover, huh? Perhaps I can accommodate you instead. I've been trying to save your virtue for you, but if you're so determined to give it away, I'll take it," Cahill said, blocking her escape.

Trying to hide the panic rising within her, JoAnna said, "What I'm doing out is my business. You are disgusting as ever and your insulting remarks don't bear answering. Now let me pass. It seems to me I heard that you were to stay away from me and that you were confined to your quarters at night."

"Yes, thanks to you and your father," he snarled.

Grabbing her arm, he said, "I've been waiting a long time to get my hands on you, Miss High and Mighty. Not only *on* you, but all over you as a matter of fact, and since it's only the two of us out here, tonight's as good a time as any."

JoAnna tried to scream, but Cahill anticipated it and put his hand over her mouth, while pulling her body into his. Then he took her mouth in a brutal, punishing kiss, cutting her lip until she tasted her own blood. One hand held her fast while his other hand began to pull open her coat and grope for her breast.

She struggled and cried her outrage and protests into his mouth, but it did no good. He was much too strong for her and before she knew it, he had tossed her to the ground and was on top of her in a flash.

Oh, why had she lingered after Notah left? Where was her father?

Cahill was going to rape her here and now, and even if he should be punished for it later, he would have gotten his revenge, and she would lose her virginity to a beast instead of to the tender lover she knew Notah would have been. A horrible thought hit her; would Notah even want her after Cahill had soiled her? Silent screams filled her head.

Notah had been torn in two to leave JoAnna as well. He had gone over the edge of the arroyo that ran behind the stable and had started up the other side when he glanced back to look at her silhouette once more. He planned to stay and watch her until she left, then he would depart as well for he would probably be shot if caught on the reservation now.

As he watched her, he glimpsed the man coming around the corner of the stable, hugging the deeper shadows created by the waning moonlight but heading straight for JoAnna. Notah's heart stopped within him when he heard Cahill speak. JoAnna would be no match for this man's lust for her, and his hatred for Notah. He could not yell out to her, either, for he did not want the captain to know he was near.

He crept back down the side of the gully and started back up the other side close to the struggling couple. Hugging the ground and using every bush for concealment, he found himself drawing out the knife he had bartered for when he floated down the stream and ran into the Navajo family. However, Cahill had a gun, so he would need to get very close to use his knife. The Apache *net-da-he*, the bloodlust to kill, was upon him, and he realized he *wanted* to be close enough to bury his knife deep in this man's black heart.

His mind had already registered this when his hand reached for the blade.

So, Notah thought, *it had finally come—the battle between Cahill and himself.*

One or both of them would be dead when it was over, but he knew Cahill would not walk away alive tonight.

On the ground, Cahill had his arm pressed across JoAnna's throat so she could not scream while he pulled up her skirt to get into her drawers. His hands were cruel as they dug into her tender flesh.

He whispered in her ear, "Yes sir, little girl, you're going to know what a real man feels like before this night is over."

He gave a dirty little laugh as she struggled harder to get away from his touch, which only aroused him all the more.

Just when JoAnna thought she would pass out from lack of air, a shadow loomed over them and an angry growl like that of a mountain lion sounded above her. She felt Cahill's body being lifted off her and tossed to the ground away from her.

She realized then that Notah must have seen Cahill attack her and come back to rescue her. What should she do? She watched in horror as the two men grappled on the ground in front of her.

The army would not tolerate Notah's trespassing on the compound again without permission, and he was attacking an officer. She stuffed her fist in her mouth to stifle the scream that was threatening to erupt.

Oh, God, what should I do? she cried silently.

Could she get her father back here in time to stop this fight? Yet she could not bear to leave with Notah battling for his life, for she knew, too, that one of them would be dead by the time it was over. She was torn between wanting to run for help and needing to stay.

If Notah killed Cahill, the army would not hesitate to hang him, and if Cahill managed to kill Notah, she knew what her fate would be at his hands. He would finish what he had started and then blame her rape on Notah, saying he had saved her from the Navajo.

The captain and Notah rolled around on the ground, exchanging punches and grunts, each trying to get the advantage. Notah had dropped his knife while they grappled, but by now he realized he wanted to get his hands on Cahill's neck and choke the life out of him while he looked him in the eye. A knife in the heart would be too quick and the *net-da-he* was in full fury now. Not the red killing haze that made you crazy, but rather the cold, deliberate calm that was deadly.

Cahill knew he was in a fight for his life and he tried desperately to get to his gun, but Notah knocked his hand away.

Notah knew he would kill Cahill and did not worry about the consequences. There was no guarantee he would live through it either as the captain had pulled his own knife out of his boot. Now it was a matter of blocking and holding off the other one's death strike.

The two men continued to roll on the ground, in and out of the moonlight. JoAnna could not tell who was winning. She just knew they were locked in a desperate struggle for survival.

Finally, Notah got up on Cahill's back, and had his head in an armlock. He knew he was going to break the captain's neck as he said, "If you have a god you pray to, evil one, say it now for you are a dead man."

Cahill knew he was facing death. With his once last ounce of strength, he rose up and elbowed Notah in his ribs, throwing him off and causing him to land on his back. The captain staggered to his feet, pulled his gun, and was about to shoot Notah when Notah got his legs in a scissor lock and toppled Cahill once more. However, they were so close to the arroyo that Cahill fell backward into the gully; arms flailing he landed with a thud, sliding down the embankment. As he reached the bottom, Notah and JoAnna heard a shot.

JoAnna and Notah both ran to the edge of the bank and looked down to see Cahill crumpled in a heap with his gun arm buried under him.

Had he shot himself or had the gun gone off when he landed on it?

They would never know . . . and neither would anyone else, unfortunately. And it would look bad for Notah no matter what they said. Everyone knew of the animosity between the two men.

"Oh, dear God, no," JoAnna breathed. She truly hadn't wanted the death of either man.

Turning to look at Notah, she saw the grief in his face and the signs of the battle he'd been in. She cried out his name and flung herself into his arms.

"Oh, Notah, I'm so sorry. I should have gone home as soon as you left. It's all my fault. Do you think he's dead?"

"Yes."

Panic set in and JoAnna voiced her fears, "You must flee, Notah. Go back to the camp. You must not be caught."

"No, JoAnna, I do not want to leave you. I will turn myself in. I did not kill him even though we fought. It was the fall that did it."

"No . . . no, you can't do that. They won't believe you. They may not even believe me. Please, they will kill you without even thinking about it. You must go."

Seeing she was becoming hysterical, he said, "All right, I'll go for now, but I will return to the fort in the morning and tell the general what happened."

Holding her close and looking into her dazed and shocked eyes, he said, "JoAnna, hurry now. Go to your father. Get away from here. I don't want to leave you like this."

Dully she knew he was right but she felt numb. Her mind didn't want to think and her body wouldn't function.

"JoAnna," he repeated her name more sternly, "hear me. You must leave now!"

Already they could hear voices coming toward them from the front of the stable.

She heard him, but she still couldn't move.

Notah wanted to shake her, but he knew she was in shock. He wondered what he was to do with her. Did he dare take her with him?

The voices were closer now and it was only a matter of minutes before they would be spotted. When Notah heard her father calling her name, he knew it would be all right to leave her.

He kissed her once more, hard, and turned her away from him, giving her a push in the opposite direction. Then he slipped over the side of the arroyo again.

As he left her, he said a prayer to the holy ones to help them. He was not sorry Cahill was dead, although taking a life was not the way of a Hataalii. However, when he knew what Cahill would have done to JoAnna if he had not interfered, there was only one decision to be made—Cahill's death or JoAnna's rape. And Notah was not about to let that happen.

So he did what he knew he would always have to do someday, and that was to *kill* Cahill. There had been no choice; yet, justified as it was in his mind, he could not feel good about it.

Chapter Twenty-Five

Rounding the side of the stable, John Lund saw JoAnna standing there, trembling with tears in her eyes. He grabbed her to him immediately and asked, "What's the matter, honey? What's happened?"

Then whispering, he asked, "Where's Notah? We heard a shot?"

Hearing her father's voice brought JoAnna back to herself.

"Oh, Father," she cried out as she reached for him. She buried her face in his neck as she said, "It was terrible."

"What was terrible, JoAnna?" John asked fearfully, taking in JoAnna's disheveled appearance and torn clothing. He felt sure Notah would not have done this, but still he had to ask.

"Did Notah force himself upon you, JoAnna?"

"Oh, no, Father, no, it wasn't Notah. It was Cahill. He came upon me after Notah left me. I waited too long to return and he caught me unawares."

"Why was he out here, he's not supposed to have

night duty anymore? Where is he?" he asked dragging her away from the guards on duty who were looking around and casting suspicious looks at JoAnna. It would only be a matter of minutes before they started asking her questions and he needed to know what happened first.

"He's dead. Down in the gully."

"Dead? Dear Lord in Heaven, how?"

"Notah saw him attack me and came back to save me from the captain as he was about to . . . to rape me. They fought and Notah was winning when Cahill drew his gun to shoot him and Notah knocked his legs out from under him. Then Cahill fell backward into the arroyo and his gun went off, killing him when he fell on it, or he shot himself. We didn't know which."

"Whooee!" John sighed. "This is bad, darlin'. Where is Notah, now? Is he still out there somewhere? He needs to come back in and give himself up. If it was self-defense, we may be able to get him a lighter sentence."

"Nooo," JoAnna wailed into his chest. "The army won't believe him, they'll kill him for sure. I told him to run away."

"Now, JoAnna, that was not smart and you know better than that," he chided her. He understood her reasoning and her fear for Notah, but she also knew right from wrong.

"I know, Father, but I love him. I could not stand it if they put him in that hole again or hung him. Anyway, he only left because I was getting hysterical on him, but he said he would be back to speak to the general in the morning."

"Well, that's good. I'm relieved to hear that. We'll see what we can do to help him, then."

The men who had come out to check out the disturbance finally gathered around JoAnna and her father.

A sergeant spoke up and said, "Miss Lund, would you mind telling me what you're doing out here at this time of night and what, if anything, did you hear or see?"

Dr. Lund spoke up, "Does she have to talk to you right now; she's had a fright. Can I take her home? You can come by and question her in the morning."

"No, sir, I'm afraid not. Captain Cahill is missing from the barracks and we need to know if she's seen him out here tonight. We all know of the captain's interest in Miss Lund and from what I can see by this torch, she looks pretty messed up. I'd like to know why," the sergeant answered.

JoAnna knew she would have to answer but her heart was breaking. She felt like she was signing Notah's death warrant if she told them what happened.

"Yes, I saw Captain Cahill tonight. He was out here and he . . . he attacked me." She struggled to get the words out without falling apart.

"What were you doing out here, ma'am? It's very late and you shouldn't be prowling the grounds at this time of night."

She looked at her father and he nodded his head, telling her she had to answer their questions truthfully; putting it off would only make matters worse. John held her close to his side to try to restore some warmth to her shocked body.

Seeing she was having trouble getting started, John answered him first.

"I have to take responsibility for some of this. JoAnna was out here to say good-bye to Notah, the holy man. You know we have been ordered to leave the fort and he was forbidden to enter it. I escorted her here to meet with him, and I left when he appeared, to give them some privacy. I had gone over to the infirmary and was talking to Dr. Benson when I began to realize how much time had elapsed, so I headed back—about the same time you heard the shot."

Turning to JoAnna, the sergeant asked, "Who fired the shot, Miss Lund?"

"No one," she answered.

"Now, wait a minute, young lady, guns don't fire themselves, and there was a gunshot."

Gripping her father's arm, JoAnna answered. "Yes, I know that. I meant no one shot it on purpose."

She knew she wasn't saying it right, but she still couldn't bring herself to betray Notah and tell of his part in it. She wondered if she could say she and Captain Cahill struggled and the gun went off while she fought him. But then, how would she have gotten ahold of his gun?

She knew there was no hope for it but to tell them the truth and trust God to take care of them all.

"Notah Begay was here and we said our good-byes and he left through the gully behind the stable.

After he left, Captain Cahill came upon me and finding me alone, attacked me. Notah heard me struggling and when he looked back, saw Cahill throw me to the ground. He rushed back to save me and he pulled Cahill off me. They fought hard. When it looked like Cahill would win because he had his gun out and pointed at Notah, somehow Notah tripped him and Cahill fell down into the arroyo, and then we heard the gun go off. When we ran to the side of the embankment, we saw him lying at the bottom with the gun under his body. We don't know if he fell on it and it went off when he fell, or if he shot himself. Truly . . . truly, Notah did not shoot him. It was a horrible accident. Notah was protecting me. It was self-defense."

While she was still talking, one of the men took another torch and leaned over the side of the arroyo and exclaimed, "Yeah, Sergeant, I see him down there."

Two others scrambled down the side and turned the captain over.

"What do you see, men?" the sergeant asked them as he peered over the side as well.

"He's shot, sir, in the chest. But the lady is right, can't tell if he did it or he fell on the gun and it went off. But he is dead, all right. He's been drinking too, he smells like whiskey to high heaven. Looks like a pocket flask broke in his hip pocket."

JoAnna and John digested that piece of information and thought it was a good omen. It might help in Notah's defense.

The sergeant wasn't happy that the private had

revealed that, so he said, "No more observations. We are not doctors and cannot make a diagnosis. Guard his body while I go inform the general. We'll take him to the infirmary for further examination as soon as the general has seen him."

Turning back to John Lund, he said, "You may take your daughter home now, but you need to be ready to answer the general's inquiries into this matter. Until then, you are confined to your quarters and are not to leave the post. You understand?"

"Yes, sir," John answered. "We will be here, and Mr. Begay has said he will turn himself in to the general tomorrow morning, as well. He wants a chance to explain his side of the story."

"That's good, for we would have gone after him anyway, but it may help his case if he comes in willingly. But if he is not here shortly after daylight, a search party will be sent out, so you better hope he comes in at daybreak," the sergeant answered. He then instructed his men to leave everything as is while he alerted the general about the suspected murder.

Upon being informed of Cahill's death, General Carleton went immediately to the site to view his body. It was obvious that he had indeed died of a bullet in the chest but whether it went off accidentally as he fell, or he shot himself it was hard to tell. Another possibility was that Notah had shot him at close range while they fought over the gun, and then placed the gun in Cahill's hand to make it look like an accident. The general knew it was not going to be easy to determine either way, and he felt a moment's regret that it had been Notah who had done the deed. Knowing the bad blood between the two men, it was not going to sit well with his higher ups or those men who were loyal to Cahill.

Dr. Benson confirmed that the fall down into the arroyo had caused contusions and a broken leg. The other bruises and cuts would have come from hand-to-hand fighting, but the ultimate cause of death was the bullet wound to the heart. The smell of whiskey was strong at the scene, too, because of the broken flask in the captain's pocket. That didn't add anything good to the captain's defense though.

Shaking his head, the general told the sergeant who had found Cahill, "I want to see the Lunds in my office at daybreak and for his sake, I hope Notah does make an appearance as well. If not, a search will be made and he will be brought in, in chains, if necessary."

"Yes, sir," the captain saluted. "I know the Lunds are still awake as they just went home. I could get them right now if you wish it."

"No," the general replied, "I need time to think about this myself, and I don't think Miss Lund is in any shape to be questioned right now, either."

General Carleton was thinking that the Lunds, and Miss JoAnna in particular, had proven to be nothing but trouble since they were commanded to come with the Navajos.

Turning to the men at the scene, he said, "Does anyone know when Captain Cahill left his quarters tonight. You all know he was not supposed to be out on the grounds after dark."

All the men ducked their heads—they knew he had bribed one of the guards to switch duty with him but they were still hesitant to speak up.

Being a good judge of body language, the general knew they were not going to open up to him.

"All right, I want everyone in Captain Cahill's barracks in my office at 0230. I will speak with each one individually, and corporately, but we will get to the bottom of this tonight."

The men looked at one another, then shrugged and walked away, except those who were ordered to carry the captain's body to the infirmary.

One trooper hung back—indecision in his every move. What should he do? Would they believe him if he reported what he'd seen? Would they go after Notah anyway? He didn't want Notah's death on his conscience, and from all he heard, everyone assumed Notah was guilty and should be hung for murder.

He decided he'd better show up at the general's inquiry, too, as he was in the same barracks as the captain and his absence might be remarked upon.

Chapter Twenty-Six

Over the next few hours, General Carleton met with the twenty men who slept in the barracks with Cahill, but to no avail. Frustrated, he told them they would all be put on report, lose a month's pay, and be confined to quarters until someone came forward with the time the captain left the barracks and any other pertinent information they had.

After checking the roster of who was assigned guard duty at the stables that night, the record showed it was Private McGillicutty. After severe questioning, he determined that either the private was guilty of something himself, or he was afraid to tell what he knew. The general was aware that Cahill had intimidated a few of the men under him, and maybe McGillicutty was one of them.

Realizing he was not going to get any more out of the men, he dismissed them and told them they were confined until further notice. If they disliked it, they knew better than to voice their opinions anywhere near the general's office, so they all left in sullen silence.

Carleton called his aide-de-camp in when they left.

"I want you to bring me Cahill's files. We need to find out if he has any living relatives that we may send his personal belongings to. Also, I want you to make the funeral arrangements. He will be buried on post grounds, but I surely do not feel like giving him any twenty-one-gun salute."

"Yes, sir," the aide answered, knowing better than to agree or disagree. "I'll get the files and handle the arrangements for day after tomorrow."

"Fine," nodded the general, and he waited for Cahill's file to be brought to him.

The Lunds, and most everyone else at the fort, spent a sleepless remaining few hours until dawn. All wondering, how this would end.

JoAnna and John were still up and finishing their coffee when a shout arose within the compound. Grabbing a shawl and throwing it over her shoulders, father and daughter ran outside in time to see the troops gathered on either side of the entrance to the fort. Many of the soldiers were in stages of dress and undress but all held their weapons at the ready while Notah walked calmly through the opening.

If he was afraid or worried, he did not show it.

It was all JoAnna could do not to run to him. She was so proud of him at that moment she thought her heart would jump out of her chest. Stoic, and looking straight ahead, he headed for the general's office.

No one made any attempt to stop him but the soldiers immediately surrounded him as he passed until he was hemmed in on three sides. He held his hands away from his side to show he had no weapons on him, but he did not hold them up in the air as in surrender, either.

General Carleton heard the commotion as well and got up to go to the front door. When he spied Notah, a mixture of respect and regret stole over him. He had begun to admire the man and did not want to be the one to put him to death. He knew that even if he did hang him, the man would not be cowed and would die a hero in the eyes of his people forever.

Right behind Notah, Carleton saw the Lunds hurrying toward his quarters, too. He wondered if he should let them all in together, or question Notah by himself first. Somehow he knew Notah would not lie to him, even to save his own life; but would he lie to save JoAnna's? He was aware, as was everyone else at the fort that the medicine man and the doctor's daughter were in love. They seemed to be the only ones not aware of it.

When Notah reached the porch upon which the general stood, he said, "I have come in willingly with a good heart to talk to the general about the death of Captain Cahill."

"I'm glad you came in, Notah, and did not make me come after you. Please, come inside."

Then, turning to JoAnna and John, the general said, "You will wait here under guard until I finish with Notah. I will question you when I finish with the holy man."

"But, General," John protested, "what we have to say will have a great bearing on the case."

"It will wait until I have finished with Notah," he answered and motioned Notah to precede him into his office.

Immediately two guards went in behind the general and Notah, and stood inside the office to guard the Navajo, and two more appeared beside the Lunds. All they could do was sit on the porch benches and wait. Each dreading what might be happening behind the general's closed doors.

The general walked around his desk and motioned Notah to sit.

Notah declined, and said, "I would rather stand," which did not please the general as it made him look up at Notah and that wasn't a commanding position for the general. But he acquiesced in this, figuring it might be a small thing compared to the grave charges that he was going to level against Notah, possibly.

The general did decide he would start the questioning though before Notah could speak.

"What were you doing on fort property last night, Notah, after you had been warned not to come here unless asked to?"

"I understood that Miss Lund and her father were leaving the fort today and I wanted to say my good-byes to them."

"To both of them, or just Miss JoAnna Lund?"

"Yes, to Miss JoAnna, especially," Notah answered.

"I got a message to her through Old Woman to meet me when the moon rose by the stables as they back up to the reservation, and I felt I could meet her there without causing a disturbance."

"And I understand she did meet you sometime before the midnight watch changed. How long were you there together?"

"A short time, then I left and told her to return to her father."

"Did she return right away?"

"No, she seemed not to be able to leave right away and so I waited in the shadows across the arroyo to make sure she stayed safe."

"Then what happened?"

"I saw a dark shadow moving around the side of the stable and I was going to warn her when I heard the voice of Captain Cahill. He grabbed her and told her she was responsible for ruining his career, and he started to force himself on her. When he threw her to the ground, I raced back to save her."

"And then you two got into a fight and you shot him with his own gun?"

"No! It did not happen that way. Yes, we fought . . . hard . . . for a good while. I had a strangle hold on him and I wanted to choke the life out of him, but he managed to break it and drew his gun. I kicked his legs out from under him. As we were close to the edge of the gully, he fell backward into it. He still had the gun in his hand when he went over the edge. When he landed, we heard the shot and ran to see what had happened. I went down and could see he was dead from his own gun."

"Why didn't you come and turn yourself in right then, instead of waiting until this morning."

"Do you have a wife, General?"

When the general nodded, Notah said, "Then you know how hysterical a woman can become. Miss JoAnna feared for my life, and would not let me come right then. She said you would not believe it was an accident because of the bad feelings between the captain and me. When her father arrived to escort her back home, I left and told her I would return this morning to tell you what happened. We fought, but I did not kill him. I am not sorry the captain is dead; I will not lie about it. But he would have raped JoAnna had I not been there, and I could not let that happen."

"Is there anyone who can prove this story, besides Miss Lund?"

"No, I do not believe anyone else saw what happened. We were alone."

The general didn't like to hear that the only other option was that Captain Cahill had taken that guard's duty and sent him away so he would not hear or see anything. But how did he know JoAnna would be out there at that time, or was it just coincidence that he found her alone.

Looking at Notah, he said, "I don't know how to prove this one way or the other, Notah. There will be a trial and you can have a lawyer assigned to you. It is just your word and Miss Lund's, and we know that a woman in love will say anything to protect those she loves," eyeing Notah as he said it to gauge his reaction.

Notah returned the general's look and said, "Yes, we are in love and although it is not thought of as proper in your society, love does not know any color, creed, or race. It just happens in the heart. This is not something I will discuss with you though, but I do not want her name and virtue talked about. Miss Lund is as chaste now as she has always been."

"I see," Carleton said. "All right, then, I will bring in Miss Lund and her father. Possibly, they will be able to shed some more light on this, but so far, it looks like I will have to hold you upon suspicion of murder. You do understand that, don't you?"

"I see that you have a problem to solve and it does not look well for me, but I did not kill him. When he fell on the gun, it went off."

The general got up and opened his office door, telling his adjunct to bring in the Lunds. He told Notah to stand over to the side where he could see him, and told the guards to come inside the room and stand at the back.

JoAnna and her father entered the general's office apprehensively. He asked them to sit in chairs in front of his desk.

When she didn't see Notah immediately, JoAnna looked around frantically and then sighed when she saw him in the corner of the room, leaning against the wall with his arms crossed over his chest. She knew her heart was in her eyes when she looked at him, but she could not help it. He nodded at her but did not speak. She could not tell from his expression if things had gone well or not. She could only hope that when she got through with her version, the general would accept it.

"All right," the general began, "who wants to start with an explanation as to what happened, and why Miss Lund was out on the grounds at that time of night meeting Notah when he had express orders not to come to the fort?"

John said he would begin.

"We knew it was against your policies but as we were leaving today, my daughter and Notah, who have formed an attachment for each other, wanted to have a chance to say good-bye in private. They made arrangements to meet behind the stables. I took her there and then went to the infirmary to give them that privacy. Dr. Benson and I got carried away on some medical discussions and more time elapsed than I realized. I had started back for her when I found her shaking and obviously in distress. Her clothing was torn and she was crying. I asked her what had happened. She told me Captain Cahill had come upon her before she left the area, and he had attempted to rape her. Fortunately, Notah had not gone very far and he saw Cahill approach JoAnna and his subsequent attack on her person. Taking the risk of being caught didn't matter, saving JoAnna from Cahill's evil clutches did. For which I am ever in his debt."

The general turned to JoAnna and said, "Would you take up the story from there, please?"

Although mortified, pale, and shaking, JoAnna told her side of it and that Cahill was definitely out for revenge against her and her father. Her, because she had scorned his attentions, and her father because he felt John's testimony about his treatment of the Navajos had cost him his standing in the army and his subsequent punishment.

"His remarks to me were vulgar and crude and I knew he would have no mercy on me," she concluded. "Had Notah not come to my aid, I might be the one dead at the bottom of the gully, and had he won the fight he would have placed the blame for my rape on Notah and said he had killed him to save me."

Notah was not surprised to hear how the captain planned to get out of being accused of killing him. He hated to see JoAnna humiliate herself this way in front of all these men and he moved abruptly in place.

His movement drew attention from the guards. They immediately raised their guns at him, and told him to stand back.

JoAnna jumped up and would have run to him, but her father pulled her back down and Notah shook his head at her. She felt like she was flying apart inside. How could she stand it if the general wouldn't believe them?

The general did not miss the emotions playing over all their faces and the tension building in the room.

Speaking to John Lund, the general said, "I'm afraid with the death of the captain, I cannot let you leave the fort today as planned. You will be needed to testify when the army tribunal convenes. Where had you planned to go when you left?"

"We were going to go to the town downriver to stay there awhile until we decided where we wanted to end up. There's not much sense in going back to Navajoland to reopen the ⸱⸱⸱ing post if there aren't any Navajos to trade with. I thought I might try to find something to do in the town."

"I see. Unfortunately, I must ask you to return to your quarters for the time being and stay within the fort grounds," answered the general, when all he really wanted was to see them gone from the post altogether.

"What about Notah?" JoAnna could not help asking.

"He will be put in the stockade until a trial is held."

When Carleton saw the alarm on her face, he said to her, "I will see he is treated fairly, Miss Lund, but you realize this is a very serious matter and he has to be judged by the army."

JoAnna could do nothing but accept what the general said. They watched as the guards tied Notah's hands behind his back and escorted him to the stockade.

The troopers milling around outside the general's office were told to clear the area. Some did so but others taunted Notah as he passed them, yet more were silent and felt sorry for the holy man. All felt he would get the death sentence for sure.

JoAnna's heart was breaking. She had to lean on her father for she couldn't even see where she was walking with the tears streaming down her face.

Notah felt her tears, for he turned and looked over

at her and gave her a brief nod of encouragement. Then looking straight ahead once more, he continued walking between his guards. As much as her tears alarmed him, he could not be distracted by them, for *if* his fight with Cahill had been one unto death, he knew the fight he was in now was truly for his life.

Upon reaching the stockade, the guards shoved him roughly into his cell. He ignored it and the snide remarks they made. At least it was not the hole, and he had survived that, so he would survive this confinement as well.

Chapter Twenty-Seven

General Carleton, meanwhile, drafted a request to Santa Fe Army Headquarters for a hearing to be held at Fort Sumner as soon as possible, detailing the death of Captain Cahill, and the subsequent arrest of Notah Begay.

Once more he found himself thinking the Lunds and Notah were more trouble than the whole Navajo nation combined. Deep down he believed their story, but protocol had to be followed, so a trial had to be held. He had no idea how the judges of the tribunal would decide but it wouldn't take half a brain to figure it out. They would find Notah guilty rather than have the reputation of the army besmirched in any way.

The general sent for Colonel Carson next and told him everything he had learned from the Lunds and Notah.

"Well, I believe their story and I would like to be called as a character witness for Notah, or even sit on the tribunal, if that would be all right."

"To tell you the truth, Kit, I wish there was some way I could let Notah go and send the Lunds on their way as well. I want them gone. I fear this could lead to an uprising on the reservation if we have to execute the holy man."

"You might be right there, General. Do I have your permission to visit and talk with Notah?"

"Yes, maybe you can discern something that I missed."

"Thank you, General, I'll go right over. I think I want to speak with the Lunds, as well."

The general nodded and waved him on his way.

When Notah heard the key turn in the lock, he looked up from where he sat on the bunk. There was no window in the seven-by-nine foot room— just a bed, a slop bucket, and a pitcher for water. He stood as Kit Carson entered.

"Ho-ta-hey," Carson greeted Notah in the Navajo language.

"Ho-ta-hey," Notah responded. "Why are you here?"

"I've come to hear from your own mouth exactly what happened. I don't need to tell you how precarious your position is right now."

"Yes, I am aware of that, but I did not kill the captain although I admit I wanted to, and probably would have, had he not fallen into the ravine."

"Well, I hope you didn't say that to the general. But please tell me everything that happened and why you risked coming onto the fort grounds when you'd been ordered not to."

So once more Notah explained everything in detail to Kit Carson; his need to say good-bye to JoAnna, Captain Cahill's attack upon her, and their subsequent fight, Cahill's fall into the arroyo, and the gun going off.

"You're sure you didn't fight over the gun and it went off in the struggle before he fell into the gully?" Carson asked.

"*No.* I had him in a chokehold when he managed to break free and I fell backward onto the ground. It was then he reached for his gun and I knocked his legs out from under him. He was close to the edge and couldn't regain his balance. He toppled into the gully. The gun went off when he landed on top of it, at least that is how it looked to me."

"That is how Miss Lund tells it, too, but she's in love with you and would say anything to save you. At least that is how the court will look at it."

"*Well, it is the truth,*" Notah answered indignantly. His word had never been questioned before and it galled him to have to explain himself over and over again.

Sensing his rising anger, Kit replied, "Calm down, calm down. I believe you. But you see how it looks and how it will sound to those who will be judging you."

"The gods will decide my fate, Kit Carson. I know the truth and I can live or die with that."

"All right," Carson said. "I will sit on the tribunal panel that is going to try you and I will ask you questions on the witness stand and call on others to bear witness in the hearing about your character, and so forth."

"If you wish to do this, that is fine; however, I want to speak for myself."

"One way or another, you will get to tell your side, I promise you that. Remember though, there are a lot of people who'll want to see you punished all the same, even though a lot of them disliked Cahill themselves."

"The truth will set me free . . . one way or another," Notah pronounced.

Colonel Carson hoped to God it would. He left Notah then to report back to the general.

Within two weeks the tribunal convened and the trial began. There were no seats left in the mess hall where the hearing was to be conducted. Men were standing all around the room and hanging in the open windows to watch the proceedings.

The panel consisted of General Sherman, an avid Indian fighter, Colonel Kit Carson, and General Carleton. Carleton was to conduct the questioning with the others having the right to cross-examine as they saw fit. They sat at a long table across the front of the room. The defendant sat by himself on one side, with the Lunds seated behind him. The sergeant who had come upon the scene first, was the prosecuting attorney and he was seated to the right of Notah at another table.

General Carleton brought the court session to order and stated the reason for the hearing as being:

to determine the cause of the death of Captain Cahill; whether Notah Begay, medicine man of the Navajo tribe, was responsible for this death; and the punishment to be meted out if he was found guilty.

The hush in the room was absolute as the general read the charges. Many held mixed emotions about the trial. Those loyal to Cahill wanted to see Notah hang, but many more were sympathetic and had come to admire the holy man. Several thought him to be of better character than Cahill—still, he *was* an Indian and they were white.

General Carleton began the questioning by calling the sergeant who had found the body. He instructed him to state *only* the facts, as he knew them.

"It was after the midnight watch had changed, possibly about 0130, when an officer patrolling the grounds heard a muffled shot and came to the officer's quarters to get me to go with him to investigate. Upon reaching the stables, we heard a woman crying and came upon Dr. Lund and his daughter out in the back."

General Sherman asked, "What were civilians doing out at that time of the night?"

"Well, I asked her the same question, and asked the doctor why he was there, as well. It appears that Miss Lund had formed an attachment for the medicine man and as the Lunds were being asked to leave the fort the next day, she wanted to say goodbye to him privately. Their answers were the same."

The general cast a long, hard look at JoAnna, as if to say, *"What could you possibly see in an Indian?"*

JoAnna felt herself blush but she refused to be cowed and looked him straight in the eye.

"Proceed," Sherman said.

Carleton asked the sergeant, "Were you aware that Notah Begay had been banned from the post grounds?"

"Yes, sir, most everyone was; but where there's a will, people make a way," he answered, amid snickers from the men listening.

Ignoring the snickers, Sherman asked, "Then what happened?"

"I proceeded to ask the Lunds if they had seen or heard anything, and if they knew who had fired the shot. Miss Lund said Captain Cahill had come upon her after Notah Begay left and made improper advances to her. The medicine man saw her struggling and came back to help her. A fight ensued between the captain and Notah and, as they struggled, the captain toppled over the lip of the ravine and then they both heard the gun go off."

"Did this Notah Begay shoot him?" the general asked.

"We could not determine that as we were not there, and when my men went down to check it out, Captain Cahill was lying with the gun under him and a bullet in his chest. Miss Lund swore that he either fell on the gun and it went off, or he shot himself. No one else could verify that though. We only have her word for it. Mr. Begay was not at the scene when we got there."

"So there were no other witnesses to this death except Miss Lund and Mr. Begay, is that correct?"

"Yes, sir."

General Carleton spoke up then and said, "I would like to hear from the accused now and have him explain, in his own words, what happened. If there is trouble in understanding him, Colonel Carson can interpret for him, if that is agreeable with you, General Sherman?"

General Sherman agreed. He was anxious to hear what the medicine man had to say and to observe him up close.

Notah was called to stand before the panel. He swore to tell the truth, chagrined that they should even have to ask that of him.

He proceeded to tell the story again for the panel exactly as he had told it to General Carleton in his office, leaving nothing out, or adding anything new.

When he was excused and had taken his seat again, General Carleton called JoAnna, and then John Lund to the stand. Each told the exact same story, but it was still only JoAnna and Notah's word about how the death had happened, and her word was suspect because of her love for the medicine man.

The general then called any others who wished to speak in behalf of Captain Cahill or Miss Lund. Several troopers came forward. One told of Notah's bravery in rescuing Private Wiley from the swollen stream, another spoke of the animosity between Cahill and Notah because of the whipping and punishment in the hole. Others said how Notah, Miss Lund, and her father had doctored the Navajos, and even some of them, on the march there. In the end, the remarks were running half in favor and half against, with no concrete evidence brought forth to sway the panel either way. But the circumstantial evidence surely pointed to Notah's guilt, most everyone agreed.

All of a sudden a commotion started in the back of the room, and Private Wiley came forward, pushing and shoving through the crowded room to get to the front.

"Permission to speak, Sirs," came a request from the man who had pushed his way to the front.

"Granted," he was told.

"Generals . . . sirs, I cannot let this man die."

"Why?" General Carleton asked.

"Because I was there, and I want to be a witness for Miss Lund and Notah."

Surprised, Carleton stood up and asked, "Why didn't you come forward before? What information do you have that has not already been told?"

Embarrassed, Private Wiley answered, "Because I wasn't sure anyone would believe me."

"Why not, Private?" Carleton asked.

"Well, it was no secret how Captain Cahill treated me, and some might have thought I had it in for the captain. Then, since I'm friends with Miss Lund and I admire the holy man, they might think I was in cahoots with them, or that I might even have shot the captain myself."

"All right, Private," General Carleton said. "Please come forward and be sworn in and tell us what you know and we will decide if it has any bearing on the case or not."

JoAnna fell back into her seat and clung to her father's arm.

"What do you suppose Toby can say, Father, to save Notah?"

"We'll find out," he answered.

After Toby was sworn in, Carleton said, "All right, please begin Private Wiley."

"Well, I witnessed the whole thing and I can vouch that everything that Miss Lund and Notah Begay said was the actual truth."

"Why were you out at that time of night, Private? You were not on duty at the stables."

"No, General Carleton, I was not. I heard Captain Cahill get up and I followed him out."

"Are you in the habit of following the captain?" Carleton asked.

"No, sir, but I had heard talk about him visiting the young Navajo and Apache girls and his sneaking out to play poker and drink with the men, so I wanted to know which it was he was going to do."

Carleton glanced over at Notah and saw the murderous look on his face and realized then that the stories about Cahill's lustful behavior as hinted at by the Lunds, and even Carson, must be true. When he looked around at the men and guards, no one would look him in the eye and that convinced him, too, that it wasn't just a rumor.

"Proceed, Private, what else did you see?"

"Well, I stayed in the shadows and I saw Notah leave Miss Lund and cross the ravine. I didn't know he had stayed over there watching her. She didn't leave right away and before too long I heard

Captain Cahill at the front of the stable telling Private McGillicutty that he was dismissed from guard duty and that he would take his place. I think he must have seen Miss Lund when she crossed the parade ground and headed for the stables because his window faces that way. Most of us know he had a personal interest in Miss Lund. He waited until everyone was asleep and then he left. As he was not supposed to be out at night, I decided to follow him."

General Sherman spoke up then and asked Carleton, "Why was the captain not allowed out at night?"

Carleton flushed as he answered the general.

"Captain Cahill was on report and confined to his barracks at night for disciplinary reasons."

He didn't want to admit what the charges were if he didn't have to. It was going to be a bad reflection on his own leadership if Cahill's treatment of the Navajos and his pursuit of Miss Lund were known to Sherman.

"So, this Captain Cahill had not behaved entirely as an officer and a gentleman, is that correct? And what are these accusations that he met with Indian girls on the side? Is there proof of this?" Sherman asked.

Turning to Wiley, Sherman said, "This is a serious charge, young man. Can you back up what you said?"

"Yes and no, sir," Toby answered. "If the men would be honest, they all knew of his poker games and drinking and his bragging about taking the young women. I know no one wants to believe the

worst about him, General, but I could not let him
hurt the girls anymore. I came across one of them
one morning as the captain was coming back from
the camp. She was bleeding and curled up in a ball
under a bush. When she saw me, she became terrified and scrambled away before I could help her. By
her condition, it was pretty obvious what had happened to her, and the captain was the only one in
the area at the time."

Sherman looked from the young man to General
Carleton and said, "I'm not sure we can incorpo-
rate that in the record. It is only hear-say at this
point."

JoAnna was beside herself. This wasn't helping
Notah! If anything, it only made it look like he had
another reason to go after Cahill.

"What else do you have to offer us?" Carleton
asked.

"Well, it was just like Miss Lund said, Captain
Cahill came around the back of the stable and
grabbed her from behind. He said awful things to
her and blamed her father for his punishment.
When he tried to kiss her, she fought him. In their
struggling, he ended up pushing her to the ground
and flung himself on top of her. I didn't know
whether to reveal myself and take a gun to him
myself, or run for help. But it was taken out of my
hands, when Mr. Begay came roaring up out of the
ravine and pulled the captain off Miss JoAnna. They
did have a fight and it looked like it was gonna be a
fight to the death."

Then, thinking how that sounded, he turned to

Carleton, and said, "But General, sir, it had been brewing for a long time, and Cahill's hatred of Notah was known by most of the men. And Notah, never that I know of, ever once tried to get back at the captain in any way."

"Go on, Private," the general said.

"Okay, well, Notah got a stranglehold on the captain, but the captain must have known it was his death he was looking at, and he heaved himself up and knocked Notah off, then stood up and pulled his gun on him. Mr. Begay knocked the captain's legs out from under him and as he was so close to the edge of the ravine, he fell over backward into it."

"How good was the lighting in the area at the time, Private? Did you see all this clearly?"

"The moon had risen and was full. It was bright enough to see them most of the time. They did roll in and out of the shadows several times, but when they were in the open, I could see them fine."

"So, what happened after the gun went off?" Carleton asked.

"Well, Miss Lund and Notah ran to the edge to see what had happened. Notah went down into the ravine and verified that he was dead, shot by his own gun. He wanted to come to you himself, right then, but Miss JoAnna was getting all worked up and begged him to leave before the soldiers found him. She thought the guards would shoot him on sight and not give him a chance to explain because of Captain Cahill's hatred for Notah."

The general was glad to hear that Notah had wanted to turn himself in, and that so far, their stories were matching the Lunds. Then he had another thought, *were they all in this together and protecting one another?*

Carleton remembered the rumors about Cahill's treatment of the young private. Had Toby finally had enough and killed the captain himself? Cahill would have beaten Toby in a fight unless he had been more inebriated than anyone knew. Had Wiley pushed him down into the ravine and when he saw the captain was not moving, gone down and shot him in the chest, then placed the gun in Cahill's hand?

He felt he had to ask, "Private, it seems to me that there were some hard feelings between you and the captain, too. Did you fire the fatal shot?"

Toby gulped, and said in a shaky voice, "No, sir, I did not shoot Captain Cahill. I admit I wasn't too fond of him. But he was my superior officer and I tried to obey the commands he gave me."

Carleton then asked, "Why then did you not come forth immediately, Private, especially when you knew I was questioning all the men in Captain Cahill's barracks?"

"Well, I was scared and confused at the moment myself. I didn't know whether you or the men would believe me since they knew I have a high regard for the medicine man . . . after all he did save my life, and I am a friend of Miss JoAnna's."

"Did you see what Notah did in the ravine? Could he have positioned the gun in the captain's hand to make it look like he fell on the gun?" General Sherman chimed in.

JoAnna's heart sank. No matter how Toby explained things, it still looked bad for Notah.

"No, sir, I did not go look into the ravine. But the gun was definitely in Captain Cahill's hands when he fell into the ravine and there was only the one shot. Notah was still on top when it went off."

"You may step down, Private. I would like to call Private McGillicutty to the stand," Kit Carson spoke up.

When McGillicutty had been sworn in, Colonel Carson asked him, "Were you relieved of guard duty by Captain Cahill on the midnight watch on the night in question?"

Shamefaced, McGillicutty answered. "Yes, sir. He said he needed to get out of the barracks for a while and he would take my watch for me. As he was my captain, sir, I did as he asked."

"Did you stay around or did you go back to your quarters immediately."

"I didn't wait around, I went straight back. I didn't want the captain mad at me."

"Did the captain get mad easily?" Carson asked.

"Well, he did get rather mad on occasions and his men knew better than to question him or cross him."

"Had you ever seen his anger in action, Private McGillicutty?"

"Yes."

"And did you witness any of this anger directed toward the medicine man?"

"Many times, sir."

"Can you tell us some of those times?"

So the private told about the times Cahill had

tried to rile Notah on the march and how when he couldn't get a reaction from the holy man, it angered him. He told about when Notah saved Private Wiley from the river, it made the captain look bad in front of his men, then when he saw Notah talking to Miss Lund one day, he brought the charges against him of making improper sexual advances toward her and had him whipped and put in the hole.

JoAnna groaned. None of this was helping. Now it made it look like there was a personal vendetta on Notah's part against the captain. Even in his death, it looked like Cahill would be the victor after all.

Notah, meanwhile, sat in stoic silence. It galled him that JoAnna must be humiliated in front of these soldiers and he could do nothing to stop their evil thoughts about her. He never looked at the witness or indicated by his actions that he was aware of what was being said. He concentrated only on maintaining his Hozho and remaining in harmony. Settling down into his spirit, he asked the gods to reveal the truth, knowing that if they did not, he was prepared to die.

General Carleton took up the questioning again.

"Private McGillicutty, did you at any time on the march here see Notah Begay incite his people to resist arrest, riot, or take up arms against Captain Cahill and his soldiers?"

"No, sir. He did not. He could not be riled in any way and that seemed to bug Captain Cahill something terrible. He provoked Mr. Begay to try to get a reaction out of him. He never succeeded until one day the captain whipped an old man because he had fallen and could not get up. When Notah went to the man's rescue, the Captain used that as an excuse to put him in chains and bind his hands."

Carleton was stunned to realize how little he had known about what was going on with the men in the fort, and all of it right under his nose. Any more talk like this and his superiors would be asking him questions about his own leadership. As Carleton looked over at Sherman, he was alarmed at the stormy look on his face. This whole thing was going from bad to worse.

The general told Private McGillicutty he could step down from the witness chair. He told the guards to return Notah to his cell and keep a strong guard around him.

General Carleton called for a recess while he and the other officers convened in his office to reach a verdict.

Chapter Twenty-Eight

Back in the general's office, the officers sat in stunned silence for a few minutes. Kit could think of nothing to add that would help Notah, although he truly believed it had happened just as he, Toby Wiley, and JoAnna had said.

No one wanted to be the first to speak, because truly, no one knew what to say at this point.

Finally, Carleton spoke.

"General Sherman, I think we're at an impasse here. I, for one, would like to dismiss the whole thing and let Notah be returned to his camp, and send the Lunds on their way. I truly fear this may have an adverse affect on the Navajos and the Apaches. We might well end up with an Indian uprising on our hands."

"Don't you think you could handle such a thing?" Sherman asked.

Kit Carson answered, "Yes, we could handle it, sir, but we are trying to convince them to become *"civilized"* and adapt to our ways. If Notah is innocent, and I for one believe he is, and that everyone has told the truth in this matter, then we are defeating our purpose for keeping them on this reservation."

Sherman, being the ranking general, said, "Unfortunately, a judgment has to be made, and if you cannot make it, I will. He will be found guilty and made an example of. Uprising or no."

Kit tried once more to intervene, "But, sir, it is all circumstantial evidence at this point."

General Sherman shook his head. "Well, I don't see any other way to show the Navajos and Apaches that they are not above the army, or our country's laws. Notah must be punished for the captain's death, whether he actually fired the shot or not."

"What should his punishment be?" Carleton asked.

"Why death by hanging, of course," Sherman answered.

Both Carleton and Carson felt sick at the general's pronouncement. It didn't look like they could change his mind. Since he was the ranking officer on this panel, Carleton being too close to the situation, they had to abide by this decision. They walked back to the mess hall, heads up and looking straight ahead.

Carson was afraid if he looked at anyone he would give away their decision, so he took his seat and kept his eyes down on the table.

General Carleton stood and asked Notah to stand, which he did, head held high looking the general directly in the face.

Carleton knew a moment of regret, but then he

was a general in the U.S. Army and he didn't shirk his duty when it was laid out for him.

"Notah, we have heard all the evidence, and since there is no way to prove or disprove your story, and even though it is circumstantial, all evidence points to you as the one who caused Captain Cahill's death. The panel finds you guilty of murder and sentences you to be hung at dawn."

Notah didn't flinch or show any outward emotion at the sentence, but he did react to JoAnna when she cried out, "*Nooo*, you can't do that. He didn't do it," and she fell into her father's arms sobbing.

Notah turned and looked at her father, and in a silent message said, "*Take care of her.*"

JoAnna was in a state of collapse. Her sobbing could be heard throughout the room.

John was just as stunned by the verdict. Even though he knew it looked bad, he had hoped that with Toby's eyewitness account, the judges might at least just give Notah time in prison instead of the death penalty.

As everyone was trying to digest what had just happened, another commotion started at the entrance to the mess hall. All turned to see what it was.

Dr. Benson was clearing the way for a petite, lovely Apache Indian girl with a baby in her arms. Behind them came Old Woman with her walking stick in her hand.

General Carleton stood up and asked, "What is the meaning of this, Dr. Benson?"

"I believe I have some new information that may have a bearing on this trial."

"What would that be, and why are these women here?"

"Swear me in and I will tell you," answered Benson.

General Sherman spoke up and said, "Swear him in. I want to hear what he has to say."

Dr. Benson leaned down and said something to the girl and motioned Old Woman to seat her near JoAnna and Dr. Lund.

Carleton swore him in and told the doctor to take the witness chair.

JoAnna was mystified. *What in the world could this mean? What was going on?*

After being sworn in, Dr. Benson began his testimony.

"Early this morning, Old Woman, as she is called by the Navajos, came to see me with Little Fawn in tow. She showed me her small child and I could tell it was a half-breed, not a full-blooded Apache. Little Fawn told me Captain Cahill had raped her before he left to go bring in the Navajos with Colonel Carson, and that her baby boy was the result of that rape. I asked her how she could prove this, and she produced Cahill's captain's bars. In her struggles with him, she had pulled them from his uniform as he raped her."

Dr. Benson then proceeded to show the two bars from a captain's uniform.

"How do you know this is from Captain Cahill's uniform?" Carleton asked.

"Check his wardrobe or foot locker and see if one of his jackets is missing any bars."

The general sent the sergeant who had found Cahill to check through the captain's belongings.

A low rumbling was heard throughout the room as the soldiers speculated about what this new evidence might mean.

JoAnna turned to Old Woman and hugged her and told her to tell Little Fawn how proud she was of her and thanked her for being brave enough to come in. She could see the young girl trembling and knew she must be scared to death.

Carleton called for silence and asked Dr. Benson to bring the girl forward with her child.

Notah was shocked and still reeling with this new development. He wanted to comfort the young girl who he knew must be terrified, surrounded by so many soldiers. He rose up in his seat as she passed by him to say a word to ease her, but was roughly pushed back down. Rage and embarrassment for Little Fawn filled him. He was sorry Cahill was already dead for he wanted to have that chokehold on him again and this time have the pleasure of breaking his bull neck with his bare hands.

Old Woman went up to the tribunal table with Little Fawn and explained to her that the Bluecoats wanted to have a look at her baby.

Sherman, Carleton, and Carson looked at the blue-eyed baby boy observing the square-jawed features and lighter skin that could only be from a white man. It did not sit well with them.

In about twenty minutes, the sergeant returned

with a blue sack coat over his arm. Everyone craned their necks to see what he had and followed his progress to the head table.

"Did you find that jacket in Captain Cahill's things?" Carleton asked the sergeant.

"Yes, sir." And he showed them the jacket and pointed out where the bars had pulled free leaving threads dangling, and also the coarse, long black hairs that had been caught on the brass buttons on the front of the jacket. They were too long to belong to Cahill's as his hair was sandy colored and all knew his eyes were definitely blue.

The generals were convinced that Little Fawn had told the truth and that Captain Cahill's conduct left much to be desired.

Looking at Sherman, Carleton asked, "Now are you convinced that Notah is innocent of the Captain's death?"

"Well, as there is no way to prove exactly what happened, I am recommending that some form of punishment still be meted out to him. I think six months in the stockade should be sufficient."

General Carleton was chagrined and at the same time relieved. He stood to his feet and called for silence as the room had broken out in bedlam again. He told Notah to stand to hear the decision of the court.

Notah stood and again looked the general in the eye.

When all was quiet again, Carleton said, "Taking into consideration this latest evidence, we conclude that Captain Cahill's actions led to his own down-

fall; however, as there is still no way to prove it was
an accident, the tribunal sentences Notah Begay to
six months in the stockade, then to be released and
never to be allowed to set foot on fort grounds
again, for any reason."

JoAnna and John sat in stunned silence. Then
JoAnna jumped up and ran around the guards to
cling to Notah.

"Oh, Notah, they should not do this to you,"
she cried.

He held her for a moment in spite of the guards
trying to pull her away. He then put her arms off
him and said to her, "JoAnna, don't make a specta-
cle of yourself. I am all right with the general's decision. I can endure this. There was no way to prove
what we said, and now because of Little Fawn's testimony, they know what a dog the captain was."

General Sherman glared at JoAnna and Notah. He
could not believe a decent white woman would let
herself fall in love with an Indian, but even to him,
the devotion between them was obvious. No matter,
he nudged General Carleton and said, "Return
Notah to his cell now, and dismiss the court."

Carleton did so and everyone filed out. Comments flew back and forth about the outcome.
Everyone felt, though, that justice had been served.

JoAnna sagged against her father, drained of
all energy. Old Woman walked over to her with
Little Fawn.

Private Wiley came over, too. He had recognized
her as the girl under the scrub brush—in truth, he
had never forgotten her. Battered and bloodied as

she had been; her beauty was still evident along with the fear he had seen in her eyes. He had hated Cahill himself at that moment for ruining such a lovely creature.

Old Woman introduced Little Fawn to JoAnna and her father. JoAnna made over the baby and hugged the young girl.

Toby told John that Little Fawn was the one he had seen and asked Old Woman to introduce him to her as well, which Old Woman did.

When Little Fawn looked up into Toby's eyes, her breath hitched in her throat. She recognized him, too. He was the bluecoat soldier who had witnessed her shame. She had been afraid of him too, but even so, she remembered the compassion in his eyes and his entreaties to let him help her. Scared and hurting, she had just scrambled away as fast as she could. As she looked at him now, she saw the same compassion in his eyes along with something else she didn't know how to name. She ducked her head in confusion.

Suddenly, JoAnna remembered where they were and her hospitality skills came to the forefront. She suggested they all go back to the house and she would fix dinner, as it was now late in the day and no one had eaten since morning. It had been a harrowing day for everyone.

Carleton watched JoAnna march her little troop out and knew he would talk to them in the morning. They would leave the fort tomorrow, hell or high water.

Turning to Sherman and Carson, he said, "I

think this calls for a drink, not in celebration, mind you, but thankfully because it is over."

Both men followed Carleton out while the soldiers put the mess hall back together for eating purposes.

Kit Carson felt almost giddy with relief at the way things had turned out. Thank God they did not have to execute Notah. He'd dreaded what the Navajos and Apaches would have done had they done so. Time penned up would be hard on the free, roaming medicine man, but at least he would be alive. He was sorry for the way Cahill had abused the little Indian maiden. Little Fawn's coming forth had turned the tide in the hearing and he was grateful for her courage in doing so.

Notah's last glimpse of JoAnna was of her herding her little group out of the mess hall. His *little warrior woman—how he loved her.* He could even be grateful to the generals in their decision and he thanked his gods they had spared his life. He vowed once again to serve them faithfully all the days he had left on Mother Earth.

Chapter Twenty-Nine

JoAnna was thrilled that Notah's life had been spared and that the truth about Cahill had finally come out. She hated to see Notah serve even one day for that evil man's death, but she was, oh, so grateful that he would live. She vowed that when he got out, somehow, they were going to be together. How, she did not know, but she was not going to be separated from him any longer.

At the house, everyone wanted to talk at once. Finally, while they drank tea and feasted on a light dinner of ham and eggs and fluffy biscuits, John asked Old Woman how she had found out about Little Fawn since she was Apache and not with their Navajo band.

Apparently, Little Fawn had kept her attack to herself as long as she could. Ashamed and scared when her time came to deliver the baby, she had sought out Old Woman who was known for her skills as a midwife. Later when she heard that they were blaming Notah for Cahill's death, she told Old Woman that she wanted to tell what Cahill had done to her and showed her the captain's bars she had saved all that time.

Old Woman picked up the story. "I knew then we had to expose that evil man for what he was. We all knew Notah did not kill him but if he had, we would have rejoiced over his death."

While they were discussing everything, Toby had maneuvered a seat next to Little Fawn. He looked adoringly at her while he tried to make small talk. If the truth were told, he could not take his eyes off her.

Little Fawn was shy in his presence. She could not help but feel his admiring glances and his desire to communicate with her. She knew a little English and could answer a few of his questions on her own. His eyes, a soft hazel, never left her face. She decided they were nice eyes and would not tell her lies, and he would not give her trinkets just to get in the blankets with her as Cahill had done. She smiled up at him, then ducked her head confused again by her own reaction to him.

Toby thought his heart would jump right out of his chest. Then, and there, he fell irrevocably in love. He determined he would do everything he could to protect her and the life of her little son. It was not the child's fault how he was conceived. He also knew what most whites thought of a half-breed child. They were usually not accepted by either side.

After they had eaten and it was getting late, Toby offered to escort Old Woman and Little Fawn back to the reservation. Old Woman told them that Little Fawn had taken up residence with her and Notah's children as the baby was colicky and disturbed her parents.

At the gate the guards allowed him to pass through when Toby told them what he was doing. He said he would be back shortly and if Colonel Carson or General Carleton looked for him, to tell them where he was. They said they would.

Toby offered to carry the boy and laid him against his chest. A feeling of such acute protectiveness came over him that he almost stumbled. He had never experienced so many intense feelings before in his life as he now felt for Little Fawn and her son.

Old Woman, watching the byplay between the three of them, smiled. It looked like it wouldn't be long before her father, Plenty Coups, would be receiving an offer for Little Fawn's hand in marriage. And, maybe, it would be a good thing for all concerned. No Apache would offer for her, and if it had to be a white man who took her to wife, it looked like this one would cherish and protect her from all hurt, harm, and danger, if he possibly could. Maybe this would end in harmony for everyone after all.

Meanwhile, back at the house, JoAnna and John rehashed all that had happened. Finally he said, "Daughter, I feel we will be asked to leave the fort very shortly, probably before the day is out tomorrow."

"I know." She sighed. "I realized that as soon as

the trial ended and I saw General Carleton staring at us. I've only got a few things left to pack. Will we go to Sumner City as we talked about?"

"Yes. We'll stay there until Notah is released, but beyond that I don't know what will happen or what we can do."

"I know, I know." She sighed again. "Do you think they would let me see Notah tonight?" she asked, brightening at the prospect.

"Probably not tonight, JoAnna. Taps have already sounded. We can try in the morning. Try to get some sleep, tomorrow might prove to be another strenuous day."

"I will," she answered, smothering a yawn as she headed for her bedroom. But she vowed to be up bright and early tomorrow morning and she *would* see Notah before they left no matter what.

She did take time to say a prayer and thank God for sparing Notah's life. "Keep him strong while in the prison and when he gets out, please make a way where there seems to be no way for us to be together," she added. "Thank you, Lord, for your mercy." Then she fell into an exhausted sleep until dawn.

The next morning as soon as roll call and breakfast were over, JoAnna and her father were on their way to General Carleton's office to get permission to visit Notah.

When the general heard them in his outer office, he beckoned them to come inside.

"I'm glad you came by this morning as I was just

about to send for you myself." He motioned them to sit down in front of his desk.

The Lunds both knew then that they were about to be given their own marching orders.

Before he started in though with what he had to tell them, General Carleton asked why they were there.

"Well, we know we will be having to leave soon and we would like to have a chance to see Notah before we leave. To say good-bye, of course, and to let him know we'll be around until he gets out."

The general couldn't help making the observation, "Wasn't it the saying of "good-bye" that started all this trouble?"

JoAnna flushed at his remark but would not be put off.

"Yes, General, we made a grave error in judgment there, but I beg you to let me see him one more time before we are asked to leave, and that is why you wanted to see us, is it not?" she asked him.

The general cleared his throat and answered, "Yes, that is correct. Your wagon has been repaired and we can lend you another if need be, and an army escort to the town nearby. You may be able to find a place to rent for a while, since you are determined to stay in the area. But hear me, I will not allow visits to Notah while he is incarcerated. When he is released, I may allow you to come back to the fort then to see him. If you send word to me where you are staying, I will think about it. But, truthfully, I am glad to be quit of the both of you. You're coming along with the Navajos was a grave mistake and has caused nothing but problems. I wish you luck in the future, and I hope you can once again prosper."

"Well, that says it plain enough," John answered. "I'm sorry we inconvenienced you as well. It certainly was not our choice to come, but for the lives we did save on the *Long Walk*, I am glad we were along."

"Yes, for that, too, I am grateful, Dr. Lund. The wagons will be at your house after the noon meal today."

"We'll be ready," John answered, and rose to escort JoAnna out. Then remembering why they came, he turned back and said, "Do we have your permission to visit Notah now?"

"Yes," Carleton answered and wrote a quick note for the guards.

Tears welled up in JoAnna's eyes but she determined not to cry in front of Notah. Oh, how was she going to stand this separation? How could she leave without saying good-bye to the children? It was tearing her apart.

At the jail, the guards read the order from the general and let them inside the anteroom. They would not be allowed in Notah's cell, but they could walk down a short hall between the only two cells and speak to him through the bars.

Notah heard them coming and stood up and walked over to the bars. His heart ached at the sight of the dark circles under her eyes, yet gloried in the love that shown in them. How he longed to be able to kiss her and hold her one more time, but he steeled himself to be strong. He knew they would have an audience and his feelings for her were too private to be exposed for ridicule.

JoAnna went up to him immediately and reached through the bars to hold his hands. He smiled at her and said, "Hello, little one."

Then turning to John, he reached out and shook his hand. "Thank you for speaking on my behalf yesterday, Doctor. And you, too, JoAnna. I would have saved you that embarrassment if I could have."

"I was not embarrassed, just mad as the devil, because they did not want to believe us," she answered.

Notah smiled at her fierce countenance. Ah, yes, she was his *little warrior woman*.

John said, "Notah, the general has asked us to leave today after the noon meal."

"Are you still planning to stay in the town down river?"

"Yes. We don't know what we can find to live in, or if I can find some work, but we plan to stay until you are released from here."

"I won't go until I know they have really set you free," JoAnna told him.

He brought her hand up to his lips and kissed it.

John, seeing they needed to be alone, excused himself and said he would wait at the door.

JoAnna was grateful for her father's understanding and moved as close to the bars and Notah as she could. She reached up and touched his face saying, "I love you so much. I don't know how I am going to survive these next six months without being able to see you and the children."

He stroked her hair, and leaned his forehead against hers, awkward as it was. He wanted to be able to pull her against him but it was impossible.

"Ah, JoAnna, my heart. I am glad you will still be in the area. If there is a way to get a message to you, I will. I told you that some of the Apaches sneak off the reservation from time to time. If I can get a message to one of them to bring to you, I will."

Just then JoAnna had an inspiration.

She told Notah about Toby being the one who had found Little Fawn after Cahill's attack and she told him how he seemed smitten with her.

"If Toby stays in touch with Old Woman and Little Fawn, maybe we can use him to get word to each other. I'm sure Toby will come around to see you. He admires you so. He once told me that you had become a father figure to him, since he could not remember his own."

"He has grown up over this past year. He is not the young, gangly boy I took a liking to," Notah answered.

"You're right. And he has developed into a handsome young man, as well. Little Fawn just might lose her heart to him, for I believe he has already lost his to her."

"That will be as hard for them, as our love is for us. No one will approve of him marrying an Apache any more than they will allow me to marry you, JoAnna," he said bitterly, realizing again how doomed this love of theirs seemed to be.

"No, we will not think like that. I want to be your wife. I don't care if it takes the rest of our lives, I told you I will wait for you."

"Ah, my love, it is not fair to ask that of you, but selfishly, I hope you will. Your face is on my heart forever."

As they tried to kiss through the bars, the guard on duty coughed and said, "I'm sorry, Miss Lund, but time is up. You have to leave now."

In spite of her good intentions, tears pooled in JoAnna's eyes.

Notah reached through the bars and wiped them away, bringing them to his lips, causing a sob to escape her lips.

"Don't cry, little one, it hurts my heart too much. This is not good-bye forever. Somehow the gods will work it out. Have faith." He smiled his heart-stopping smile at her. The one that made her weak in the knees.

"Yes, I will." She smiled back, and then turned to leave with her head high. She would not break down in front of him or the guards who were watching her.

John poked his head back in and told Notah good-bye once more and then he took JoAnna's arm to escort her to their little house for the last time.

She would have stumbled had he not been holding on to her, the tears were running so hard down her face.

John just held her close. There wasn't much he could say, only pray that in time God "would work all things together for good," as the holy book said.

Chapter Thirty

The next six months were hell for JoAnna.

Fortunately, though, with the money and supplies the army had given them, they were able to find a place to rent in the town of Sumner, and John had been able to buy into a dry goods and hardware store on the main street.

Toby, who was seriously courting Little Fawn, had been able to get messages back and forth when he was off duty and allowed a weekend pass to come into town. He told the Lunds that Notah was to be released the next week and the general had agreed to let them come to see him and visit the reservation for a few hours.

JoAnna was grateful and shed tears of joy at the news. She wondered if she had any tears left to shed. It seemed like that was all she had done these past six months. The women of the town had not befriended her once they found out that she had let herself fall in love with an Indian. She learned the hard way that prejudices ran high on that subject. However, she didn't care. Her love for Notah was pure and good. He was a wonderful, intelligent, humble man and it did not matter to her what they thought.

On the day of Notah's release, she dressed with special care, wearing a blue sprigged muslin dress that matched her eyes, and a big straw picture hat. She'd washed and brushed her hair until it gleamed and left it down because Notah had once said he liked it hanging softly around her face. She was so excited she could hardly sit still on the wagon seat.

"This is a red-letter day, isn't it?" John smiled down at her restlessness.

"Oh, yes," she breathed. "It has been the longest six months of my life and I am so glad the wait is over. I must remember to thank the general for letting us come today."

They arrived at the fort around noon and when General Carleton heard they were on the grounds, he invited them to have lunch with him. The release would take place after the meal.

They acquiesced and thanked him for his kindness, both for the meal and for letting them see Notah.

"I knew you would probably come anyway," he answered smiling, "when I found out you had stayed on in town and were doing well. He has been a model prisoner, but I can tell you, I will be glad to have him out of my jail. I have let Old Woman come to see him from time to time because of the children. They will probably come to escort him back to their camp. You may visit the reservation for a few hours, but then I must ask you to leave. No civilians are allowed there anymore."

When they finished and the general had extracted their promise to leave by four o'clock that afternoon, he led them over to the stockade.

It seemed the whole fort had turned out to see this event. All wanted to see how Notah had survived and if he was still as assured of himself as ever.

JoAnna was on pins and needles. She did not know that the general had ordered that Notah be allowed to bathe that morning or dress in clean clothes that Old Woman had brought to the fort the day before. She hoped he would not be embarrassed to come out like he had been to let her see him in the hole.

When the door opened, everyone gasped, including JoAnna. Some marveled at how well he looked, some grumbled he hadn't been punished enough, but most were glad he was free.

There he stood in the doorway, tall and proud, looking none the worse for his time in jail. He blinked a few times until his eyes adjusted to the bright sunlight of a fall day and then his gaze collided with JoAnna's. His heart swelled to see her there and for the first time in his life, he was unsure how to act.

JoAnna took that decision out of his hands by flying across the space that separated them and jumping into his arms. She threw her arms around his neck and buried her face in his shoulder, laughing and crying at the same time. Her hat got knocked off in the process but she did not care. She didn't care what anyone thought, either, of her seemingly outrageous behavior. This was her own true love, and if the world didn't like it, it did not matter.

Notah set her down and walked over to John and shook hands. He turned to the general and said, "I thank you for allowing the Lunds to come today. I have no hard feelings toward you, General Carleton. You are a leader who has to give, as well as take, orders. I will say I am happy to be free and I will abide by your decision to stay away from the fort."

The general acknowledged his thanks, and said, "I have given the Lunds permission to visit the reservation for three hours and after that, they must leave. I feel I can trust you to see that they comply."

Nodding, Notah took JoAnna's arm and followed by Dr. Lund, headed out between the gates.

Dr. Lund thought for a moment, and then said, "JoAnna, you and Notah go ahead. I think I have something I want to discuss with the general. I will drive over in an hour and meet you at the camp."

As soon as they were out of eyesight of the fort, Notah turned JoAnna toward him and kissed her passionately. Her knees turned to jelly as she clung to him. He pressed her so close she felt the rising of his arousal against her.

"Oh, Notah, I thought this day would never come. I have missed you so. I've died a thousand deaths since you were locked up."

"I had no idea the general would let you come. I could not believe my eyes when I saw you there.

Your face was the last thing I would see before I closed my eyes to sleep while in there, and the first thing I thought of in the morning. I burn for you, little one. I don't know how I'm going to keep my hands off you, but we must go on. I need to see Bella and Bacca and hold them, too."

"Yes, yes, of course. I want to see them, too. I missed them as much as I missed you. Did they let Old Woman visit you often?"

"Once a week, she was allowed in. But it was enough. She kept me informed of what was happening in the camp, and Toby would come by and let me know when he had seen you. He is certainly in love with Little Fawn, and from what Old Woman says, she returns his love. Toby also said his enlistment is up and he plans to get out of the army and marry her, and take her somewhere where they can make a life together."

"I envy them that ability." JoAnna sighed. "Do you think a time will ever come for us to be married?" she asked wistfully.

"I've thought of nothing else, JoAnna, but so far, I have not been able to see a way to do it."

Although she knew that was the truth of the matter, and the way things were, she still felt let down. Against hope, she had thought he would come up with a plan.

When they arrived at the campsite, Bella and Bacca threw themselves into Notah's outstretched arms and clung to him, just as she had. Then they turned and hugged JoAnna, too.

JoAnna was shocked to see how much they had

grown until she realized they would be entering into their teen years soon enough. And they had seemed so young when they first met.

Notah turned to Old Woman and embraced her frail old body as well, although she tried to act as if it were nothing to see him home again. Then Little Fawn stepped out of the dwelling, with a chubby little two-year-old clinging to her hand.

"It is good to have you home, Hataalii," she told him.

"Thank you, Little Fawn. And, a very late *thank you* for coming to my trial and putting yourself out there in front of the soldiers to tell your story. It was a brave and courageous thing to do."

"Old Woman helped me to do it. I was only too glad to hear that the captain was dead at last and would not hurt any other young maidens."

When they finished exchanging happy words, Old Woman got their attention by announcing, "Now we will all have a celebration under Chief Manuelito's arbor. Everyone wants a chance to welcome you back, Notah. I hope you do not mind."

"How could I mind? I am anxious to see my chief and greet the others. I have missed being a part of my people's lives. I could perform no sings in the jail cell."

While he had talked to Little Fawn, JoAnna had reacquainted herself with the children. They were equally as glad to see her, especially Bella. JoAnna had become a mother figure to her and she was happy to have her with them again.

They all walked off in a group, Notah holding

Bacca's hand and JoAnna's, and JoAnna holding Bella's. It almost felt like they were a family already. In JoAnna's heart, they were.

When the chief heard the commotion outside, he immediately went to see what it was. As Notah had walked through the camp, he had picked up his people along the way. JoAnna smiled as the picture of the Pied Piper flitted through her mind. Everyone was singing and yelling their "Ho-ta-heys" at him as the drummers walked along beating out a chanting rhythm.

Chief Manuelito took Notah by his forearms and greeted him with misty eyes.

"We have sorely missed your presence, Notah Begay. Welcome home."

Notah was equally moved and glad to be home.

For the next hour and a half, eating, singing, dancing, story-telling went on until, finally, Notah told the Diné that he needed some time with JoAnna before they made her leave the fort and reservation grounds.

Old Woman told them to go on, she would take the children home and they would see him at the evening meal.

JoAnna was glad he had spoken up at last, for she longed to be alone with him. She did not begrudge his people giving him the warm homecoming, but she had her own welcome she wanted to give him.

They wandered down to a spot along the Pecos River and sat down under some willow trees. When Notah sat down and leaned up against the tree, JoAnna settled in front of him between his legs, content just to be near him. They sat like that for a while—just taking in the nearness of each other, listening to the water running by, the birds chirping, and rustling of the leaves overhead.

"I could stay like this forever," JoAnna sighed.

"Umm, yes, but I know some other things I would like to do to you forever, my sweet little one," Notah said as he nuzzled the side of her neck, trailing little kisses down to her shoulder.

She turned in his arms and lifted her face to his to receive the kisses she had longed for, for six agonizing months.

One kiss turned into a dozen and they were both breathless when he pulled her dress off her shoulder and bared the tops of her breasts. His hungry gaze melted her. When he bent his head and kissed one breast, taking the nipple into his mouth even through the cloth, while palming the other, JoAnna felt the shock all the way through her body as her womb clenched.

Laying her down, he ran his hand up her skirt to her thigh and felt her open her legs wider for him. Groaning deep his throat, he tried to control his raging desire. He could feel her moist heat radiating into his hand as he palmed her woman's portal. At his touch she tensed, then closed her legs around his hand.

Kissing her once more, he said, "JoAnna, we have to stop. I cannot last much longer."

"Oh, Notah, don't stop, my love. I want to belong to you in every way. I don't care whether we are married or not. I feel married to you in my soul, no words will make a difference."

Her words almost broke his willpower, but he was determined they would be married either in the Navajo way or by her father before he took her. But he could relieve the pressure for her, so he lovingly caressed the petals of her entranceway and the little nubbin at the top.

JoAnna writhed beneath his hands, not knowing what to do or what to expect, but just knowing something had to happen to set her free from this spiraling whirlwind of heat he was creating.

Notah broke out in a sweat as his body clamored for the same release he was trying to bring to JoAnna. Everything in him wanted to be inside of her. Just when he thought he would break and give in to his own body's demands, JoAnna cried out and grabbed on to him as the throes of her climax took her.

JoAnna thought she was floating somewhere above her body. Never . . . never . . . had she known there were feelings like this. Afterwards, she drifted back down to earth, replete and safe in Notah's arms.

He held her close and savored her fulfillment.

"Is it always like that?" JoAnna finally asked him, stunned at the power of such emotions.

"Only with someone you love, I think," he answered her. And yet, he had *loved* Squash Blossom, but she had never come apart in his arms the way JoAnna had just now.

Knowing the hours were quickly slipping away, he reluctantly sat up and said, "We best be getting back, love. Your father will be here soon and may already be looking for us."

"But you couldn't have been satisfied. Doesn't something have to happen to you, too?" she asked innocently.

"Yes, you know it does, but I am content to know you are content. There will be a time for me to show you what pleases me and then you will see my reaction," he laughingly told her.

He pulled her to her feet and they started back, arms around each other, her head resting on his shoulder.

"I don't want to leave you," she murmured.

"Don't think about it for now. You have never been away from me even though you were not here physically. I even visited you once in your dreams. I will be hurt if you tell me my powers didn't make you feel me there with you."

She looked up at him amazed, and then said, "Yes, about a month ago. I thought you were in my room. It almost felt like I was having a vision, you looked so real. I reached out to touch you and you vanished. So I assumed I had dreamt you."

"I told you that our spirits can travel. I did visit you but I could not hold it very long. But it was a comfort to see you."

"Well, I'd rather have you in person than in spirit," she quipped.

He laughed out loud, delighted with her witty answer.

"You will have me, I promise."

When they got back to Notah's dwelling, John

was there and so were the children. Old Woman was stirring something in the cook pot and Little Fawn was gazing up into Toby Wiley's eyes, who had come along with John after he got off duty.

JoAnna greeted her father with a hug. She thought she saw something twinkling in his eyes. He seemed excited and restless. *I wonder what is going on with him,* she thought.

As they were finishing up the last of the coffee, John said, "I have something to tell all of you. I hope you will be pleased; I worked on it all afternoon with General Carleton and Colonel Carson."

I knew it! thought JoAnna. He's been up to something. She could always tell when he had a "bee in his bonnet," as the saying went.

"Well, out with it, Father. You've got us all curious."

He beamed like the fabled cat from Alice in wonderland. They were going to like his surprise, he was confident.

"The general and the colonel both feel that there is no simple solution to the problem of you and Notah, and the army will not countenance you living on the reservation with him."

"And you're smiling about that?" she asked incredulously.

"Yes, because we worked out a plan so that all of us can be together."

"How?" both JoAnna and Notah asked at the same time, grasping each other's hands.

"Well, it seems that the army feels Notah, and you JoAnna, have caused considerable upset since coming here. The general thinks there will be no peace until you two are settled. He cannot let the whole Navajo nation go back to the four corners area, but he has decided to let Notah, his children, Old Woman, you leave at the end of next week. He doesn't want any more trouble on the reservation."

JoAnna and Notah looked at each other, then laughed out loud and hugged each other.

"But how can this be?" Notah asked. "I don't see how he can just let us go. Won't there be repercussions?"

"Yes, if the army knew about it. And there is a possibility that there still may be some repercussions, but the general and the colonel thought that if you all just slipped away one night and disappeared, no one would be the wiser, and it would not be reported; not on his watch at least."

"You mean sneak away from the reservation?" JoAnna asked.

Turning to Notah she asked, "Can we really do this and return to your homeland? I'm willing to risk it, if you are."

"Yes, it could be done. Are you sure, John, that you wish to come too? How about your business dealings in Sumner town?"

"I can sell my interest back to the owner, and we can leave whenever you like. I'm for it. Maybe I won't open a trading post again, but I want to be around to play with any grandchildren you two give me." And he smiled at both of them.

"Whoopee!" shouted Toby Wiley. "That is the best news I've heard in a coon's age. Congratulations to you all. Boy, do I envy you."

"Well, Toby, isn't your enlistment up this month?" John asked him.

"Yes, it is, and I plan to get out of this man's army pretty darn quick and marry my Little Fawn," he said, smiling and reaching for her hand.

"Then how about you joining up with us and coming along for the ride? We can wait long enough for you to muster out, and then we'll all set off together," John said.

Looking over at Old Woman and seeing her crestfallen face, he realized he might not have told her she was included.

He walked over to her and said, "Hey, Old Woman, don't think I mean to leave you behind. This deal includes you, too. It was all or nothing when I spoke to the general."

Her face lit up like a thousand candles and she kissed his hand.

"Now, don't go doing that. Let's plan how we're going to do this. And while we're at it, I want to officiate at both your weddings. I'm afraid we can't make a big deal out of it, or invite all the Diné, but I want to see you all start out as married people."

"Oh, Father, I don't know how to thank you, or how you did it, but we are so grateful. And, yes, we'll let you marry us the first day out. How does that sound to you, Toby and Little Fawn?"

Toby beamed from head to toe. "It is sure all right with me. What do you think, sweetheart?" he asked Little Fawn.

"I would be honored to be the wife of Toby Wiley," she answered shyly.

Toby let out with another loud "whoopee!" and swung her around in the air as everybody laughed and hugged.

JoAnna was delighted. She said a silent "Thank you, Lord, for your mercy and goodness." Who would have ever thought it would turn out this way?

They had to hurry to leave by their curfew, so they hugged all around once more before parting. Toby said he would be the go-between for their plans and they would be ready to go by the end of the month.

Praise God. They were going to be free to follow their heart and their loves to wherever life would take them.

Chapter Thirty-One

They had been married by her father on their first day of the trip, but had decided to wait until they got here to have their special time alone. Toby and Little Fawn were off somewhere on their own as well, while Old Woman and John kept all the children and the home-fire going.

Notah had chosen their honeymoon site well. It was a mile away from where their family dwelled at Canyon de Chelley, yet close enough to be easily reached if needed. They had not gone all the way back to Dinétah, but had stopped off here in this pleasant valley where some of the peach trees, and other things that Carson had destroyed on *The Long Walk,* had reseeded or come back to life.

A slow-flowing stream, not too wide or too deep, was within easy reach of the brush arbor shelter he had built. The banks gently sloped down to the water and were covered with soft sand and willow trees.

He'd covered the floor of the lean-to with woven Navajo blankets and sheepskins, fleece side up. A fire pit was dug in front and lined with stones around the sides. A tripod hung over the hole, holding an iron kettle to cook in. Although they were limited in the provisions that could be spared from the others, he knew they would not go hungry. His skill as a hunter would provide them with the small game needed to supplement their diet.

For now, his hunger was only for one thing—JoAnna.

His need for her had been building for a long, long time and he had dreamed of making sweet passionate love to her for months. Now, at last, they would be free to share and express that love without hindrance from their gods, other people, the U.S. government or its army.

They had ridden double to this site on one of the army horses given to them as they left the fort. Notah had never expected to be let go by General Carleton, but he was grateful that the man had looked beyond the color of his skin and listened to John's argument for his release from reservation life. He vowed he would never take *freedom* lightly again. He still hoped, eventually, that General Carleton would see the system had failed and let the rest of his people return as well.

Upon reaching the site, Notah gently lifted JoAnna down from the horse, letting her slide slowly down his chest. They just stood there gazing into each other's eyes, too filled with emotions to speak. The look was filled with the love they shared, the pain they had gone through to get here, and the hope for the future that lay ahead of them. The spell was too precious to break immediately, so they just stood there, hearts beating as one, drinking in each other's face.

Finally, JoAnna sighed and buried her head under his chin. Notah leaned down and kissed the top of her head, clasping her tightly to him.

"Ah, JoAnna, I have dreamed of this moment more than you'll ever know."

"I have, too, Notah, but despaired of it ever coming to pass. You kept your distance from me until I thought I would never be able to make you love me."

"Oh, little one, I think I fell in love with you the first day we met on the trail, but my training and plans for my life didn't include love or another marriage—ever. But you changed that, and soon I could not think of you without thinking marriage. The thought of you marrying someone else of your own race, which I kept telling myself was best for you, warred with my own desire to have you for myself."

"No one else would have sufficed, Notah," JoAnna told him, raising her head to look into his eyes once more. "You captured my heart and my imagination that first day also."

"Then enough with this talking. Let us begin our new life together now. I don't think I can wait a minute longer to claim you as my wife."

JoAnna found she was feeling the same way, but last-minute modesty claimed her and she blushed and ducked her head.

Taking her chin in his fingers, he raised her face

back up to his and eased her self-consciousness with a slow, searing kiss that left her breathless and wanting more.

Notah took her by the hand and led her into their shelter. It was the middle of the day; still warm enough to undress in the open. Should she become chilled he would quickly and easily warm her with his own body.

Once inside, he asked her to sit on the lamb's fleece that lined the floor of the hut. She did so willingly and reached up for him to follow her down.

Instead, he knelt in front of her. Taking her face in his hands, he kissed her tenderly, moving from her mouth over her cheek, to her ear, and down the side of her neck as he frustratingly undid the buttons on the front of her blouse. He thought he would teach her to wear the tunics of his people after this. They were much easier to get in and out of.

As each new expanse of skin was exposed, he kissed that as well. When he reached the top of her breasts that peaked at him above her camisole, he could see her nipples had already pebbled in arousal. They seemed to be asking him to kiss them, too. So he did, right through the cloth covering them.

JoAnna gasped and grabbed at his head, holding him to her so she could experience more of the pleasure he was giving her.

Odd, but she had never thought of her breasts being used for anything but nursing babies. Who knew a man's touch on them could be so thrilling.

She moaned low, and Notah reacted immediately with his own growl of arousal.

"You have too much cloth between us, JoAnna. I want you naked before me. Help me get you out of these wrappings. Do all white women feel the need to wear so much covering? How do their men ever get close to them to make love?"

She had to smile at that remark. JoAnna felt the same way about him, too. He had much too much on, as well.

"If I undress, you will have to do so, too!" she told him boldly.

"You want me naked before you?" he asked, holding his breath. He knew she was not as innocent about the mating act as she had once been, but he had not wanted to rush her.

"Yes, I want to see you," she answered, blushing as she said it.

That was all the motivation Notah needed. His moccasins, leggings, and tunic were off before she could change her mind, leaving him wearing only his breechclout. He still didn't want to shock her with his rapidly increasing desire.

JoAnna had seen his naked chest before, but still she stared at him in awe. She knew he was heavily muscled and beautifully formed, but seeing him practically nude took her breath away. She also knew what the protrusion pushing at the front of his breech-clout meant. He was definitely aroused and wanting her.

She began peeling off her skirt and petticoats, agreeing with Notah that white women wore way too many clothes, until she was down to camisole and bloomers.

"No, JoAnna," Notah told her. "Leave nothing on."

"But you're still covered," she exclaimed, her face flaming red at her forwardness.

He chuckled low. "Yes, but I can have it off in a heartbeat. I was trying not to make you self-conscious with the depth of my desire."

JoAnna didn't know where her boldness came from all of a sudden, but she answered, "Well, if I have to undress completely, so do you."

With a flip of the cloth covering his private parts, Notah's breech-clout fell away.

Once again, JoAnna stared in awe and trepidation at the large and firm piece of flesh before her.

"Oh my," she whispered. She knew the rudiments of sexual intercourse, but now she wondered if *that* would fit inside her.

Raising her eyes to his, she could not help but notice the proud and satisfied gleam in his eyes because he knew she found him appealing.

Tentatively, she reached out her hand as if to touch him, then drew it back hastily, not sure she should do that.

"It's all right, little one. If you want to touch me, do so. I would like it," he said, as his manroot jerked in response to the thought.

"See, he wants your touch as much as I do," he reassured her.

Glancing down at him, she could see he was right. *It* did seem to be thrusting in her direction, begging to be touched.

JoAnna reached out carefully and tenderly. As she touched the tip, it jerked once more. Startled, she looked up and asked, "Did that hurt you?"

He smiled at her and said, "Not the kind of hurt you mean. Go ahead, touch me again."

She did so. This time noticing how soft the skin felt at its head, and how rigid the rest became. Gaining boldness, she wrapped her small hand around it and felt it stiffen even more in her hand.

When Notah gasped in response, she knew it was in pleasure this time, and not in pain. It gave her a certain feeling of power to know she could elicit such a response from him so she began stroking up and down his shaft.

This time Notah's whole body jerked and he covered her hand to stop her movements, saying, "Enough! No more or I will embarrass myself in your hand. Now it is your turn to be touched. Let me take off the rest of your clothing. It is my turn to feast my eyes, and feel my hands on you."

By this time, JoAnna knew she wanted to be undressed in front of him, too, and gladly helped him rid her body of the rest of her clothing.

When she stood up naked before him, he stared in awe of her, as she had of him. She was so small, yet so perfectly formed. Full breasts on such a tiny waist, fitted over gently flaring hips and shapely legs, sent his senses reeling. He guessed it was good that she kept herself so bundled up; any man seeing this would keep her undressed forever, for it was his own thought as well.

How she could ever have thought no one would

want her was beyond him. Yes, her foot turned in, it was as perfectly formed as the rest of her.

Gently, he laid her down on the fleece and ran his hands down her legs, soothing her as he felt her nervousness return. Then, picking up her deformed foot, he kissed the top and side of it as he held it in his hands. He kissed the arch underneath and then took her big toe in his mouth and sucked on it.

It was JoAnna's turn to gasp as sensations ran from her toe to her womb as it clenched in response to Notah's action. *How in the world were those two parts connected,* she wondered, dazed by the feelings emanating from such a curious touch.

Notah left her foot, laying it down, smiling at her shocked expression. All along he had had ideas of how he could make her a better-fitting, corrective moccasin that might help her walk better. When they returned from their honeymoon, he would talk with her about it.

For now, he hoped he had shown her that her deformity would never matter to him.

And, indeed, for JoAnna, it had. She knew she would never view her foot in the same way ever again without remembering how his kissing it had made her whole in a way he would never know.

Oh, was there ever such a tender, thoughtful, loving man as this, she wondered. *No . . . never,* she decided. And she was so glad he was hers.

JoAnna started rubbing her hands absently up and down his back when all of a sudden she realized she was feeling the welts and scars left from Cahill's lashing. She felt him stiffen as if he didn't want her to touch him there. Sensing his unease, she told him to turn over and lay on his stomach. Maybe she could erase the feelings he had about them, as he had done for her about her foot.

She straddled him, sitting on his backside and started running her hands all over his back.

Leaning down, she kissed each welt and scar as she ran her hands over it. His intake of breath told her she was affecting him, but how she did not know. She wanted to show him his scars didn't matter to her. He would always be handsome in her sight.

When he could stand no more, he rolled her under him saying, "Ah, JoAnna, truly you have healing in your hands. I am sorry you have to look upon those marks, but you have shown me by your loving touch, they do not bother you. Thank you, little one. I love everything about you."

JoAnna answered, "You will always be beautiful and perfect in my sight." Then her thoughts scattered as he started kissing his way back down her body as he stroked her stomach and breasts.

Notah kissed her behind her knees, the inside of her thighs, skipping over her woman's core to kiss her stomach and stick his tongue in her belly button. He smiled to himself when he felt her stomach muscles quiver and jump within her.

When his mouth reached her breasts, she was a bundle of nerves, trembling and aching for more. At the first touch of his mouth, she breathed his name in wonder.

"Notah . . . Notah. What are you doing to me?"

"Loving you," he replied. "All of you."

She sighed and clutched his head closer as he took her nipple between his teeth and tugged on it.

She had never known passion before Notah and she was only now beginning to understand its power. There was a fire building inside her lower regions that needed to be quenched, and she knew this time that Notah would quench it, but not like before.

"Notah, help me. I don't know how to control these feelings," she pleaded.

"Just let yourself go, little one. Trust me. Put your body into my keeping. I won't let anything happen to you until you're ready to experience all that I can teach you about the ways of a man with his woman."

"Oh, yes, teach me, Notah. I'm ready to learn," she responded.

That was all the invitation Notah needed. Positioning himself over her but supporting his weight on his forearms, he cradled her face in his hands and asked her a question.

"You do know that with the first time a woman is taken fully, there can be some pain and discomfort for her?"

Swallowing, she answered, "Yes. Will it hurt very much?"

He kissed her quickly, and said, "I will make your first time as sweet as I can, JoAnna, with as little hurt as possible. Do you trust me in this?"

"Yes. Yes, I trust you. I know you would not willingly hurt me."

He nodded and lowered his whole body on top of hers with his rod lying in the apex of her thighs.

JoAnna's body instinctively adjusted to accommodate his, and even arched into him.

Once more he kissed her senseless while his finger trailed over her stomach to her woman's entrance.

She was writhing and gasping, begging for release. She didn't know what to call it, but something had to happen, she knew.

When Notah felt her dampen with the moisture of her own excitement, he positioned himself to enter her.

Her legs fell open to let him in and he pushed until he reached her maiden's barrier. He waited a minute to let her body accustom itself to his being inside her stretching the walls of her woman's passage. It was almost more than he could stand—the blood was pulsing in his head and in his man-part, wanting to push through to completion, but he held still until he felt her move. Her head was thrown back and she was actually lifting herself up to meet him.

"Notah," she sighed. "Is that all? There was no pain."

Chuckling, he answered, "No, dear one, it is nowhere near done. I'm just trying to give your body time to adjust to my invasion of it. You are so tight and snug. I feel like I've come home from a long journey and I want to nestle down inside of you."

"Then, nestle," she told him as she experimentally moved her body and was shocked at the reaction moving against him caused in her. At his intake of breath, she knew he'd felt it too.

That clinched it for Notah. As innocent as her moves against him had be. . .was now time for a full penetration. He couldn't hold back any longer. With one hard thrust, he pushed past her barrier and planted himself deep inside her.

"Ohhh," was all JoAnna managed to get out at the sting of it.

"It will not hurt anymore, I promise you," Notah told her, as he moved slowly back and forth in little tantalizing slides inside her that soon had her mimicking his moves.

She arched her hips against him and wrapped her legs around his waist when he showed her how.

Carefully taking her bottom in his hands and holding her tight against him, he started moving faster and harder inside her.

JoAnna felt the pressure and the rising crescendo coming but still didn't know how to handle it or what to do with it. She moved with him until she thought her heart would fly right out of her chest, it was beating so hard. When she cried out his name as her climax took her, Notah let her finish before he took his own release, collapsing on top of her, then rolling over and pulling her alongside of him.

"Oh my," JoAnna breathed. "That was *it*, wasn't it?" she asked Notah. "Sorta' like a fireworks explosion on the Fourth of July."

Notah chuckled again and said, "That was *it*, but I'm not sure what the Fourth of July explosion is."

JoAnna smiled when she realized he would not

understand the reference to the Independence Day celebrations and the fireworks that were used.

"Oh, it is an American holiday where they set off things called firecrackers filled with gunpowder that make loud noises when they explode and sends colors like lightning into the sky."

"Well, I guess it could be compared to that. Some people claim to see stars and lights when they come into their release. Are you feeling all right? Did I hurt you in any way?" He was concerned that he might have been too rough at the end.

"No. It stung for a moment but after that it felt so good, I could think of nothing else. Will it always be like that?"

"It will only get better over time. I will never tire of loving you, and showing you how many ways there are to make love to you."

"There are different ways?" she asked, rearing back to look up at him from under his arm.

"Yes, little one, many more, and I will enjoy showing as many of them to you as you desire to learn," he answered her.

Then, fearing her first time had made her too sore to continue for now, he sat up, got to his feet and reached back down to pull her up, too.

"What?" she asked confused.

What did he want to do now, she wondered. She became self-conscious when she looked down at her nakedness and realized it was still daylight.

"Nothing," he answered her. "We are going to take a cooling dip in the stream. I want to ease any discomfort you've experienced from our joining."

Looking down at her body once again, she saw the evidence of the loss of her virginity and thought a bath might be a good thing, so she let him lead her outside, hesitating for a moment when she looked around. She'd never been naked in the sunlight before and it unnerved her.

Sensing her doubt, he said, "No one is around for miles. I am the only one who'll see you like this . . . ever," he added.

So saying, he led her off again in the direction of the stream.

Even though she felt self-conscious, JoAnna felt somehow liberated at the same time from the shame and the morals of her time. She told herself that she was with her lawful husband and no one was around to witness her state of undress.

When they reached the water's edge, Notah picked her up and carried her into the middle of the stream. He let her slide slowly down his body until her feet touched bottom. He was getting hard again, but he knew it was too soon for her.

JoAnna yelped once when the water covered her bottom and midriff but then shivered in delight when it cooled her heated body and eased the soreness between her legs.

Notah cupped his hands and slowly dribbled the water over her shoulders, down her back, and then gently washed the blood and semen from her thighs.

JoAnna wondered if such intimacies were allowed between a man and a woman, but again she reminded herself that he was her husband and her body was his, as his was hers, so there was nothing to be ashamed of. She then started sluicing water over his shoulders, too.

He laughed when he saw her relax and splashed her. Then lying on his back, he pulled her off her feet to float with him. Thank the gods, she did seem to know how to swim and wasn't afraid of the water.

They played around some more, swam a little more, and then came up out of the water facing each other.

Notah took her into his arms and kissed her tenderly.

Soon their kisses intensified and JoAnna realized she wanted more than just his kisses. She wanted to experience that *oneness* again. Wantonly she started caressing him and pressing herself into him.

Immediately Notah was aroused.

Taking hold of her shoulders, he said, "Careful, little one. Keep this up and it will only lead to one end. You'll be flat on your back on that bank over there."

Smiling enticingly, she asked him, "How quickly can you get me to the bank?"

Growling low in his throat, he picked her up and showed her how fast he could be. Where she had been shy and reticent before, she was learning fast to be a seductress. And he liked it.

Within seconds he had pinned her to the grassy bank and was inside her.

"Ahh," she sighed. Never had she known she could feel so whole having a man inside her.

"I may not be able to be gentle this time," Notah

warned her as the blood lust rose within him. "I want you too much."

"It will be okay," she answered him, for she found her desire had intensified to meet his own.

All at once, he pulled out of her and flipped her over, slipping into her woman's passage from behind as he raised her up on her knees.

Shocked at first, JoAnna thought, *This is how animals do it,* but then she found that she must have a little animal in her when she felt herself rearing back to meet each of his thrusts.

By the time they climaxed, both were breathing hard as they collapsed together on the bank.

When Notah could speak, he rolled her into his arms again and said, "Ah, JoAnna, I do not think I can ever get enough of you. I hope I did not shock you that time."

"Nooo . . . I just never thought humans did it that way," she answered.

Chuckling again, he realized that he had laughed more with her lately than he had in years. JoAnna was good for his bruised soul. She would never quite understand how her love had set him free from the hurt and pain of the past.

Gathering her up in his arms, he walked back into the stream for another wash-off, and then carried her back to the shelter. They would sleep for now and when they awoke, he would feed his woman, and meet all her needs.

As JoAnna drifted off to sleep in his arms, Notah planned ahead for a future for them all—JoAnna,

Bella and Bacca, John Lund and Old Woman, and, hopefully, a few little ones of their own.

They would make a new life beginning from here and, perhaps someday, help to bridge the gap between the white man and the red man—at least in this little corner of the world.